In Moonlight and Memories:

VOLUME TWO

JULIE ANN WALKER

From *New York Times* and *USA Today* bestselling author
Julie Ann Walker comes an epic story about sacrifice,
friendship, and the awe-inspiring power of love.

To my three older sisters, the strongest women I know.

Aren't you glad I didn't turn out to be a tumor?

"Life can only be understood backwards;
but it must be lived forwards."
~ Søren Kierkegaard

CHAPTER THIRTY-ONE

Cash

Dear Cash,

I went to Audubon Park today and sat on the bench beneath our weeping willow. The katydids have hatched. They're looking for mates, and for some reason their clicking and clacking reminded me of the time last summer when you and Luc cleaned out Old Man Murphy's shed for $100. Y'all came back covered in chiggers and spent the next week looking like walking advertisements for calamine lotion, pink head to toe.

The memory made me smile.

I think it's the first time I've smiled since you left. And honestly? It felt weird on my face. Like it had no business being there. Like I shouldn't have the right to smile. Not after... everything.

But I can't think of that. If I think of it, I might scream.

Oh, Cash. WHY did you go? WHY won't you answer any of my emails? And WHY did you change your phone number?

I've called you every day, hoping to hear your voice, CRAVING the sound of your voice. But all I get is the recording telling me your number is no longer in service.

I don't understand.

Please, help me understand. Send me an email, a letter, a note in skywriting. I don't care. Just...please.

Love, Maggie

Sometimes you don't know what you need until someone gives it to you.

Didn't know I needed Maggie's letters until I read some of them this morning. After last night, I was waffling on…well, just about everything. Now I have my head on straight. Back to working *The Plan*.

Only problem?

That kiss. That deep, wet, wonderful kiss.

"Top o' the mornin' to ya!" Luc bursts through the front door, bringing the crispness of the November air and the rich smell of freshly brewed coffee with him.

"You pick up that Irish brogue from watching too many Jamie Dornan interviews?" I don't bother getting up from the folding chair parked in the middle of the room. "I know how much you loved those *Fifty Shades* movies."

"Come on now." He sends me a pitying look over his shoulder as he shrugs out of his leather jacket and hangs it on a hook by the front door. "More like the Lucky Charms commercials during Saturday morning cartoons."

He walks over and hands me a paper cup of steaming coffee. Flopping into the vacant chair, he stretches out his legs. Then he pops the top off his own coffee and blows across the surface to cool the liquid.

Spying the blue three-ring binder sitting on the milk crate between us, he says, "Your letters from Maggie?"

I frown. "She told you about them?"

"Got a set of my own."

Numbness. A time-honored self-defense mechanism when someone or something scratches at my feelings.

Maggie didn't mention she'd spent a year writing to Luc too. Although, I guess I should've known. And I guess I should be happy.

"You read any of them?" I ask.

He nods. "The first six."

"That's an odd number."

"Actually, it's an even one." He mimes a three-beat drum solo with his coffee still in hand.

I roll my eyes. "I mean it's oddly precise."

He shrugs. "Reckon I'll read six a day for the next coupla months. It'll gimme something to look forward to in the evenings."

"Getting lonely out there in that swamp house?" I ask. It's never occurred to me he might feel isolated in the bayou. He's always seemed so at home there. Plus, if ever there was a man comfortable in his own skin and happy with his own company, it's Luc.

I envy him that.

My skin has always felt too tight, as if I'm stuffed inside a body suit that has shrunk in the wash. And left to my own devices, I get restless. Time alone allows a person to think.

Thinking can be tricky since it inevitably opens the door to old hurts and regrets and…self-reflection—perish the thought.

"Not really," he says. Then he seems to reconsider. "Sometimes, I guess. But it's more like I wanna savor her letters, you know? They *sound* like her, all thoughtful and vulnerable and a bit heartbreaking. Or at least they sound like she did back then."

"She hasn't changed much," I say. She's still thoughtful and vulnerable. She for damn sure still breaks my heart. And last night proved she still smells the same, still feels the same, still…*kisses* the same.

Maggie has a way of using her mouth so deeply and thoroughly I feel like I'm falling. One touch of her tongue, one taste of her sweet breath, and I'm Alice chasing the White Rabbit through the hole in the ground and plunging into a new world. Colors are brighter. Smells are sweeter. Everything is so much *more.*

Wasn't until this morning—and a quick read of those first few letters—that reality came crashing down again. Although, maybe it wasn't the letters so much as the relentless pounding of my head that brought me back from Wonderland.

"So." Luc sets his coffee on the milk crate and turns to me. "You wanna start tackling the cornices in the front bedroom? I reckon we should—" He stops midsentence, narrowing his eyes at my jawline. "What the hell happened to your face?"

I test the bruise with my fingers. It's painful. But not nearly as painful as the bump on the back of my head. That thing throbs like a second heartbeat.

"Had a visit from Rick last night." Saying the bastard's name makes the whiskey in my back pocket send up a siren's call. Taking out my flask, I add a drop of Gentleman Jack to my coffee.

Luc sits forward, his eyes drilling me. "What did he want?"

"To warn me."

"About what?"

"About steering clear of you and Maggie. He says Sullivan is coming for you both, and he doesn't want me getting involved and dragging our good family name through the mud."

Luc snorts. "Like his shady-ass business deals haven't done that already?"

I spread my hands. "That was pretty much the point I made."

"And that made him sock you?"

"Nah." I shake my head. "He socked me because he's a sadistic sonofabitch who's always enjoyed ending conversations with his fists."

After a brief silence, Luc asks, "You need me to help you get rid of the body?"

He's completely, dead-eye serious.

I laugh, then wince. It feels like my skull is packed with Semtex, seconds away from detonating. I hate to admit it, but... "Didn't get in a single punch."

His jaw drops open.

"Maggie showed up with her letters," I explain. "You should've seen her, coming to my defense like a momma bear, roaring at Rick to get out."

"Though she be but little, she is fierce," he quotes Shakespeare. Then he adds a more homespun adage. "When it comes to those she cares about, that woman would charge hell with nothing but a bucket of ice water."

"Amen, brother." I salute him with my coffee cup. "It's one of the things we love most about her."

He doesn't say anything to that. Instead, he sits back and stares at the ceiling. "So, it wasn't all bluster the other morning at the café. Sullivan really is gunning for us."

"Sounds like it." I add another drop of whiskey to my cup.

"Damn." He lowers his chin and tugs at his ear, giving away his agitation.

"What do you want to do about it?" I ask, ready and willing, despite Rick's advice, to jump in headfirst. Because, you know, fuck Rick. And besides, I'd do anything and everything for Luc and Maggie. They're the only two people I have left in the world.

"Don't rightly know," Luc muses thoughtfully. "Needa think on it for a spell." Then his lips twist. "'Course, the easiest thing to do would be to leave town, I reckon. It was our coming back here that stirred up this stink."

My scalp prickles at the mere notion. Leaving in no way fits in with *The Plan*.

"Wrong," I'm quick to tell him. "Our making it out of the army alive is what stirred up this stink. Even if we moved halfway around the world, don't delude yourself into thinking Sullivan would back off."

He grimaces. "Yeah. You're probably right."

"Besides, could you really run out on Maggie again?"

A muscle ticks in his jaw as he stares at me through narrowed eyes. "Could you?"

"No," I immediately admit.

"Me neither." He's quick to agree. "We're in this thing for better or worse. Question is, how we aim to make sure it's for the better. So, like I said, I need to think on it."

I glance out the front window. A couple of tourists looking worse for wear stagger down the uneven sidewalk across the street. It's early, and they appear to be suffering the effects of a late night. Probably going in search of a good cup of coffee, footloose and fancy-free, except for their hangovers.

How long has it been since I felt that way? Not hungover. Lately, that's a weekly, sometimes *daily* occurrence. But not having a care in the world? When was that? Ten years ago? More?

"None of this would be happening if I'd stayed," I concede quietly. "I fucked up everything by running off that night."

"Stop it." Luc points at me. "You did what you had to do. The only person to blame for what happened in that bayou is Dean Sullivan."

CHAPTER THIRTY-TWO

Luc

Dear Luc,

It's nearly midnight and I'm sitting on Aunt Bea's front porch swing. The air is sweet with the smell of tea rose begonias and there's a full moon out. It's big and yellow and reminds me of the one that shone down on us in the bayou last month.

Lord, that feels like forever ago. So much has changed since then, changed in the worst possible ways so that most days it takes everything I have just to get out of bed. Then again, staying in bed isn't really an option, is it? No doubt Sullivan is watching me, waiting to see how I'll behave.

So I pretend. I pretend to care about the long, hot summer days. I pretend to enjoy Auntie June's cooking even though everything tastes like ash. And I pretend that the only thing weighing on my heart is the desertion of my best friend and my boyfriend.

Maybe "desertion" isn't the right word. At least not for you. I understand why you had to go, but I don't agree with that email you sent. I don't agree that we need to leave the past in the past and just get on with life, especially if that means we can no longer be friends.

Oh, Luc, please know if I could take it all back, I would. If I could go back in time and undo everything, I would.

Unfortunately, I don't own a time machine. Which means all I can do is sit here and miss you. Sit here and wonder where you are.

Is it possible you're looking up at this same yellow moon?

I hope you're taking care of yourself. I know you're taking care of Cash.

Forever and always, Maggie May

There are some things that happen in life that change you to your core.

That night in the bayou obliterated the green and gullible teenager I was. Then, whatever speck of innocence left in me was stomped out by the army faster than a knife fight in a phone booth.

I know I have to strike first when it comes to George Sullivan. I have to find a way to make him back off. But to do that, I need Maggie's help.

So here I am, standing beneath her balcony, peering up at the yellow glow inside her apartment. It looks cheery and welcoming. Too bad the thing I need to discuss with her is neither.

Pulling my cell phone from my hip pocket, I dial her number.

"Luc?" Her sweet, clear voice has goose bumps popping up on the back of my neck. "Are you done at Cash's for the day? Did you get the cornices in the front bedroom finished?"

I don't answer her questions. Instead, I say, "I'm standing outside your front gate. You got a minute?"

"Uh…" She hesitates.

An unsettling notion occurs. "Are you…entertaining someone?"

She laughs. "*Entertaining?* Lord, you sound like Aunt Bea. *No,* I'm not entertaining anyone. Well, there's Jean-Pierre, but he doesn't count."

"Hey now!" I hear an offended male voice in the background.

"I'll be right down." She cuts the connection.

Rubbing my hands together, I glance around the quiet street. The sun has long since set. But before it did, the sky overhead was covered by a thick blanket of battleship-gray clouds. Even though it's too dark to see them now, I know they're still there because the moon and the stars are nowhere to be found.

"I had a dream about you last night." Maggie appears on the other side of the wrought-iron gate. She's wearing a loose hooded sweatshirt, black yoga pants, and a pair of red house slippers stitched with the iconic Harry Potter lightning bolt.

"You and Sally Renee were sitting in my living room," she says. "And Sally Renee said she was hungry. You said, 'Here. Eat my finger.' And she *did*. There was so much blood." She shudders. "But Sally didn't stop. She ate all five of your fingers, then started snacking her way up your arm. You just sat there with this stupid grin on your face while I screamed my head off."

"And good evening to you too, Maggie May," I say.

She opens the gate. I wince when it squeaks torturously on its hinges. (The humidity in New Orleans is brutal on anything metal.)

"That's all you have to say? You don't want to speculate about what my dream means?"

"It's no big mystery." I give her a quick hug. "That night at the bachelor auction, I said I thought Sally Renee was gonna do her best to eat me whole. Your subconscious took that statement and ran with it."

"Hmm." She threads her arm through mine as we make our way into the courtyard. "And here I thought dreams were supposed to reveal deep, dark meanings."

"Sorry, Sigmund. Sometimes a banana is simply a banana."

"Did you just make a dick joke?"

"Me?" I feign shock. "Never."

She eyes me askance and then sighs. "I suppose you're right. Still, I was beginning to come around to Sally until I saw her gnawing on you like a stick of beef jerky. Now I think I'm back to square one where she's concerned."

Maggie's insistence on butting into my love life would be annoying if I didn't know she was doing it because she cares. It's impossible to be sore at her for wanting to see me happy and settled.

"I'm not here to talk about Sally," I tell her.

"No?" She drags me toward the steps leading to her apartment, but I stop in my tracks. Peering up at me in confusion, she says, "Then you stopped by to see how I look on a Waistband Monday, is that it?"

That startles a laugh from me. "A what?"

"A Waistband Monday. You know, that night of the week when you put on pants with an elastic waistband, order pizza, and binge Netflix with your upstairs neighbor?"

"That's a new one on me," I admit with a smile. "But, Maggie May, you know I always think you're beautiful. Waistband Mondays included."

I'm not lying. With her face scrubbed clean of makeup and her hair in a messy topknot, her allure (while unassuming) is impossible to miss.

She slaps my arm. "Don't you dare turn those dimples on me, Lucien Dubois. Save them for the fun-and-done ladies you waste your time with."

She's in a playful mood. I can't bring myself to burst her bubble right off the bat, so I play along. "You can't blame me for the dimples. Got 'em from my dear ol' daddy." I give her an exaggerated wink.

"No flirty winking either." She feigns a frown as she once again tries to pull me toward the stairs.

"Mind if we stay out here for a bit?" I ask.

Her pretend frown becomes a real one as she studies me. "If it's about last night, I already told Jean-Pierre what happened. You don't need to worry about talking in front of him."

"It's not about last night," I say. Then I reconsider. "Although, I guess it is in a way. I heard it was pretty bad."

The white twinkle lights wrapped around the rails of the galleries cast a fairy glow over her face and highlight the wrinkle

12

that appears between her eyebrows. "Cash said it was bad? And here I thought he jumped up and insisted on walking me home because he was trying not to take advantage of the situation."

Confusion has me shaking my head like a dog shaking off water. "Wait. What're you talking about?"

She gives me the side-eye. "No, what are *you* talking about?"

"Rick," I say.

"Oh yeah. *Him.*" She shivers. "That *was* bad. I couldn't believe it when I saw him haul off and punch Cash like that. Although, I'm glad I *did* see it. It opened my eyes. *Finally.*"

She peeks up at me, her face full of chagrin. "Y'all must've thought I was a real idiot not catching on way back when. My only excuse is that Cash *was* always getting into scrapes, and I was such a sheltered girl that the idea of that kind of abuse was more unfathomable to me than a whole slew of dementors showing up at my door and... Goodness gracious! Luc, are you okay? You've gone completely white."

Holy hellfire. After all this time, she knows. A weight I didn't realize I was carrying lifts away so fast it leaves me dizzy. I lift a hand to my head.

"Cash didn't mention he told you about..." I have to swallow. It feels like all the sand in the Registan Desert has been dumped down my throat. "That he finally came clean about his dad," I manage to finish.

"Oh, he didn't want to. And I don't think he would have if I hadn't pieced things together on my own and come right out and confronted him."

"I wanted to tell you," I swear to her. "There were so many times I wanted to say something, but he made me promise never to breathe a word."

She steers me toward the metal table and chairs set up beside the tinkling fountain and takes a seat. Her chin wobbles a bit when she says, "I don't understand why he didn't want me to know."

"Shame," I say, dropping into the chair next to her.

She lifts her hands and lets them fall. "See? That's what I don't get."

"You don't get how he could be ashamed of sharing the blood of a bastard who could beat his own child? You don't think an eighteen-year-old kid who's trying his damnedest to be a man could feel embarrassed that he gets his ass handed to him on the regular by a middle-aged bastard?"

She looks at me for a long time. Then she says, "But if he'd just *told* me, I could've helped him. Aunt Bea and Auntie June could've helped him."

I have nothing to say to that, and as the silence stretches between us, it's broken only by the chatter of the water in the fountain and the *clip-clop* of a carriage mule passing by outside.

The French Quarter is oddly quiet tonight. Maybe it's because it's Monday and everyone is recovering from the weekend. (Although, here in New Orleans, where drinks and dancing can occur anywhere at any hour of any day, Mondays are more similar to Saturdays than in other places.) So perhaps it's something else.

There's a feeling in the air. I can't put my finger on it, but it's there. Like something is stirring far in the distance. Something aggressive and slightly sinister.

Or maybe this whole mess with George Sullivan has me imagining things.

"What did you mean when you said you thought Cash jumped up and walked you home 'cause he didn't wanna take advantage of the situation?" I ask.

"Oh, well..." A small grin flirts with her lips. "I told him I still love him. And then, you know..." She makes a rolling motion with her hand. "I kissed him."

I sit back in my chair, shocked not only by her words but also by the feeling skittering through my chest like a prickly legged centipede. I should be happy. Two people I love more than life are finally making progress toward each other. Except...

No. Not *except*. I should be happy. I *will* be happy.

Her expression turns tentative. "I probably shouldn't be talking about this stuff with you now that...now that..." She swallows, unable to finish.

"Maggie May." I take her hand. "I *wanna* hear anything and everything you have to tell me. So please, *please* don't stop. Okay?"

She searches my eyes. Her face betrays her skepticism even as she says, "Okay."

I open my mouth to assure her that I mean what I say, but before I can get a word out, the door to her apartment opens and Jean-Pierre appears on the gallery. He has Yard on a leash and is shrugging into a suede jacket.

"Me, I'm takin' dis dumb dog for a walk," he calls. "He been eyein' me and whinin' for da last five minutes. Y'all come inside dis house before you freeze to death."

"You don't have to do that." Maggie hops up from the chair and makes her way to the bottom of the stairs. "I'll put on some shoes and get my coat."

"Need to walk off dat pizza anyway, *cher*." Jean-Pierre bends to kiss her cheek as he and Yard step off the last tread.

She snorts. "So you'll be walking until next Sunday?"

The Cajun pats his flat stomach. "'Bout thirty minutes should do it."

"I hate you and your metabolism," she jokingly gripes.

Jean-Pierre flashes a smug smile before turning his attention my way. I stand from the chair and shake his hand when he offers it to me. "When you goin' to come play with me again, yeah?"

"First chance I get," I promise him.

Disregarding the run-in with Todd the Tool, that night playing with Jean-Pierre at Maggie's bar was one of the best I've had since I came back. The only place where past troubles and current worries can't touch me is onstage. There, I'm able to focus on the music and nothing else.

"Dis Thursday?" Jean-Pierre asks. "Me and mine are havin' a birthday party for my uncle. Come join us."

"Done and done," I say, happy to have a distraction to look forward to. "Should I bring a gift?"

"Bring yourself, your guitar, and your appetite. Oh!" He snaps his fingers. "And a stiff constitution. It'll be a true *fais do-do*." With an ornery laugh, he makes his way toward the gate.

After watching him go, Maggie and I take the stairs to her apartment. Once inside, I give Leonard a scratch beneath his whiskered chin, then I settle into the corner of one of her sofas. She doesn't grab the spot next to me. Instead, she chooses the wingback chair across the way, perching awkwardly on the edge of the cushion.

"Y'okay?" I ask with a frown.

Instead of answering, she pulls her locket from inside her sweatshirt and worries the filigreed heart with her fingers at the same time her teeth worry her bottom lip.

Here's the thing you need to understand about me. Thanks to my daddy, I have the patience of Job. He (my daddy, not Job) taught me early on that I should take my cues on how to live life by watching the bayou. And the bayou knows there's no hurry. It'll get where it's going. Don't try to rush it.

So I sit quietly and wait for her to work up to admitting to whatever's got her knickers in a knot.

Eventually, she does.

"I'm glad you told me what you did on Halloween. But now I don't know how to..." She stops and spreads her hands in a helpless gesture. "I don't know how to *be* when I'm around you."

Pulling her out of the chair, I situate her next to me on the sofa and throw an arm around her shoulders when she looks ready to bolt. "Just be yourself, Maggie May. You're still you and I'm still me. Only difference is there aren't any more secrets between us."

16

When I feel her relax against me, I ignore the warmth that spreads through my blood. For a while, we silently watch the candles burn in the fireplace. Then Sheldon slinks from beneath the sofa in that watery, sinuous way of a feline. He sniffs my boots before rubbing his whiskered cheek across the worn laces.

"It's the darnedest thing," Maggie says, scowling at her cat. "You're the only person on the planet he seems to like, which is super unfair considering *I'm* the one who keeps him in Fancy Feast and fishes his giant turds out of the litter box."

I chuckle. "Can't blame him for having impeccable taste. I mean, have you seen me lately?"

She shakes her head in mock disgust. "What happened to that shy, humble teenager I used to know?"

"He grew up and got crazy-hot."

She laughs, as I'd hoped she would. It'll take time for things between us to get truly comfortable again. But I don't regret telling her the truth. I feel like I've shed the skin of my past. What's growing back in its place is thicker, tougher. More *me*.

"So? You told Cash you still love him, huh?" I prompt, proving to her (and to myself) that I truly am still the guy she can talk to about anything. "What'd he say to that?"

She wrinkles her nose. "I didn't give him a lot of time to respond. Which, in retrospect, probably wasn't the smartest move. Like I told Jean-Pierre, now I don't know how to interpret the kiss that followed. I mean, on the one hand, I felt all the old feels. On the other hand, Cash hopped off that mattress like it was covered in poisonous snakes and nearly dragged me home by my hair. So, now I'm wondering..." She trails off and shrugs. "Well, now I'm just left wondering. He hasn't called or texted today, so what does *that* tell you?"

When I don't immediately answer, she continues, "My mind's been jumping like hot grease in a skillet, and the result is a Waistband Monday and two too many slices of pizza." She rubs a hand over her belly. "I'm capable of eating my feelings at a professional level, in case you were wondering."

"I'm sure you're winding yourself up over nothing," I reassure her. "Given all that's happened, Cash is probably just aiming to take things slow."

"You think? Did he mention anything to you?"

"No." I shake my head, shifting awkwardly because it's time I say what I came to say. "But I reckon that's only 'cause we were too busy working out how we aim to deal with this bad business with Sullivan."

I hate the fear that makes her brow pinch. "Did something happen after he came at us in Café Du Monde?"

"That's what brought Rick 'round to see Cash last night. He wanted to tell Cash to keep his distance from us 'cause Sullivan has declared war."

"*War?*" Her eyes go as wide as pie plates.

"Little does Sullivan know, I'm pretty damn good at war," I assure her. "And if there's one thing I've learned, it's that the best defense is a good offense. We're gonna hit him where it hurts. You think you could set up a time for us to talk with Miss Bea?"

She blinks. "What does Aunt Bea have to do with this?"

"If we're lucky, she'll have the information we need."

Once again, she unconsciously grabs her locket, squeezing it in her fist. Every time she does that, it feels like she's hanging on to a piece of me. Which gives me a thrill even though it shouldn't.

"I wish I could undo what I did that night," she whispers.

I tighten my arm around her. "All you did was defend yourself. There's nothing wrong with that."

"Tell that to George Sullivan. Or more like, tell that to *Dean* Sullivan. Oh, wait. You can't. He's *dead*."

I blow out a weary sigh and glance out the window at the starless night. I'd planned to go stag to my senior prom and meet Cash and Maggie at the dance. But when Cash stopped by on his way out of town, beat to shit and with a savage look in his eyes, I did as he asked and took Maggie in his stead.

In hindsight, it was the biggest mistake of my life.

"I shouldn't have dragged you to that stupid prom," I grumble, remembering the destroyed look on her face when I handed her the letter Cash had written and explained to her that he was gone. "I shoulda sat with you on that porch swing until your aunt Bea called you to go inside."

"I *wanted* to go to prom," she insists. "Cash had just broken my sixteen-year-old heart. I needed a distraction, and you provided it. I've never thanked you for that, have I?"

"Considering how things turned out, there wasn't much time or much call for thanks."

"Well, now there's time and call for it now. Thank you." She lifts her hand as if to tug on my ear, then hastily drops it, curling her fingers into a fist on her lap.

I hate that she second-guesses herself when it comes to touching me. But I have faith she'll get past it. I just have to give her time to realize I wasn't kidding when I told her nothing's changed for me.

"You were always there for me when I needed you." Her voice is soft when she emphasizes, "*Always.*"

"Still"—I shake my head—"dinner and the dance shoulda been enough. We never shoulda gone to that party afterward."

"As I recall, you didn't want to. I was the one who insisted. By that point, my heartbreak had morphed into pure-D fury. I was going to *show* Cash I didn't need him. Show him I could have a grand ol' time without him."

She had been crazed that night. Wild-eyed and single-minded in her pursuit of fun.

"Yeah, but as soon as I drove up and saw Dean's truck there, I shoulda turned right back around."

"You couldn't have known what he'd do."

"Maybe not. But I knew he was bad news." Thinking about Dean, even all these years later, still makes my teeth clench. "I shoulda known he'd try something after Cash beat the living shit outta him. He was the sort to nurse a grudge."

Maggie shivers, and I know she's reliving those hellish moments in the swamp. If someone ever invents brain bleach, the first thing I'll do is use it to wash her clean of the memory of what happened there.

"Whose place was that anyway?" she asks. "Do you remember?"

"Cory something-or-other. It was his dad's fishing house."

"That's right." She nods. "Cory Jackson. He was in the marching band."

"Not a day goes by that I don't regret dragging you outta that house and into the swamp," I admit.

She gives me a disbelieving look. "The baseball team was getting baked in the corner. Half the girls on the cheerleading squad were bonging beers; the other half were getting felt up by drunk teenage boys. And Dean and his butthole buddies were looking to fight anyone and everyone. That place was a powder keg waiting to explode. You got me out of there because it was the smart thing to do, and I'd gone way past making smart decisions. And besides, for a while afterward it was…nice." She nudges me with her elbow. "You taught me how to waltz, remember?"

My mind drifts back to that clearing in the swamp…

A cool breeze stirred the air. The bullfrogs and bugs and gators were in fine form, singing their lament in the moonlight as I led Maggie away from the house on stilts and down a narrow path into the heart of the bayou.

"What should we do now?" she asked me, the stars above twinkling in her eyes. Even though she'd fixed her mascara after crying her heart out on the porch swing, there were still smudges below her bottom lids. Her hair had slipped a little from its fancy updo. Tendrils of black curls fell across her shoulders, flirting with the edge of her sweetheart neckline.

She looked like a temptress in that red sequined prom dress. A temptress who didn't yet know her own power.

"Wanna dance?" I offered her a hand. We could still hear the music from the house party, even though we had to be a hundred yards away.

"To this?" She wrinkled her nose.

Someone had tuned the radio to a zydeco station. The fiddles whined. The accordion wailed. And the lead singer opined ever leaving the black water of the bayou for the sun-baked hills of Texas.

"Sure. You know how to waltz, right?" When she shook her head, I winked. "Come on, then. Let this swamp rat teach you a thing or two."

"I can't dance here in these shoes." She pointed to her strappy high-heeled sandals. "The heels will get stuck in the dirt."

"So kick 'em off."

"And have a twig stab through my foot?"

"You can stand on my feet. No more excuses, woman. I'm teaching you to waltz."

"So bossy," she accused, even as she bent to undo the clasps on her shoes.

Her innate coordination had her learning the steps to the waltz in no time. We moved around that little clearing as one, and I tried not to notice the feel of her soft hand in mine, or the way her hips twisted in that slinky dress.

It was different dancing in the middle of nowhere than it had been dancing in the festooned school gym. There, two hundred sets of eyes had watched us, wondering what happened to the combative blond-haired boy who was *supposed* to be her escort. But out in the bayou, it was only us.

And yet she was still my best friend's girl.

Wasn't she?

Someone switched radio stations, and David Archuleta started singing about having a crush. Shaking my head, I thought it couldn't get any more appropriate. Although, what I felt for Maggie went way beyond anything so trite or trivial.

It wasn't love at first sight. Even at eighteen years old, I knew that concept was complete and utter horseshit.

Lust at first sight was certainly possible. But *love* required getting to know a person. All the good parts and bad parts, all the weird parts and sad parts.

Luckily, the hours we'd spent together in the school library reading and talking about Harry Potter, and the days and weeks and months we'd been friends since, had afforded me the rare honor of getting to know Maggie. I no longer thought of her as the pretty girl with the sky-blue eyes and gap-toothed smile. (That was simply packaging.) I thought of her as *Maggie May*. And *Maggie May* epitomized the look and feel, the smell and taste of…love.

Out in that bayou, dancing with her in my arms, I finally admitted to myself that I was ass over teakettle for her. Like a fruit fly, I'd buzzed around the notion for months, landing occasionally only to flit off again. But there was no more denying it.

Pulling her close, I swayed with her to the lilting melody of Archuleta's crooning tenor, reveling in the way she fitted against me like a puzzle piece clicking into place. There were no electrical storms on the horizon, and yet the air around us crackled with an expectant sort of energy.

I let my hand drift up her back until my thumb brushed along the top edge of her dress. I never knew skin could feel so satiny.

"Luc?" She tightened her grip on my waist. "Why did he leave? Was it something I did? Something I said? Did he not want to—" Her voice hitched on a sob, and the spell between us snapped as easily as the stick beneath the heel of my rented patent leather shoe.

"It's got nothing to do with you, Maggie May," I assured her.

"Then why, Luc?" She stopped dancing to hold me at arm's length. Her eyes were big and wet with unshed tears. "Why did he leave tonight of all nights?"

I swallowed and turned away, torn between my loyalty to Cash and my love for her. "He had to go. That's all I can say."

"W-will he come back?" Her gaze beseeched me.

I hugged her close and gave her the only truth I could. "I don't think so."

A terrible whimper escaped her then. All I could do was try my best to hold her together even as she fell apart. It was odd to want her for myself at the same time I wanted Cash to come home and stop her from hurting.

I have no recollection of how long we stayed there in that clearing, her crying her heart out and me hanging on to her for dear life. But eventually her tears subsided, and she heaved a deep sigh that sounded like resignation.

When she looked up at me, I used my thumbs to wipe the tears from her cheeks, marveling at the warmth of her, the softness of her, the vulnerability and strength of a sixteen-year-old girl on the cusp of womanhood.

"Luc?" Her voice was tremulous.

When I stared into her eyes, she must've seen the hunger in mine, the need I had spent so much time hiding.

"Luc, I—" She swallowed but didn't shake her head *no* when I bent toward her.

Slowly (so slowly I died a little with each passing second) I closed the distance between us. When I felt her hot breath brush my lips, I shuddered.

"Maggie May?" Every question in my head was wrapped up in those three syllables. In her *name*.

She began to tremble. With sorrow? With passion? I was too inexperienced to tell.

"I'm cold," she blurted, jerking from the circle of my arms and taking three steps backward. It felt like she reached inside my chest and took my heart with her.

In that moment, I knew.

She would never be mine.

"I'll run back to Smurf and grab my jacket," I told her, trying to be the gentleman my momma raised me to be despite my aching heart. I hoped that the few minutes it would take to make the round trip to the truck and back would be enough for me to come to terms with the loss of something I never even had. "You stay here."

With those three words, I sealed our fate.

CHAPTER THIRTY-THREE

Cash

Dear Cash,

The weatherman warned we should brace for a storm tonight. The rain isn't here just yet, but already the wind is crazy. That old pine tree growing beside my bedroom window keeps tapping on the glass, reminding me of all the times you climbed the silly thing.

How many hours did we spend talking with eight feet of air between us, me sitting on my windowsill and you clinging to the trunk of that tree? Through all those long, lazy nights, what in the world did we discuss? Can you remember? I can't. But I suppose we must have talked about everything and nothing at all.

That's the way of those kinds of conversations, isn't it? They don't seem important or particularly memorable at the time. But now I wish I could recall every word.

It's been two months since you left me. Two months since I had someone to talk to about my feelings, my fears, the nightmares that jolt me awake in the middle of the night.

All that seems to remain for me now is this pen and this paper and that pine tree outside my window. But to be honest, none of them are much company.

Lord, I'm lonely. Lonely like I used to be before I met you and Luc. So lonely I feel it in my bones. Do you know what that's like? Maybe not, because you have Luc there with you.

Sometimes I think I hate you for leaving me with nothing and no one. I hate you for it, and yet I still love you.
    Love, Maggie

I'm lucky. I've known true friendship and true love. Not everyone can say that.

So even though fate has kicked me in my ball sac with this whole head thing, I woke up this morning with a can-do attitude.

This will work. Everything I have planned *will* work. I just have to make sure Maggie understands a few things first.

For a moment, I allow myself to stand outside Bon Temps Rouler and watch her wipe down the bar. Her hair is pulled into a high ponytail and the silver band on her watch catches the morning light streaming in through the windows. It plays peekaboo with the tattoo on the inside of her wrist. The tiny memorial to the purity of our young and impulsive love.

Although, maybe it wasn't so impulsive. Maybe it was the opposite of impulsive because, after more than ten years, it still survives.

The thought has melancholy trying to sneak up on me, so I quickly square my shoulders and push into the bar. Or...at least I attempt to. The door is still locked.

Frowning, I check my watch. She should've opened ten minutes ago.

The rattle of the door handle catches her attention. She skirts the bar and heads toward me with a skip in her step.

Years ago, when the ice bucket challenge for ALS was a thing, I did my part and let Luc douse me. The shock of the icy water made me gasp and shiver. Her smile makes me feel the same way now.

After turning the dead bolt, she holds the door wide and flips the closed sign around until it reads *Entrez, C'est Ouvert*. The fancy French version of *Come in! We're open!*

"You're here early." Her unique New Orleans accent sounds particularly juicy this morning.

Never understood why people from up North sneer at the way folks from down South talk. It's like they think slow speech is an indication of a slow mind.

They're dead wrong, of course. The sleepy pace of conversation allows for thoughtfulness. And round, elongated vowels are soothing to the ear.

"Getting a late start, aren't you?" I step inside. The traditional smells of corner bars the world over accost me: booze, bleach, and fresh urinal cakes. The volume of the jukebox is turned down low so that the sound of Kermit Ruffins blowing his trumpet drifts through the air, sweet and soft as a memory.

My instinct is to kiss her, to take her in my arms and squeeze her tight. So I hasten toward a barstool.

"You know business hours are flexible here." She slips behind the bar. When she lifts a pot of freshly brewed coffee, I nod.

"You're telling me. Places seem to open late or close early with no rhyme or reason." I blow across the top of the joe she hands me until steam swirls in front of my eyes. It makes her image look slightly witchy.

With her black hair and angel eyes, I can *totally* picture her stirring a cauldron and casting spells over the hearts of unsuspecting men. She certainly beguiled me the first time I saw her. And she's been enchanting me ever since.

She shrugs. "I mean, sure, I get the need for consistency. And business is business. But more importantly, life is *life*. I don't understand folks who can't seem to grasp that."

"That's 'cause you were born and raised here."

"And thank the good Lord I was," she declares with emotion. "I don't think I'd have made it anywhere else."

"You'd have made it. You're tough."

Her expression remains doubtful. "I don't know. A couple of years back, I stayed with Eva up in Chicago for a few days.

She was there doing a photo shoot, and oh my gosh, Cash, there were so many *people*. Everyone seemed to have someplace to go and be in a gosh-darned hurry to get there. Every taxi driver was meaner than a mama wasp. And the *cursing*." She holds a hand to her heart as if her delicate sensibilities have been offended. "They drop the F-bomb like nobody's business. By the time I was finished having a conversation with someone, I felt like I'd been knocked into next week looking both ways for Sunday. When I got back from my vacation, I needed a vacation."

I chuckle. "If you think Chicago is bad, you should try New York City."

"No, thank you very much. I'm happy here in my soft, slow corner of the world."

Soft, slow corner of the world…

That pretty much sums up this city. It isn't ambitious. Not like Atlanta or LA or even Houston. It has no need to look outside itself for signs of progress. It is what it is and makes no excuses for it.

Taking a sip of coffee, I eye her over the rim of the cup. "Never think of leaving?"

She shakes her head. "I'm a hometown girl when you get right down to it. I like the familiar."

"It's one of the things I've always admired about you. You know who you are and where you want to be."

She studies me. "That means you're lucky too, right? You know exactly who you are. And you bought that Creole cottage, so you must know exactly where you want to be."

I neither agree nor disagree. Instead, I take another sip of coffee and welcome the warmth in my belly. The brisk wind on the walk over nipped at my nose and the tips of my ears. They still feel the bite.

"The weatherman said this cold snap is supposed to blow over by tomorrow," I say.

She blinks myopically. "And now we're talking about the weather? Next time, switch on your turn signal so I'm prepared to change lanes."

I grin. "My point is, I feel like this weather has kept me inside too much. I know we're supposed to wait until our brunch on Sunday to plan our next excursion, but I was wondering if you'd have time in the next couple of days to check something off the list."

She frowns. "Just me and you?"

"Shit no. This is a job for the Three Musketeers."

Her expression softens. But then she makes a face of regret. "I'm pulling a double tomorrow."

"What about Thursday?"

"I'm working the afternoon shift, and then I'm going with Jean-Pierre to the *fais do-do* his family is throwing for his uncle's sixty-fifth birthday."

I lived in New Orleans for six months before I learned a *fais do-do* was a Cajun dance party. It was a year before I was invited to one and realized exactly what that entailed.

A true *fais do-do* is a raucous event filled with belly-busting food, a band that inevitably includes one or two fiddles, Mason jars overflowing with home brew, and more foot-stomping and tall-tale-telling than a Yankee such as myself knows what to do with.

"And then on Friday, we're all meeting with your aunt," I say.

She lifts a brow. She's always had particularly talkative eyebrows, and right now they ask a question without words.

"Luc called me after he left your place last night," I explain. "He told me you green-lighted bringing Miss Bea into this."

"If he called you last night, then you understand why I was late getting started this morning. He and Jean-Pierre played music until almost two a.m. Actually..." She snaps her fingers and points at me. "He agreed to play at the *fais do-do*. It won't exactly be an excursion, but if you're there, then it'll kind of be like one.

We can dust off the rust that's grown on us these last few days. Let our hair down. Cut a rug."

"Stop." I hold up a hand. "Any more clichéd idioms and my brain will turn to mush and leak out through my ears."

She chuckles. "I'm serious. You should come."

I shrug. "Wouldn't feel right crashing the party without an invitation."

"Are you kidding? The more the merrier. Besides, Jean-Pierre's uncle will have a field day with your Jersey accent. He thinks anyone born north of the Mason-Dixon Line should be hogtied and shot. Or at the very least, teased to death. Give Uncle Homer a target to aim his wit at. Consider it your birthday gift to him."

I flatten my lips into a straight line. "Well, when you put it that way."

She reaches across the bar to pat my forearm. Her cool fingers set my skin on fire. "Come on. It'll be fun."

"Will there be jambalaya?" I ask.

"You can bet on it." She nods.

"And a table set up in the back with a bunch of grizzled old guys chewing tobacco and playing poker?"

"Of course."

"And an old woman with no teeth who'll get drunk and pinch my butt?"

"Wouldn't be a *fais do-do* without one of those."

"All right. I'll go."

"Good." She winks before grabbing the dish towel lying atop the bar and going to work polishing a pilsner glass.

Glancing out the window, I'm struck by the empty sidewalk. "Quiet this morning," I muse.

"It's too cold for the locals and too early for the tourists," she says.

My mind isn't really on the lack of foot traffic. It's on the second reason I headed here. No use putting it off any longer. "So, about the other night…"

Her hands fall still. When I don't immediately go on, she sets the pilsner glass aside and tosses the towel over her shoulder. "What about it?"

"I shouldn't have kissed you."

Her chin jerks back. Did I mention she has a particularly expressive chin too? "I seem to recall that *I* kissed *you*," she says.

"But I kissed you back."

"Which is pretty much what every girl hopes for in that situation."

"I shouldn't have."

Her frown deepens. "For heaven's sake, *why*?"

"Because..." I swallow. There's no easy way to say this. "I think it gave you the wrong impression."

Her expression is the facial equivalent of a chalkboard that's been wiped clean. "And what impression would that be? That you still want me?"

"No. I mean, yes. I mean, no. Dammit!" I'm more addled than that time I woke up with Luc's dick in my face.

We'd been bunked down in a mud hut seventy clicks from friendly territory. A deathstalker—an especially gnarly species of scorpion—had crawled into Luc's pants while he was sleeping. He woke up in time to shuck his drawers before the fucker could sting him, but his striptease in the tiny hut meant I had the dubious honor of getting up close and personal with his nightstick.

"You're an incredibly attractive woman, Maggie," I admit slowly. "But—"

"Do you still love me?" she interrupts.

"I..." The words strangle in my throat.

That's Magnolia May Carter for you. One minute, she's the picture of easy Southern manners. The next, she's in your face, demanding you cut the crap and give it to her straight.

"I mean..." I shake my head, my thoughts stumbling over themselves like they have two left feet. This isn't how I envisioned this conversation going. "Yes. I still love you. In fact, loving you was the easiest decision I ever made. You've always been the best thing about me."

A slow smile stretches her mouth and makes her eyes twinkle. There she is, my sparkly, shiny girl.

The ache in my heart translates to my head, and I reach for my flask. After adding a generous shot to my coffee, I take a long sip and try to arrange my thoughts into order.

"But that doesn't change anything," I mutter. "This thing with my head, it's—"

"We'll get through it."

I close my eyes. *We'll* get through it. *We.*

I have to stop this crazy train before it goes off the rails. "There's no *we* about it. It's *me*. I don't want you involved."

"Too bad. I already am." She grabs the dish towel and goes back to polishing. She might look like a sweet, pink cupcake, but she can be as stubborn as a jawbreaker.

"I mean with *me*," I clarify. "I don't want you involved with me. I don't want—"

The door bursts open, and Earl blows into the bar like he's been shot from a cannon.

"You're late," Maggie declares.

"Woke up this morning with my old bones frozen stiff." His mustache twitches with distaste. "This weather has me fit to be tied."

"It's supposed to warm up tomorrow." She pours him a cup of coffee, but hesitates with the half-and-half. "I hate to ask, but...are you back on dairy?"

"Yep." Earl pats his flat belly at the same time he hops atop his usual stool. "I been adding prunes to my diet for the last two weeks. It's been hit or miss for the most part. But they came on with a vengeance this morning and really got things moving. I swear, when I stood up from the toilet, I felt ten pounds lighter."

Maggie turns to me, and her expression is priceless. "This is my life," she says. "I can see you turning green with envy."

Despite my annoyance at Earl's ill-timed arrival, one corner of my mouth twitches.

Taking a sip of coffee, Earl closes his eyes and hums. "That's good enough to make you want to slap your granny." Then he pins me with a look. "So what brings you here this morning? Don't tell me you had the bad sense to stand Maggie up again."

"No, sir." I shake my head.

"Good to hear. I was beginning to think you ain't got enough brains to pour piss out of a boot."

Before I get a chance to respond, the door opens, and a quintet of tourists pushes in. They're all middle-aged women, bundled up as if a nor'easter is set to blow through.

I don't know what it is about this city, but you *feel* the cold here so much more than in other places.

"Brrr." The woman leading the pack shivers. She has that quintessential mom hairdo, a short brown bob that frames her face. "Please tell me you serve coffee." She looks at Maggie beseechingly.

Maggie holds up the pot. "Freshly brewed."

"Oh, thank God," Mom 'Do gushes. "Make mine Irish. I need a little hair of the dog."

My cell phone vibrates in my pocket, an indication that Luc has arrived at the house and is wondering where I am.

Damn. Hell. Piss. And shit. But it's not like I'm going to get a chance to talk with Maggie alone again anyway.

Taking out my cell, I shoot off a quick response to Luc. Then I wiggle the phone at her. "And that's my cue. Thanks for the coffee."

She looks up from arranging four mugs on the bar. "So I'll see you Thursday night?"

I nod. "Should I catch a ride with you or Luc?"

"I'm driving. I told Luc I'd be the DD since he's never sampled Uncle Homer's moonshine and is sure to get browbeaten into giving it a shot. Or *many* shots. Pick you up at six?"

"Looking forward to it."

The smile she gives me is so bright and sweet that I use the excuse of hopping from the barstool to look away from it.

"Leave your wallet at home!" she calls to my back as I head for the entrance. "You remember what happened last time we went to a *fais do-do*?"

"I lost sixty bucks at the card table," I admit with a put-upon sigh. "In my defense, those old men cheated."

"They always do." She waves as I push through the door.

Turning up the collar on my leather jacket, I walk by the front window and peek inside to see her laughing at something one of the women is saying. I've never known anyone so animated. Or anyone who seems to possess the ability to listen with all her senses. I could spend all day watching her.

Unfortunately, I have a list as long as my arm of things I need to do. Not the least of which is coming up with a way to dissuade her from thinking we can pick up where we left off. You know, since my idea to simply talk her out of it just crashed and burned like the Hindenburg.

CHAPTER THIRTY-FOUR

Maggie

There are two kinds of folks in this old world. Those who know how to throw down, and those who don't.

In my experience, Cajuns in general, and Jean-Pierre's relatives in particular, fall into the first category. This is the third Marchand family *fais do-do* I've been to, and it's as boisterous and rowdy as the first two. Maybe more so since this one's a celebration of Uncle Homer, who happens to be one of the more colorful characters in a clan chockablock *full* of colorful characters.

After the initial howdy dos, after he blew out the candles on his hummingbird cake, and after everyone filled their bellies with jambalaya, butter beans, and corn fritters, Homer cornered Cash by the beer coolers lined up along one wall of the barn.

He started out giving Cash what-for for having the bad sense to have been born a Yankee. Then he launched into a joke that went something like, "Know why Northerners are like hemorrhoids? Because they're a pain in the butt when they come down, and it's always a relief when they go back up." And he ended it all by listing the ancestors he lost to enemy fire during the Civil War—although, he kept referring to it as the War of Northern Aggression.

At one point, Cash looked at me with big Bambi eyes and mouthed, *Help me.*

I shook my head and told him, "I warned you."

Now the band—including Luc—is wailing on the small wooden stage built into the corner. Forty or so members of the Marchand family are out on the dance floor, which is nothing more than a handful of plywood sheets nailed together and covered in sawdust. And Uncle Homer is sitting beside me, swinging me through the branches of his family tree.

"Now, ya see dat one der?" He points to a woman in tight leopard-print Lycra pants and a red polka-dot shirt. I wish I could say her outfit is the zaniest thing about her, but her dance moves hold that title. While everyone else is two-stepping, she's doing a pretty mean moonwalk. "She's my brother Leroy's youngest daughter. Poor woman done gone plumb crazy on account of a bad batch of moonshine her old man cooked up a coupla years ago."

"Please." Homer's friend Isaac, who's sitting on the other side of me, rolls his eyes. Considering he has a beard that belongs to a *Duck Dynasty* cast member, his eyes are the only part of his face I can actually see. "She was lookin' at crazy in da rearview mirror *long* before dat business with da moonshine."

"Mmm, maybe." Homer shrugs.

"Ain't no maybe about it," Isaac insists.

"Moving on." Homer hitches his chin toward a group of men standing inside the open barn door. All of them seem to be eyeing the bevy of pickup trucks parked outside. From this vantage point, I can't tell if they're appreciating the shotgun racks mounted on the back windows or the tailgates full of bumper stickers with sayings like, *Mawmaw told me you gotta suck da head!* and *Honk if you love Jesus!*

About thirty miles outside the city, Jean-Pierre's granddaddy's land is set way back in the middle of nowhere. It's accessed by a five-mile dirt road through a loblolly pine forest, but once you break into the clearing where the homestead sits, you're presented with a charming vignette. There's a two-story wood-sided farmhouse painted bright white, two acres of well-manicured lawn, and this massive barn that doesn't seem to perform any function except to hold the family's parties.

"Next up is da man in da overalls," Homer says.

"Which one?" I laugh. About a third of the men here look like they popped out of an episode of that old variety TV show *Hee Haw*.

"Dat one." Homer points. "Da one dat looks like he fell on hard times from one hell of a great height."

"Da one as ugly as a three-eyed pig," Isaac adds unhelpfully.

"The one missing his two front teeth?" I ask.

"Nah. Not him. Da one next to him with da stumpy arm and da bowed legs."

"Yep." I nod. "Okay, who's he?"

"Dat's my cousin's second husband. Her first husband done gone to glory after an accident on a shrimp boat, but dat's a story for another time. Anyway, dis here husband's name is Armand. He lost dat arm to a gator back in ninety-two. Biggest damn beast you ever did see."

"Never trust a one-armed man." Isaac shakes his head vehemently.

I've noticed he likes to offer these bombastic statements at regular intervals. So far I've heard him say, *Always check da back seat for rattlers.* And, *Der be more dan one way to skin a cat, but dat don't mean you should.* And my favorite, *Ain't nobody in New York City worth a fart in da wind.*

"Oh, I don't know," Homer says now. "Armand ain't so bad once you get past dat mean streak of his."

I glance at Armand askance.

"And dat's it for me and mine," Homer declares. "Da rest of dese fools are friends, or friends of friends. And speakin' of, tell ol' Homer 'bout your men. Which one ya love, *mais* yeah? Dat one up on da stage? Or dat one losing all his money to my kinfolk?"

I glance at Luc. He's in heaven as he strums and picks, keeping time to the music with a tapping toe. His dark hair is matted to his forehead with sweat and curling in the most beguiling way. It seems every woman in the place, from seven to seventy, is raptly watching him play.

Then there's Cash. Despite my warning, he's once again found his way to the poker table. If the grin he's wearing is any indication, he's being taken for all he's worth. But he's having a heck of a good time doing it.

My heart warms at the sight of them both having fun. If there were ever two men who deserved a little happiness, it's them.

Obviously, I've been quiet for too long. Isaac nudges me. "You can tell us if it's both, *cher*. We don't judge."

I slap his shoulder. "What is it with you men of a certain age thinking I'm the type of girl to go in for that sort of thing?"

His beard sets at an obstinate angle. "Who you callin' a man of a certain age?"

I laugh. "If you must know, I *do* love them both."

"See?" Isaac leans around me to grin at Homer. "Told ya. Pay up. Twenty bucks." He sticks out his palm.

I smack it away. "You didn't let me finish. It's *platonic* love for the one onstage. I'm *in* love with the one getting fleeced by a bunch of Marchands."

It feels good to say that. To admit it out loud. When I told Eva and Jean-Pierre about finally figuring out why Cash left ten years ago and when I made the decision that instead of forgetting about the past and just being his friend I was determined to jump in whole hog, Eva muttered, *Be careful. Sometimes you get what you want only to find out it's not what you need.*

But that was just Eva being Eva. I'll let her worry about me all she wants because I'm done worrying about myself. I'm in. All the way. Even if Cash seems to need more convincing.

"Huh," Homer muses now.

"Huh what?" I frown at him.

"Me, I would've said it was da other way 'round."

"Really?" I blink, surprised. "Why?"

"Dunno." He shrugs. "Just a vibe. Guess my antennas got crossed." And then, in a sudden change of subject, he extends his hand. "Let's dance. Don't think 'bout sayin' no to me neither. Not on my birthday."

"Why would I say no to the best-looking man in this place?"

He wiggles his shaggy eyebrows. "I took one look at you da first time Jean-Pierre brought you 'round and said to myself, 'Homer, dat der is a woman with impeccable taste.'"

He drags me out on the dance floor and proves that age is only a number. Homer can scoot a boot with the best of them. An hour and eight dance partners later, I'm sweaty, my feet ache, and I'm happier than I've been since Luc told me his plan to go on the offensive with George Sullivan.

Speaking of Luc...he's left the stage and is surrounded by a group of women over by the dessert table.

I look toward the poker table for Cash, but he's glaringly absent. No doubt he ran out of money and the Marchands ejected him from the game. Walking over to the cooler stocked with water bottles, I let my eyes take a journey around the barn, my brow wrinkling when I discover he's nowhere to be found.

Probably headed inside the house for a bathroom break, I tell myself.

Myself answers back, *Maybe. But the last time you saw him, he had a Mason jar full of moonshine.*

I wait a couple of minutes, draining the water bottle and trying not to let it show that my concern is growing like a wisteria vine, all thick and twisted. Then I can't stand it a second longer. I have to go in search of him.

Stepping outside, I'm struck by the beauty of the night. The weatherman got it right. The cold snap moved on, and now the warm breeze wicks the sweat from my skin.

The smell of the pine forest is tart and dry inside my nose, and the sky overhead is filled with a million stars. They shine brighter here, away from the city lights, and I'm reminded of the dance Luc and I shared under a sky that looked just like this one.

What would've happened had I let him kiss me?

He'd been so intense, so...*focused*. And I remember being confused because he was *Luc*. Part of me had wondered if he was simply taking pity on me, trying to be a good friend and make me feel pretty and wanted. Another part of me couldn't help imagining what it would be like to kiss him.

Soft and soulful like his poetry? Studied and intense like his guitar playing?

But I shoved that part of myself aside because I recognized it was the selfish part. The vengeful part. The part that wanted to hurt Cash for hurting me, and I could never use Luc that way.

Stepping from the comforting circle of his arms, I told him, "I'm cold," even though that was the furthest thing from the truth. Sweat slicked the back of my neck, and my heart punched my breastbone like a frightened fist.

I thought I saw relief in his face when he told me to stay put while he ran back to Smurf to fetch his rented tuxedo jacket. But knowing what I do now, I realize that maybe what I saw was resignation.

Watching him disappear into the trees, I recall being relieved, because it meant I had a moment to gather my wits. But my relief was cut short when a disembodied voice drifted to me from somewhere in the woods. "Didn't anyone ever tell you the swamp is no place for a girl?"

"Who's there?" The full moon, which had seemed plenty bright when Luc and I were dancing, didn't penetrate the canopy. "Come out where I can see you!"

My voice sounded tremulous instead of strident. I hated that.

"With pleasure." A dark shadow disengaged from the forest, and the first thing I noticed was a set of broad shoulders. The second thing was the slight sway of the figure, like the ground beneath his feet wasn't quite steady. And the third thing was the change in the air.

Danger!

Every fiber of my being recognized it.

Unfortunately, at sixteen I hadn't learned to trust my instincts, and I was naïve about the terrible things men could do to women. Even the whispered rumors coming out of St. Bernard Parish didn't seem real enough to make me turn tail and run, or climb the nearest tree, or scream bloody murder. In my mushy teenage brain, violence was something that happened to people on the news or in movies. It didn't happen to *real* people like me.

Lifting my chin, I demanded, "What are you doing here, Dean?"

The girls at school swooned over him. With dark hair, a square jaw, and deep-set eyes, he embodied the teenage dream. Plus, he had that quintessential state-champ quarterback's physique. None of that interested me, however, because beneath his pretty packaging, he was snake-mean all the way through.

"The better question is, what are *you* doing here?" he said with an ugly twist of his lips. "Sucking that bayou bastard's dick? If so, I'm next."

His words repulsed me and sullied the sweetness of the friendship Luc and I shared.

"Go away," I told him, standing my ground even though he took a step toward me. He wore the look of a predator searching for prey. I knew if I ran, he would chase me. "Luc will be back any second and—"

"And until then," he cut me off, "you and I can have some fun. Come on." He extended a hand toward me. It was a big, square paw, and for the first time in my life, I realized how small I was and how that made me intrinsically vulnerable. "Come dance with me like you were dancing with him."

"You were watching us?"

He sneered drunkenly. "You looked so *sweet* staring up at him, and so...slutty. Here we all thought you were this Goody Two-shoes hiding behind the bravado of that dick hole from New

41

Jersey while stringing along that poor son of a whore from the swamp. But all this time, you been banging them both, haven't you?"

The accusation stung even though it wasn't true. "No." I shook my head. "You have no idea what you're talking—"

"If you're giving it away to both of them," he interrupted me again, "I don't see why you shouldn't give me some too."

I was a split second too late in realizing his intention. I'd barely taken a step backward before he lunged. He grabbed my shoulder in a cruel grip, but I managed to twist away.

And then, even knowing he would chase me, I ran.

I couldn't stop myself.

I started toward the house where Luc's truck was parked, but had to zigzag in a new direction when Dean gained on me. I could feel the heat of his dank breath on my neck. His inhuman snarls were loud in my ears as he pursued me into the trees.

The sticks and stones and sharp-bladed grass stabbed into the bottoms of my bare feet. Tree limbs and bushes snagged the hem of my dress. And the dark water of the swamp glistened under the moonlight.

I ran toward it.

But before I could plunge into the dangerous water, he grabbed my arm and flung me to the ground as easily as a cranky child tossing aside a rag doll. I landed on my back. Lights flashed in front of my eyes as my breath was knocked out of me.

Still, I had the wherewithal to roll over and scramble onto my hands and knees. That's as far as I got, however, before Dean landed on top of me, flattening me to the ground and grinding my face into the dirt and leaves. When he flipped me over, I was able to suck in enough oxygen to whimper.

It was a weak sound. A sound of surrender.

That pissed me off. With anger galvanizing my airways, I raked in a lungful of night air and screamed for all I was worth.

CHAPTER THIRTY-FIVE

Cash

Dear Cash,

I got an afternoon job scooping ice cream at this cute place on Magazine Street. I like having something that occupies my mind because...well...ever since you left, it tends to go to a dark place unless I'm distracted.

Did Luc tell you what happened? Did he tell you that I...

No. I won't put it into words even here in this private letter that nobody will read, including you. I'll keep it locked up tight inside like I promised I would. And I'll pray to God it doesn't eat me alive.

Anyway, back to my new job. There are two things I really like about it. The first is I get to ride the streetcar to and from work. Considering George Sullivan has his police officers pulling me over and giving me a ticket almost every time I get behind the wheel, having an alternative mode of transportation is key. The second is I get to spend time with the old folks and the young kids who come in for sundaes and single scoops. It's so nice hearing small talk and big stories. It's like, for a little while, I'm part of their lives.

Which means, for a little while, I can forget about my own.

Wow. That sounded self-pitying, didn't it?

I don't mean it that way. I just mean, it feels good to pretend, even for a second or two, that night never happened. To pretend I'm not weighed down knowing I dragged Luc into my *mess. To pretend I'm not lonely and scared. And don't hate me for saying this, Cash, but it even feels good to pretend I don't miss you.*

Love, Maggie

There are so many lines in life.

There's the line of people waiting to get into Walmart on Black Friday. The checkout line at the grocery store on a Saturday morning. The dotted line on legal documents showing you where to sign. And all those pesky invisible lines.

The problem with *them* is that sometimes you don't know you've crossed one until you're standing on the other side. At that point, it's too damned late.

Last night I stepped over a line.

Not sure how. Not sure which one. Most of what happened after the poker game is a blur. But I seem to remember a brunette with a big rack and then a look of horror on Maggie's face.

Even though she and Luc showed up at my house this morning at the prearranged time, they've barely spoken two words to me. Considering my head feels like a watermelon that's been cleaved in two, I should be okay with that. Unfortunately, my mind keeps touching on that look on Maggie's face.

I want so much to take out my flask and down the contents, but it was overindulgence that led them to give me the silent treatment, so I satisfy myself by raking in a deep breath of damp fall air.

Luc dropped Smurf off at a shop in the Tremé neighborhood for an oil change and a lube, so we're riding the St. Charles streetcar to Miss Bea's house. Maggie is sitting beside me on the old-fashioned wooden bench, doing her best impression of a two-by-four. And when I glance at Luc, seated in front of us, I'm met with a view of his tightly hitched shoulders.

Okay, then. Breaking the ice is up to me.

"Either of you plan on telling me what the hell happened last night?" I ask. "Or would you both prefer to continue giving me the cold shoulder until I die from frostbite?"

Luc spins in his seat and tries to burn a hole through my forehead. Right. So his shoulder might be cold, but there's fire in his eyes.

"You don't remember?" He snorts. "Well, that's convenient."

"Not for me," I protest. "Since I can't recall what happened, I don't know where to begin my apology. And I get the impression a blanket 'I'm sorry' isn't going to cut it."

"Lemme roll out the timeline for you." He lifts a finger. "Sunday night, Maggie May tells you she still loves you and the two of you snog." I roll my eyes at the Harry Potter patter, but that's only to hide the impact of his words. I've been replaying Maggie's confession over and over in my mind and falling asleep every night with the taste of her lips lingering on my tongue. It's been torture. "And then on *Thursday* night"—he lifts a second finger—"barely four days later, she finds you out behind a barn, gorked outta your mind on rotgut and feeling up some chick with boobs as big as my head."

The milk I drank this morning to try to ease my woozy stomach curdles. I turn to Maggie. To my surprise, her expression isn't accusing. It's kind.

"To be fair"—she searches my bloodshot eyes—"you weren't feeling the woman up so much as using her to *stand* up."

Her defense of me makes everything so much worse.

"Maggie..." I blow out a shaky breath. "I don't remember any of that." Maybe I should stop there. But I can't pass up this opportunity. "And I'm sorry if seeing me with that woman hurt you. But I told you that kiss on Sunday night was a mistake."

"Good God Almighty." Luc looks at me in slack-jawed disbelief. "Are you kidding me? Is your dumb bone connected to your stupid bone?"

I lift my chin and stare him down. "The last thing I want is to hurt Maggie." I turn to her to reiterate. "The last thing I want is to hurt you. But this thing with my head is—"

"I emailed the best neurosurgeon in the country," she blurts, making me blink in confusion. "I've asked him to look at your scans and records and stuff." She grabs my hand. Her grip feels frantic. "I'm waiting to hear back."

I close my eyes, unable to look at the hope and desperation in hers. "You shouldn't have done that," I grit between clenched teeth.

Fuck it. I need a drink.

She watches me uncap my flask and let the Gentleman Jack slide down my throat. "There's *got* to be something more that can be done for you," she insists after I wipe the back of my hand over my mouth.

"There's not," I assure her. "You heard the doctors."

"I heard them. But they don't know everything. You haven't tried—"

"I *have* tried!" I realize I'm shouting when the guy across the way turns a disgruntled look on me. "Maggie." I squeeze her hand. "Thank you. Thank you for trying. But this is me now. This is as good as it gets. And when you and Luc hassle me about my prognosis, all it does is makes me remember that I'm broken, that I'm so much less than I should be."

"Oh, Cash."

I have to look out the window to escape the pity on her face. We're almost to our stop. Thank God. I want this conversation to be over. I *need* it to be over. But not before I make sure she understands.

"We can't have what we had," I say after turning back to her. "We can't be what we were."

Her jaw sets at an obstinate angle. "We could if you'd stop feeling sorry for yourself and pull your head out of your ass."

That makes my lips twitch. But I immediately sober. Ha! *Sober?* As if. "I'm serious, Maggie."

"So am I, Cash."

"We're *friends*."

"Of course we are."

I search her face. Usually, I can read her like an open book. But she's closed herself off. Shuttered her thoughts behind a blank expression.

Before I can say anything else, the streetcar screeches to a stop—I wince because my brain vigorously protests the noise. When Luc and Maggie make their way out, I manage to follow them.

"You're an idiot," Luc grumbles once we cross the street. His face reminds me of the landslide that brought down the side of the mountain in Afghanistan.

"Never claimed otherwise." I flash him a shit-eating grin that I hope looks more real than it feels.

As we head up the street toward Maggie's aunt's house, I recall something I read once. Apparently, it takes seven years to replace every cell in the human body. Which means we're a completely new organism every seven years. Different. Changed.

Despite my doctor's dour predictions, I've been using that bit of trivia to hold on to a glimmer of hope. Hope that my broke-ass brain cells might somehow repair themselves. Hope that all the good and wonderful things in life could still be mine.

Hope that there might be a way for me to have Maggie.

But it's time for me to let go of that hope.

It's the only way she will.

CHAPTER THIRTY-SIX

Maggie

The most powerful motivation is rejection.

Cash doesn't know me very well if he thinks I'll give up on him without a fight. If he thinks I'll give up on *us* just because this problem with his head means things won't be easy. Once I'm in, I'm *in*.

He wants to be friends?

Fine. I'll be his friend. I'll be so friendly he won't know what to do with himself.

Hiding a secret smile, I ring the doorbell before turning the knob and stepping inside Aunt Bea's house.

"Who the Sam Hill is that?" Auntie June calls from somewhere upstairs.

"How am I supposed to know?" Aunt Bea hollers back. "And stop caterwauling at me from the upper floor!"

My mouth twitches as Aunt Bea rounds the corner from the library and stops when she sees us gathered inside the front door. "Oh my lands!" She presses a hand to her skinny chest. "The skin I just jumped out of landed somewhere in Mississippi."

I'm quick to apologize. "Sorry, Aunt Bea. I didn't mean to scare you."

"Why are you ringing the pea-pickin' bell like some stranger?" Auntie June demands from the landing. Her thermal shirt and green cotton overalls tell me she's already been gardening this morning. No doubt digging up her fall bulbs to save and replant for next year.

"I thought since I brought company with me, I should signal our arrival," I say.

"Well, so you've signaled. Come in all the way and close the door behind you. You're letting out all the good air." Auntie June makes her way down the stairs, white-knuckling the handrail. She's getting unsteady on her feet, and it makes my heart hurt.

Losing the people we love is life's greatest injustice.

Cash is quick to skirt me and meet her at the bottom step. He places her hand in the crook of his arm and dutifully presents his cheek when she motions for it.

Her kiss is loud and smacking. She licks her lips and chuckles. "You smell like a distillery, and I can taste the alcohol coming out of your pores. What'd you get up to last night, Cassius?"

"A *fais do-do* at Jean-Pierre's family's place," I'm quick to say, determined to make light of the fact that he looks like a roadkilled raccoon. The circles under his eyes are so big and dark, when I first saw him this morning, I thought he'd gotten into another fight with his dad.

"Well, then, I'm not sure *he* should be the one escorting me," Auntie June says. "With the arthritis in my knees giving me fits on account of all these changes in the weather, we're both likely to end up face-first on the rug. Dance on over here, Lucien. Let me kiss your face and then you can take my other arm."

Luc is in the process of bussing Aunt Bea's cheek, but he's quick to do as instructed. Once Auntie June has a man on either side, she glances up at them and whistles.

"Even hungover, y'all are still finer than a frog's hair." She wiggles her eyebrows at me and hitches her chin toward the masculine arms she's clinging to. "See, honey? Getting old has its perks."

"Auntie June," I scold playfully, "you're a terrible flirt. Were you always this way?"

"*Yes*," Aunt Bea answers before Auntie June can. "Now, Maggie, you said on the phone y'all needed to ask me some questions. Are these questions the front parlor sort? Or should we head into my office?"

"How about we go into the kitchen instead?" Auntie June suggests. "I made some fresh-brewed sun tea yesterday, and I think we have some leftover black bottom pecan pie from Galatoire's."

Luc's stomach rumbles so loudly Aunt Bea chuckles. "I think that settles it." She turns toward the hallway leading to the kitchen.

We haven't taken more than a few steps before Auntie June remarks, "Boy howdy. Those Cajuns sure know how to party, don't they? Makes me miss my Jack."

When I glance at her over my shoulder, I see she has a dreamy, faraway look in her eye. I've been told Auntie June's husband was as ornery and jolly and Cajun as they come.

One of my favorite family videos is of her son's eighteenth birthday. It's grainy and shaky—like home videos were back then—but the three-minute clip shows Good Time Jack in middle age, still fit and handsome and manning the grill. In one hand he has a set of tongs. He uses them to turn ears of corn. His other hand is around young Auntie June's waist. And even though he's wearing an apron that reads: Kiss me, I'm Cajun, it's Auntie June who keeps getting the sugar. He can barely keep his lips off her. Every thirty seconds or so, he smooches her cheek or the top of her head, and she absolutely glows from his easy affection. Throughout the entire video, they're smiling ear to ear, so obviously head over heels in love even after two kids and two decades of marriage.

"I wish I'd met him," I tell her.

"Me too, honey. Me too."

We continue down the long hallway with its expensive wainscoting and rows of black-and-white photos of family members long dead. When we step into the kitchen, the comforts of time and place, home and hearth wrap around me. Exposed-brick walls, copper pots and pans hanging from hooks, huge ceiling beams, Spanish-tile floors, and wooden countertops that have been scrubbed so often they're as soft as silk pay homage to the history of this house. The only nods to modernization Aunt Bea allowed in here are the appliances and the island she had built in the center of the room.

Auntie June bustles toward the refrigerator, and Aunt Bea motions for us to grab the stools pushed up against the island. She doesn't join us. Instead, she remains standing. After folding her manicured hands atop the countertop, she says, "Something tells me we should forgo the small talk and get right down to it."

She's always been a shrewd woman. She's had to be. Her husband left her with a not-so-small fortune to manage. And with great wealth comes great swindlers. Over the years, plenty have tried to scam her out of her millions. None has managed to get as much as a dime.

Just like her, Luc doesn't hold back. "Maggie May and I are in trouble, Miss Bea."

Auntie June stops filling glasses with Louisiana Kool-Aid, more commonly known as sweet tea, and demands, "What kind of trouble?"

"The *worst* kind." Luc makes a face. "The superintendent of the New Orleans Police Department blames us for the disappearance of his son."

Hearing the words aloud makes my mouth go dry.

"What?" Auntie June squawks. "Why in tarnation would he do that?"

"Because of me," Cash is quick to admit. "Sullivan never forgave me for standing up for Maggie and putting a hurt on his precious boy out behind the school gymnasium. I didn't just stomp Dean's face in, I stomped his pride in too. Which means I stomped his father's pride in by extension. Sullivan would love to see me behind bars for that. But since I have an airtight alibi for the night Dean disappeared, he's going after Maggie and Luc. He knows taking them down would hurt me worse than going down myself. And he's cooked up some crazy scenario where I held a grudge against Dean and had Luc and Maggie do my dirty work for me by doing away with the dickhead out in the swamp. Uh...excuse my French."

"Sweet Jesus on the john," Auntie June whispers.

Aunt Bea is more acerbic. "The nut did not fall far from the tree when it came to Dean Sullivan."

"Some crazy scenario is one thing," Auntie June insists. "Proof is quite another. I'm assuming he doesn't have any?"

Aunt Bea and Auntie June know I was at the same party as Dean the night he disappeared and that Sullivan has pulled me in for questioning over the years regarding my recollections of that night. They didn't see me come in after prom, but they know I jumped straight in the shower, and then stood in my robe as I burned my dress in the fire pit outside.

They think I did that because I was righteously pissed off at Cash for standing me up—and truthfully, even had that bad business in the swamp not happened, I probably *would* have burned the dress. Still, that rise in Auntie June's voice makes me wonder if they've ever suspected anything. Is it possible I didn't hide the bruises as well as I thought I did?

"Sullivan's got squat because there's nothing there," Luc says. "But we all know he won't bat a lash at fabricating what he needs."

"Lord have mercy." Auntie June's hands are shaking as she finishes pouring the teas and slides them across the island countertop toward us.

I take a quick drink, hoping it'll wet my cotton mouth.

"Why now?" Aunt Bea asks. She's fingering the pearls around her neck. It's the only indication she's agitated. "Why wait over a decade before coming after you?"

"Sullivan hoped Cash and I would bite the dust over in Afghanistan," Luc explains. "He figured that was better than the two of us sitting here in a nice, cushy jail cell. But instead of getting our heads blown off by the Taliban, we turned back up, whole and hale."

"So now he's after his own warped brand of justice," Auntie June muses.

"Or so we've been told," Cash says.

"By whom?" One sleek, gray eyebrow climbs Aunt Bea's forehead.

"My father," Cash admits. "He was good enough to pay me a visit and advise me to keep my distance from Luc and Maggie. You know, so I wouldn't take the fall with them and put a blight on our family name."

My aunts are silent. While Aunt Bea is pretty good at hiding her emotions, Auntie June is not. She looks like she's sucking on a lemon.

"Go ahead and say what you're thinking, Miss June," Cash tells her. "I'm sure it's not half as bad as what *I'm* thinking."

"Your daddy and George Sullivan are both egg-sucking dogs," she snarls. "But in your case"—she takes Cash's hand—"the nut *did* fall far from the tree."

"Thank you, Miss June." His voice sounds misty. "It means a lot to hear you say that."

"Simply speakin' the truth, honey pie." She grins at him affectionately.

Aunt Bea shakes her head. "I'm confused, Cash. If George Sullivan thinks you had it out for Dean and were the one behind his disappearance, then why on God's green earth is he still bosom buddies with your father? And why would your father remain friends with Sullivan if Sullivan thinks you're responsible for what happened to Dean? Seems like it'd be an awful conflict of interest between them."

"Not when you realize they share a mutual hatred of me," Cash says.

I cringe at the thought of the deep psychological scar he must bear knowing his only living parent loathes him.

Auntie June's rosy cheeks bleach of color. "How in the world can a man hate his own child?"

Cash shrugs. "You got me. Maybe because I remind him of my mother? Maybe because he never wanted a kid in the first place, or because he was born with a bitter heart that finds pleasure in others' pain? I gave up trying to figure him out years ago."

"What do you need from me?" Aunt Bea gets back down to business.

Luc twists his lips. "Before I get 'round to the asking part, lemme first say I know you gotta lot of pull in the city, but that's only 'cause folks admire and respect you. So don't feel like you hafta answer my questions if it's gonna hurt your standing within the community."

Aunt Bea bats the notion away. "If you know of a way I can help Maggie, then I'll do whatever it takes."

Aunt Bea looks like an ice queen, but she's got a heart of melted butter. There's a lump in my throat when I give her a shaky smile. "Thank you, Aunt Bea."

"No thanks necessary, my sweet girl. Family is family. Luc"— she turns back to him—"get to asking."

He immediately launches into the heart of what brought us out today. "I don't think it's any secret that to keep his job through one scandal after another, Sullivan has been blackmailing some of the more influential citizens of New Orleans into supporting his reappointments."

Aunt Bea's gaze sharpens. "The folks you're talking about may have some skeletons they want kept in the closet, which is how Sullivan is able to get them in a bind, but having skeletons in the closet and being bad people aren't one and the same. These are good folks."

He pulls a face. "I don't doubt it, Miss Bea. And the last thing I want is to hurt anyone. But the only way I can see to stop Sullivan from coming after me and Maggie May is if I bring him down first. And the only way I reckon he can be brought down is if some of the people he's been blackmailing go to the authorities about it. I'm hoping they only need some coaxing."

Even before Luc is finished speaking, Aunt Bea is shaking her head. "They won't agree to have their secrets exposed just because you ask them."

"They might if we promise their secrets will *remain* secrets," I say. "If we can find a way to bring Sullivan down without outing them."

"And how do you plan to do that?"

"With the help of the police."

She scoffs. "No one trusts the police, because no one knows which of the officers are under Sullivan's thumb."

"I know one," I'm quick to say. "Rory Ketchum. You met him and his wife, Jackie, and their two little girls at the Rex parade two Mardi Gras ago, remember?"

"Twins, right?" Aunt Bea's eyes narrow in memory. "They were wearing matching yellow dresses with about a hundred braids in their hair all secured with sweet little duck barrettes."

"That's them. And Rory's told me on more than one occasion that he thinks George Sullivan is lower than a snake's belly in a wagon rut. He's discreet. You can bet on it. And he also knows who's in Sullivan's pocket and who isn't. He can help us find the right people to go to with any information folks give us."

Aunt Bea fingers her pearls again. "I suppose it could work. But..." She turns to Cash. "Everyone knows your daddy and Sullivan are as thick as thieves. They'll never agree to anything if you're the one doing the asking."

A look of disgust passes over Cash's face. "Damned by my own blood."

"I'm not saying it's fair." Her expression is full of sympathy. "I'm only saying it's true. You need to let Luc and Maggie be the ones to approach them."

Luc pulls out his cell phone and slides it to Aunt Bea. "The names, if you don't mind, Miss Bea," he says. "I'll memorize your list and then delete it."

She takes the phone, but hesitates before typing. "You understand I don't know anything with complete certainty. Everything I've heard is through the grapevine."

"Give us a few strings to pull," he assures her. "Maybe it'll be enough to unravel Sullivan's web."

She takes a deep breath and starts typing.

To lessen the tension, Auntie June dishes up slices of pie and pushes them our way.

Usually, I wouldn't have much of an appetite after this conversation, but black bottom pecan pie from Galatoire's isn't your average fare. This stuff would've tempted Gandhi to break his fast. Forking a bite into my mouth, I close my eyes as the sweet, nutty flavor explodes on my tongue.

"This here pie's got me thinking on Thanksgiving," Auntie June says around a mouthful. "What're you boys planning for the holiday? You going to see your momma up in Shreveport, Luc?"

"No, ma'am." He shakes his head. "She's coming down here to see me and Cash."

"Is she now? Well, isn't that nice. And where will she be staying?"

"Out at the swamp house with me."

Aunt Bea looks mortified. "Won't that be cramped?"

Luc laughs. "There used to be *three* of us living out there, Miss Bea. We managed just fine."

"Well, I think y'all should come here for Thanksgiving dinner at least," Auntie June declares. "Bea and I would love to have you, especially seeing as how I always cook way too much food."

"It's true," Aunt Bea mutters at the same time I say, "She does."

Auntie June dons her most persuasive expression, all twinkling blue eyes and wrinkled cheeks. "What do you say?" she cajoles.

"Well, I don't rightly know what Momma has planned," Luc equivocates. "But I'll run it by her and see what she says."

"Do that." Auntie June nods.

"There." Aunt Bea hands Luc's phone back to him. "Those are the folks I've heard talked about in connection with supporting Sullivan's appointments. Take them all with a grain of salt."

"Thank you, Miss Bea." Luc flashes his dimples, and darned if my aged aunt doesn't color up like a schoolgirl.

"Yes, thank you, Aunt Bea." I reach across the island to give her bony hand a heartfelt squeeze.

She smiles, but it slips from her lips like they're greasy. "I hate this for you, honey. I hate everything about it."

I don't sugarcoat my response. "I hate it too, Aunt Bea. More than you know."

CHAPTER THIRTY-SEVEN

Luc

Dear Luc,

School has started again, which means the late-season azaleas and camellias are blooming. Aunt Bea's entire backyard is festooned in fuchsia flowers that remind me of that horrible hot-pink T-shirt Cash wore the week after we first met him.

Do you remember? It read, "I'm from Jersey. Go fuck yourself!"

The principal nearly had a stroke. She made him turn it inside out, but you could still read it if you squinted.

Funny, at the time I couldn't understand why he was always raising such a ruckus. Now I kind of miss it. Without the ruckus, I have time to think.

When I think, I worry.

I worry about where you are. I worry if you've been sent to some faraway place filled with men who want to kill you. I worry the only reason you're there, the only reason you felt you had to follow Cash, is because of what happened.

By the way, the kids at school look at me funny. Like they're waiting on me to... I don't know. Confess to something? Break down into tears? Run screaming through the hall, tearing out my hair?

I feel like a fish in a glass bowl most days.

But I'll keep on keeping on. I won't let the depression I was suffering from two years ago get a foothold on me again.

I never told you about that, did I? Well, I'm telling you about it now, even though I'm ashamed to admit it. I was contemplating the worst, Luc. Then you came along and saved me.

You're a hero. You're MY hero.

And that worries me too. Because heroes do heroic things by putting themselves in dangerous situations.

Wherever you are, please don't think you need to be a hero. Please...just be safe.

Forever and always, Maggie May

Sometimes, to be a lover and writer of words is to know the limitations of the language.

Take the word *love*, for instance. It's four little letters that don't begin to encapsulate the enormity of the emotion.

There are other words that are similar. *Pain, hate, faith.* All of them are too small to embody the entirety of their meaning. But I think *love* is the worst. Love is massive and staggering. It's convoluted and complex.

Just look at the three of us.

On the one hand, I want to strangle Cash for telling Maggie that kiss was a mistake and all he wants is to be friends. I love her, and I don't want anything to hurt her. But I also want to hug the life out of him and tell him to stop pushing her away because I know that more than anything in the world, he loves her. He just won't allow himself to have her on account of what's happening with his head.

On the other hand, because I love Maggie, I want to warn her that any path she chooses that includes Cash is bound to be a rocky one. No. Not rocky. It's going to be a trek over the damned Himalayas because (there's no easy way to say this) Cash is screwed up. And he seems to get more screwed up every day. I hate the idea of her suffering alongside him. But then I hope she *does*, because I know he'll do better with her than without her.

See? Enormous. Convoluted. Complex.

"Miss Bea said his name is Billy Joe Summerset, the president and CEO of Fidelity Bank. But a quick Google search shows he goes by BJ," Cash says, glancing at his phone.

He and Maggie are sitting in front of me on the streetcar heading back toward The Quarter. After we drop off Cash at his house, Maggie and I plan to walk over to the shop where I left Smurf. From there, we'll make our way down the list of folks Miss Bea gave me. (A list I quickly memorized and then just as quickly deleted. As a Green Beret, I'm leery of having anything in writing. I mean, what if Sullivan somehow convinced a judge to subpoena my phone?) Maggie and I are going to ring doorbells, knock on doors, and *hopefully* persuade someone to help us take Sullivan down. (Something that should have happened years ago.)

"*BJ*," Cash emphasizes with a twist of his lips. "I mean, seriously? That's worse than *Todd*."

"Maybe he thinks it's subliminal advertising," Maggie suggests. "Like, he hopes every time a woman says his name, she'll be unconsciously considering giving him a blowy."

Cash snorts. "A *blowy*? What are we? Twelve?"

She laughs, and it's a bright sound.

Cash catches my eye and winks. He's trying to keep her mind off what lies ahead. And maybe, just maybe, make up for what happened last night.

"You know," he ventures, "it's almost lunchtime. You guys should hold off trying to talk to people until after they've eaten. My hunch is they'll be a lot more receptive on full stomachs."

Maggie turns to frown at me. "He's got a point."

"How about we stop by the Tomb of the Unknown Slave before you head out?" he suggests. "There's time to kill. And it's something easy we can check off our list."

"Where is it again?" Maggie asks.

"In the churchyard of St. Augustine up in the Tremé. It's only a block from the shop where Luc left Smurf."

"Luc?" She lifts an eyebrow at me. "What do you think?"

What do I think? I think I'm not feeling adventurous. I think we need to get this George Sullivan shitshow on the road. But if Cash is aiming to smooth things over with her, who am I to get in his way?

"Sure." I nod. "Sounds like a plan."

That's how I find myself standing outside the brick wall of a Catholic church thirty minutes later. The three of us are looking at a large rusted chain that's been welded into a cross. It's tipped onto its side and partially buried in the ground. Hanging from the links of the chain are several slaves' shackles.

Listening to them sway and creak in the gentle breeze has a ghostly finger drifting up my spine. Despite the soft warmth of the noonday sun, goose bumps break out over my arms.

There are a lot of things about New Orleans that make me proud to have been born and raised here. Its history as a major port for the slave trade isn't one of them.

"Are there slaves buried here?" Maggie asks, her voice low and reverent.

"I don't think so." Cash's head is bowed. Sunlight shines on his chin stubble, making it look like gold dust. "I think it's only a memorial to them. All twelve-point-five *million* who were shipped from Africa to the New World."

Maggie shudders. "To think of them surviving the Middle Passage only to get here and then suffer horrible atrocities at the hands of white men. And to think those white men actually looked at them and didn't see human beings but pieces of property. It's too awful to comprehend. What is *wrong* with us as a species?"

"When you think about this country being built on the backs of enslaved Africans, it makes you proud to be an American, doesn't it?" Cash's tone is dripping in sarcasm.

After that pronouncement, none of us speaks for a while. Instead, we allow the gravity of the site to seep into us. Another light gust of wind blows through the churchyard, pushing at the slaves' shackles and bringing with it the smell of a garden—fresh-cut grass and newly turned dirt.

Ever notice how a garden and a graveyard smell the same? Odd considering one is a place of birth and growth and the other is a place of death and decay.

Or maybe it's not so odd. We come from the earth and return to it. Maybe the beginning and the end *should* smell the same.

Low, melancholy blues drift toward us from somewhere nearby. When I recognize the tune, I smile.

"Uh, Luc?" Cash frowns at me. "Why is your face making that face? This is supposed to be a solemn affair."

"You hear that?" I point in the direction of the music. "It's "Hymn to Freedom." Pretty damned appropriate, I'd say."

"Mmm." He nods. Then, "You ever think about what you'd want played at your funeral?"

I frown at him. First it was a Viking funeral, and now it's funeral music? "You've become obsessed with funeral arrangements lately. You realize that, right?"

"'Don't Worry Be Happy,'" Maggie interjects. "I mean, it makes sense. Once I'm dead, there's not a darned thing anyone will be able to do to bring me back, so…*don't worry*. And instead of mourning my passing, I'd much rather people celebrate my life and *be happy*."

Cash chuckles. "That's perfect, Maggie." Then he turns to me. "How about you, Luc?"

"I've never given it much thought," I admit.

Truth to tell, we were so close to death so many times in Afghanistan that I decided it was better to ignore the subject entirely. To think about death might've gotten its attention and invited it to turn its malevolent eyes our way.

Not that I'm a believer in any of that woo-woo nonsense. But better safe than sorry.

"I want "Hallelujah" by Leonard Cohen played at my funeral," he says with an emphatic jerk of his chin.

Maggie frowns. "I thought you weren't religious."

"It's not religious," he declares. "Have you ever listened to all the lyrics?"

"I don't reckon anyone's listened to *all* the lyrics," I say. "It was originally eighty verses long, or something like that. Most folks only know about seven or eight of 'em. The more popular ones. But you're right. It's not religious at all."

"But it says *hallelujah*," Maggie insists. "That's pretty much the entire chorus."

"I think Cohen's whole point is that there are a lot of things to praise and ways we should praise that don't have anything to do with a higher power. I think he was trying to tell us that although some things are 'cold and broken'"—I make air quotes—"that doesn't make 'em any *less*. He's saying flawless hallelujahs have the same value as shattered hallelujahs."

"Wow." Cash shakes his head. "Deep. And here I just thought the song was pretty."

Maggie and I look at each other and laugh.

"For such a complicated man, you have moments of surprising simplicity," I tell him.

He shrugs, and I look at my watch. It's nearly thirteen hundred. The lunch hour is over. Time to get down to business.

As we make our way out of the churchyard, Maggie takes hold of Cash's arm. Ostensibly, she needs support over the uneven ground since she's wearing a pair of wedge ankle boots. But when we make it to the sidewalk, she hangs on.

Cash glances at me over his shoulder, his face begging for my help.

She catches his expression. "What? Because we're only *friends* I'm not supposed to take your arm? I mean, I take *Luc's* arm all the time."

Her tone is pure innocence, but I know better. She can't out-argue Cash when it comes to his decision to put the kibosh on their romantic relationship. So she'll do her best to undermine his position by touching him. By putting herself next to him every chance she gets.

I feel for Cash. I really do.

Maggie *does* take my arm. But she doesn't know how it makes my chest swell with pride. She doesn't know how the feel of her cool fingers makes my heart race. And she certainly doesn't know how the two of us moving together, side by side, feels oddly... *intimate*.

But Cash knows what I'm talking about. Oh yeah. One look at his face tells me he *definitely* knows.

He pulls out his flask and empties it down his throat.

CHAPTER THIRTY-EIGHT

Maggie

Fear is a strange thing. It's weightless, and yet it can crush you like a ten-ton boulder.

"It wasn't a total loss," I venture hesitantly. "Was it?"

Luc leans against Smurf's tailgate and crosses his arms. The light from the streetlamp makes his hair look as glossy as mink's fur. He's always been able to say a lot with his eyes, those warm, liquid-brown eyes. But right now, they're the polar opposite of warm and liquid. Right now they're hard enough to stop bullets. And nothing they're saying is reassuring.

"Cowards," he spits. "The lot of 'em."

I guess it's possible everyone we spoke with *is* a coward. But I suspect what truly happened is that they are so bogged down by the weight of their fear that they can't manage to crawl out from under it.

"At least that BJ guy had the gumption to tell us we're barking up the wrong tree, right?" My tone sounds desperate, even to my own ears. "We have a new lead, right?"

Hunger, and the disappointment of so many wasted hours, is getting to me. Well, it's more like hunger, disappointment, and an insidious, polluting *unease*. If we can't find anyone who's willing to stand up to Sullivan and help us bring him down, how the heck are we ever going to stop him from coming after us?

"Luc?" I say when he's been quiet for too long. A hard shiver shakes me from head to toe. I didn't realize we'd be out this late, or I'd have brought my coat.

He unzips his leather jacket and pulls me against him. I hesitate to thread my arms around his waist. I'm still not sure how to *be* when I'm around him. So I simply curl into his heat, grateful for the solid feel of him.

"You know this makes everything much more difficult," he says. "And it means we're gonna hafta involve Cash."

"He's already involved."

"Yeah, but now he'll hafta be *involved* involved. We'll need him to take an active role."

"You say that like it's a bad thing."

"He's a drunk, Maggie May." There's censure in his voice, but also sadness and defeat.

As hard as it is for me to watch Cash spiral downward, it must be doubly hard for Luc. They've spent the last decade depending on each other day in and day out. I can't imagine the bond that forms.

"Drunks are rarely reliable," he finishes.

My heart rebels against his words. "He's not that bad."

"He *is*. He just doesn't show you the worst of it."

"I'm going to get help for him," I swear. "I'm just waiting to hear back from that neurosurgeon."

"And what happens if this guy can't do anything more than Cash's current doctors? Are you still willing to walk down this path with him?"

"What are you talking about?" I shake my head. "What path?"

"You *know* what path, Maggie May." I try not to flinch at the rebuke in his tone. He's turned into a man of hard truths. There's no longer any give in him when it comes to prevarication. "You're throwing caution to the wind and jumping back into a relationship with him 'cause you've convinced yourself he can be saved. But what if he can't? What if he's right? What if how he is now is as good as he's gonna get?"

The thought of Cash continuing to suffer is too awful to contemplate. "You heard him." I firm my chin. "He won't *let* me jump back into a relationship with him. He's plunked me firmly in the friend zone."

Luc's mouth twists. "That may be where he's put you, but you have no intention of staying there. You're gonna tempt him with gentle touches and sweet words and soft glances until he gives in."

I blink in astonishment. "How do you always know what I'm thinking?"

"'Cause I know everything about you. How your breath catches when you see fireflies. How you get goose bumps anytime you hear "The Star-Spangled Banner." I know you so well I could find you in the pitch black in a crowd of people."

Good. Lord.

I'm suddenly aware of the steely feel of his thighs against mine, of the clean, woodsy scent of his aftershave.

"None of that matters right now." I pull from his embrace. "Because right now, we have bigger fish to fry. We need to go tell Cash what we found out from BJ."

I skirt the side of the truck and buckle myself into the passenger seat. Luc's quiet as he climbs behind the wheel and stays that way the entire drive to Cash's house. After pulling next to the curb, he cuts the engine and turns to me. "You know I'd do anything for you, right?"

"Yes." I nod. He proved that in the swamp that night.

"But I can't hurt you to help Cash. And vice versa, I can't hurt him to help you."

"I don't understand."

For a long time, he stares at me. The only sound in the truck is the *tick-tick* of the cooling motor. Eventually, his voice so low I strain to hear it, he says, "I think you do."

CHAPTER SEVEN

Cash

Dear Cash,

I was walking through the French Market today, and the Joan of Arc statue caught my attention. No wonder, right? Could the thing BE any more gold? Plus, someone has festooned her and her horse in Mardi Gras beads. So now she's gold AND gaudy.

For the first time, I stopped and read the inscription at her base. "Joan of Arc, Maid of Orleans, 1412-1431." Did you know she was only nineteen when she was burned at the stake? Nineteen.

That's so young. I mean, that's how old YOU are. Or at least that's how old you'll be next week.

I can't believe I'm going to miss your birthday. It seems so surreal not being able to hug your neck or send you a card.

I know you're not one for celebrating, but I hope you'll do something nice for yourself. Or if you can't do that, then let Luc do something nice for you. You know he'll try.

After the French Market, I went into Café Du Monde and sat at our favorite table. It wasn't the same without you and Luc. Nothing feels the same, actually, and I'm trying to figure out if that's because y'all aren't here, or if it's because I'm different now.

I AM different, by the way. But I guess after what happened, I should be. If I wasn't different, if I wasn't changed by it, what sort of person would I be?

Anyway, I miss you. Still. Always.
Happy early birthday.
Love, Maggie

Part of being human is sucking it up and carrying on even when you're the emotional equivalent of a damned tire fire.

Ever since Luc and Maggie went on their hunting expedition, I've been thinking back to how Maggie held on to my arm in the churchyard. She claimed it wasn't about anything more than friendship. But the way my body reacted to her touch certainly hadn't felt friendly. Or, more like, it'd felt *too* friendly.

Beneath her palm, my skin had heated. And then, when I'd looked over to find her smiling that siren's smile, the world had gone pear-shaped. I'd been seconds away from chucking my good intentions to the roadside, from chucking *The Plan* to the roadside, and kissing her.

Damn it all! It's going to take more than words to convince her to steer clear of me. It's going to take action.

I know what I need to do. The idea has gotten inside me like a tapeworm, and all afternoon it's been eating at me, leaving me with a terrible ache in my belly that the Gentleman Jack can't help.

Although...may as well keep trying.

Popping the top on my flask, I swallow two mouthfuls, welcoming the warm buzz that softens the edges of too many sharp thoughts.

"Put that shit away." Luc comes through the front door with Maggie in tow. The sight of her makes my heart squeeze like a fist. And when she walks in my direction, I drink in each hip-swinging step. "We got good news and bad news, and we need you sober to hear both."

Capping the flask, I send it to its home in my back pocket.

"Took you guys long enough." I dust the sanding grit off my hands. Stripped ten layers of paint from the baseboards last week.

Today I've been sanding them down. "I expected you back hours ago." I motion to the two folding chairs and grab a seat atop the milk crate.

"New Orleans's upper crust can't be bothered to turn on a dime and lend us their ears." Luc holds Maggie's chair for her and takes his seat only once she's situated. Here in the South, chivalry is alive and well. "We spent most of the afternoon sipping sweat tea in front parlors or sitting in reception areas waiting for folks to deign to speak to us."

Maggie reaches over and pats his shoulder, saying to me, "You'll have to forgive him for being grouchy enough to make a hornet look cuddly. Today didn't go as planned."

"Shoulda known better than to hang my wash out on someone else's line," he grumbles. "Not a one of 'em was willing to stick their necks out and confess to being blackmailed by Sullivan. They all lied straight through their too-white teeth."

"Reputation means everything to most of these families," Maggie explains unnecessarily. "But you're making it sound like it was a total waste of time. It wasn't. BJ gave us something to go on."

"So despite the nickname, he's not such a blowhard after all?" I ask.

She cracks a smile, but when Luc continues to frown, it falls off her face.

"What did BJ... I can't say that with a straight face." I shake my head. "What did he give you guys to go on?"

"He said that if folks *were* being blackmailed to support Sullivan, then they'd be hesitant to try to bring him down unless we could assure them that we'd also bring down..." She trails off, and a sinking feeling pulls at my stomach.

In a flash, I know what she's not saying. "Rick?" I say, and her expression is pained. Luc tugs on his ear. "Hey." I hold up my hands. "I know what an asshole my sperm donor is. Don't hold back on my account. Give it to me straight."

"BJ said the only way people will risk coming forward is if they know George Sullivan *and* Richard Armstrong will be brought to heel. BJ indicated that Sullivan was originally the one to go around threatening folks into supporting his reappointment as superintendent. But he said in the last ten or so years, it's been your father doing the strong-arming. And not only to support Sullivan."

"He's extorting them for money." I don't pose it as a question. I already know it's the answer.

Maggie spreads her hands. "It was implied."

I let my head fall back. The single bare bulb hanging from the center of the ceiling glows dull yellow and seems to pulsate. Not sure if it's an electrical surge, or if this thing with my head is beginning to affect my vision.

"If Rick's taking their money, then he's putting it somewhere." I lower my chin. "And I don't mean he's burying it in Mason jars in his backyard. Maybe he's funneling it into an offshore account. Or it could be he's laundering it through his other businesses. Regardless, he's leaving a trail. Money *always* leaves a trail. If taking down Sullivan means having to take down Rick, then we need to start by finding that trail."

"But how?" Maggie asks. "Where would we even begin?"

"He still lives in that house on Prytania in Uptown." When Luc gives me a weird look, I admit, "Got curious a few Saturdays ago when you stayed out at the swamp house to do some work and took myself to have a look-see. Same address as always. Same asshole at that address."

Maggie frowns. "So what? Like you said, it's not like he's burying the money in the backyard."

"Since I was old enough to know what was what, Rick's stored a big ledger inside a safe. He's old-school that way. Doesn't like electronic bookkeeping when it comes to his nefarious endeavors. Too easily tracked or hacked. The ledger lists all the records and transactions he *doesn't* let his accountants see. If he's squeezing these folks for money, you can bet your sweet ass he's recording the payments there."

"So then what's the plan?" She looks incredulous. "You're going to walk in and say, 'Hey, Dad, mind if I—'"

"Rick," I interrupt. "Never Dad."

"You're going to walk in and say, 'Hey, Rick, mind if I take a peek inside your safe?'"

"More like wait until he leaves and then break in."

For a second, she says nothing. Then, "B-break in? Like, *break* in? Anything we find would be inadmissible."

"Gather the evidence first." Luc nods. "Find a way to make it work for us later."

She gulps, struggling with the itsy-bitsy ethical dilemma of committing a crime in the name of bringing down a couple of criminals.

"What kinda safe is it?" Luc asks, already on board with the plan.

"The kind I know the combination to." I wink. "Rick wasn't careful about opening the thing around me when I was young. I'm sure he figured I'd never have the balls to open it myself, since he'd beat me to within an inch of my life if I did."

"Good. Does he still go into the office every day?"

"Hell if I know."

"So we need to do recon first." Luc rubs his chin thoughtfully. "Check out his security system. Learn his schedule so we know the best time to go in. I say we start surveilling his place on Monday."

"Wait until the weekend is over and he's back to his regular work schedule. Yep." I nod. "We're on the same page."

Maggie throws her hands in the air. "Do I even need to be here?"

Luc has the grace to look chagrined.

"We have a particular set of skills," I say, lowering my voice to a guttural growl. "Skills we've acquired over long careers. Skills that make us a nightmare for people like—"

"Please." She rolls her eyes. "I recognize *Taken* when I hear it. Liam Neeson is an Irish god."

Busted.

"It's been years since you've been inside that house," she points out. "What makes you think he still has the same safe? And if he *does* have the same safe, what makes you think he hasn't changed the combination?"

"Because he's an egomaniac," I explain with a snort of derision. "Considers himself the big man in town, above the law, untouchable. He won't have changed the safe or the combo. It won't have crossed his mind that he might *need* to."

She seems to chew on that for a while. Then she rubs the back of her neck and lets out a long, tired-sounding sigh. "Man, I feel like ten miles of bad road. Listening to people lie like dogs all afternoon really took it out of me."

"I'll drive you home." Luc stands from the folding chair now that our plan is set.

"Wait. I'm hungry. Aren't y'all hungry?" She looks from Luc to me. "What do you say we head over to Willie Mae's Scotch House for fried chicken?"

"I ate an hour ago," I tell her. I don't mention that by *ate* I mean I slapped some squares of American cheese onto crackers because that's all my stomach would allow. "But you guys should go."

I can tell she's disappointed, even as she plays it off by standing. "Suit yourself."

The truth is, I want nothing more than to go with them. Go with *her*. Spend every minute of every waking hour being close to her. But that's part of the problem, and it's *not* part of *The Plan*.

First order of business, bring down Sullivan and that piece of shit whose name is on my birth certificate. Second order of business, prove to Maggie once and for all that what we had is well and truly gone.

After the front door closes, I shuffle to the kitchen and grab a new bottle of Gentleman Jack. Then I take my liquid relief and my heartbreak to bed with me.

Chapter Forty

Maggie

Life has a familiar beat. A rhythm. And your body knows it and can keep on dancing even when your mind is splintering into a thousand pieces.

Somehow, despite everything going on in—and going wrong with—my life, I pulled a double yesterday. And I managed to laugh and carry on like always. But I woke up this morning feeling the side effects of all the stress and worry.

My head aches. My back hurts. My stomach is in knots. As Auntie June says, I feel like I've been chewed up, spit out, and stepped on.

Even my quick trip to the animal shelter this morning to drop off an extra bag of dog food and my nice chat with some of the regular volunteers weren't enough to lighten my spirits. Nor was the walk from my apartment to Café Du Monde despite the rays of the sun melting into my skin like Vaseline. I'm hoping a delicious cup of coffee will do the trick.

Waving to the waitress, a cutie pie whom Cash will no doubt flirt with once he gets here—*grrr*—I say, "Can I get a café au lait when you get a chance?"

"Coming right up," she says cheerfully. Her rosy cheeks and bright smile scratch at my frayed nerves as the door opens and Cash pushes inside.

"Oh my," the waitress says breathlessly when he grabs the seat next to mine. Her name tag identifies her as Jessica, but she's quick to introduce herself to Cash as Jess.

He has the temerity to gift her with his most devastating pirate's smile.

"He'll have a black coffee. And we'll both take a plate of beignets," I say without my usual tendency toward small talk or politeness.

Ugh, ugh, *ugh!*

Maybe I should've stayed home with the covers over my head. I'm not fit for company. Especially pretty, chipper, waitressy company.

And yes, it's true that Cash is an equal-opportunity flirter. Young or old, rich or poor, homely or pretty, *everyone* gets the benefit of his charm. As a general rule, I don't let that bother me. But it seems that *everything* is bothering me this morning.

After Jess turns toward the kitchen, Cash frowns at me. "You wake up on the wrong side of the bed or what?"

"Well, a happy howdy-do to you too, Cash."

He turns that smile on me and mimics my accent. "Howdy-do. You look especially beautiful this morning."

I didn't bother with makeup, and my hair is pulled into a sloppy bun on top of my head.

"You're a liar and a tease," I accuse, but darned if some of my bad mood doesn't melt away.

"You lack the ability to discern the subtleties of my character. I'm an idealist and a complimenter."

"*Complimenter* isn't a word."

"Neither is *grumpy-wumpy*, but that's you in a nutshell. Why are you scowling like someone kicked your dog?"

I fidget in my seat. "I don't know. It probably has something to do with me not being able to stop thinking about tomorrow. The thought of you and Luc going over to—"

He reaches across the table and grabs my hand. "There's no need to worry. It's nothing but recon. We won't engage."

"*Recon*," I parrot. "*Engage*. I feel like I'm a character in a movie. A fugitive on the run from the law with two covert operatives as my sidekicks. How the heck did this become my life?"

Regret peeks through his genial expression. "Because I used my fists on Dean all those years ago instead of using my head."

"Or because"—I make sure my voice is barely above a whisper—"I hit him with a—"

I was so engrossed in our conversation I didn't see Luc arrive. He startles me into silence when he pulls out the chair to my right and takes a seat. Bending to press a quick, perfunctory kiss to my cheek, he sets a red polka dot gift bag on the table.

"What's this?" I eye the present.

"I saw 'em online and couldn't resist." He grins. "And in case you're wondering, yes. I bought a pair for myself."

Glad for a distraction from the current topic—it was beginning to make my stomach hurt—I dig past the tissue paper and come up with red plaid pajama bottoms and a matching T-shirt printed with the Gryffindor Quidditch Team logo.

"For when you wanna lay 'round and get waited on by a house elf." His grin widens. "Or, you know, for your Waistband Mondays."

Luc has a way of making even the darkest day brighter.

"I love them." I hug the pajamas to my chest before carefully refolding them into the gift bag. "I've always said the Sorting Hat would've put us in the same Hogwarts house."

Cash rolls his eyes. "If you two start quoting *The Big Bang Theory*, I'm out of here."

I shake my head sorrowfully before turning to mock-whisper to Luc, "It's sad to be sitting next to such a lost cause, isn't it?"

"It's not like we didn't try with him," Luc laments.

Cash's expression says his exceedingly magnanimous patience is being stretched to its limits. "Maggie's in a mood this morning," he tells Luc. "She's worried how tomorrow will go, so I say we take her mind off things by checking another excursion off our list. The Voodoo Museum is open today. We could swing by after we're finished here."

"You're sure in an all-fire hurry to finish that list." I frown at him.

"Life's short." He shrugs. "Why wait?"

Jess reappears with our coffees and two plates of beignets. The sweet smell of powdered sugar fills the air, and I distract myself with settling the gift bag next to my chair so I don't have to watch Cash flirt.

"This seat taken?" A familiar voice with an accent as thick as bread dough sounds above me.

"Eva!" I jump up to give her a hug. She's been in Atlanta modeling clothes for an online catalog for the past week. I didn't think she was supposed to be back until later this evening. "What are you doing here?"

"I changed my flight to first thing this morning," she says. "And the minute the plane landed, I started jonesing for something sweet and calorie-laden. Molly's booked me for three runway shows this spring, so I'm determined to indulge over the next couple of months before I have to start starving myself come the New Year."

Molly Van Buren is Eva's hotshot New York agent. Eva credits Molly for getting her all the best gigs. But I think Eva's long, slim beauty does the heavy hitting for her.

"Sit, sit." I retake my seat and shove a plate of beignets her way.

She greets Luc and Cash. And after Jess reappears to take Eva's and Luc's drink orders, Eva picks up a beignet and stares at it like it's a lover. "Come to Momma, you wonderful doughy nugget of deep-fried glory."

Taking a bite, she closes her eyes and hums in ecstasy. I swear, every male head in the place turns to watch her enjoy her food. But she's oblivious when she opens her eyes and says around the beignet, "Thanks for the fingernail polish, Maggie. You don't have to leave me a gift every time you come over to water my plants, you know. *I* should be giving *you* gifts."

I hitch a shoulder. "I just think it's nice to come home to a welcome-back present."

I don't add that I understand how lonely it can be to walk into an empty apartment. That loneliness—coupled with my love of animals, of course—is why I have Sheldon, Leonard, and Yard.

"How did you manage to get your hands on a bottle?" She eyes me curiously. "I thought that color was discontinued."

"It was." I wiggle my eyebrows. "But I have my secret ways."

When I heard her favorite polish was going to stop being made, I stocked up on six bottles of the stuff so I could surprise her with it in the months and years to come.

"You're a wonder." She leans over and busses my cheek. Then she rubs at a speck of powdered sugar she left behind. "Isn't she a wonder?" She turns to Luc and Cash.

They agree that I am, and I make dismissive sounds while shaking my head. It doesn't take much to whip out my credit card and put in an online order at Sephora.

"We're headed to the Voodoo Museum after this," Cash says around a bite of beignet. "You should come with us, Eva."

"You *should*," I enthuse. "With your family history, it'll be a hoot."

Cash frowns. "What family history?"

"I never told you?" He shakes his head, and I rub my hands together, relishing the tale to come. "So..." I lower my voice to an appropriate storytelling octave. "Eva's great-great-too-many-greats-to-remember-grandfather was a Voodoo priest. He fled Haiti during a slave revolt at a sugar plantation sometime in the middle of the 1700s."

I must've made Eva's grandmother tell me this story a dozen times. I used to sit at Granny Mabel's feet for hours listening to her talk about how people in her neighborhood would sprinkle red brick dust across their stoops to protect themselves against curses and hexes and how they could buy love potions and gris-gris from the local drugstores.

"According to Eva's family lore," I say, "he hid in a clothing trunk and was smuggled into New Orleans by none other than Anne Bonny herself."

"Anne Bonny?" Cash asks.

"Famous female pirate," Luc explains.

"What a bunch of hooey." Eva laughs. "Every Creole family worth their salt has a story about an ancestor who came from Haiti and was a Voodoo priest or priestess."

"Are you saying you don't believe it?" Luc asks.

"Oh, I believe in a lot of crazy things. Fat-free chocolate cake. Exercise that's fun. Honest men. But I think Granny Mabel could spin a yarn like nobody's business, and I *know* she recognized when she had a gullible audience." She angles a thumb my way.

"Fine. Make fun. But I'll be the one laughing when the spirit of your Voodoo ancestor speaks to you once you're inside the museum." I wiggle my fingers spookily.

She pulls a face of regret as Jess arrives with the coffees. "Wish I could come," she says. "But I have a mani scheduled in an hour. Tomorrow I'm doing a shoot for a new brand of dish soap."

Did I mention Eva does body-part modeling too? She's pretty all over. Even her hands and feet are in high demand.

The beeyotch.

As we settle in with our morning joes and beignets, the conversation turns to food and music, natch. Eva tells us she has a cousin who'll be filling in for the regular pianist at Fritzel's, the only true-blue jazz club left on Bourbon Street, and that we should stop by to have a listen if we find the time. And Luc tells us he's been aiming to perfect his mother's oyster casserole, but hasn't managed to get it right just yet.

"How much nutmeg are you using?" Eva asks around a sip of coffee.

"A teaspoon," Luc says. "Mom's recipe says 'a pinch,' so…"

Eva shakes her head. "That's way too much. Quarter of a teaspoon at most."

Luc smiles at her bemusedly. "So besides being beautiful and smart and kind, you can cook? Why hasn't some man snatched you up and made an honest woman of you?"

"Hey, I'm as honest as they come!" Her laugh is deep and throaty, and I swear once again every male head in the room turns to get a better listen. "But the truth is…" She makes a face. "I intimidate men. I don't know if it's the height or the hair or the job or what."

"You don't intimidate me." Luc leans forward and whispers something in her ear that makes her catch her bottom lip between her teeth and smile.

I feel like I'm watching foreplay. The kind that leads to wild, unbridled sex. That's sex with a capital S and triple X.

When he pulls back, my bad mood reasserts itself, and I hear myself asking him, "So what's the deal with Sally Renee? I haven't heard you mention her lately."

His eyes narrow. "She's taking a three-month tour of Europe, hoping it'll help her get over the death of her husband."

I lift both eyebrows. "I thought *you* were helping her with that."

"I was only a stopgap measure."

I shake my head. "So y'all called it quits? Just like that?"

"We figured we should get out while the getting was good."

I turn to Eva. "Take note. He looks sweet and wholesome, but don't let the dimples fool you. He's grown into a rake and rogue. I'd give him a wide berth if I were you."

After that pronouncement, an uncomfortable quiet descends. Luc tugs at his ear. Cash gives me a strange look. And Eva shifts uncomfortably in her chair.

Good Lord! Why did I say that?

CHAPTER FORTY-ONE

Cash

Dear Cash,

It's Carnival season again. And you know what that means. Parades. Krewes. Throws. And cheap, plastic beads covering the entire town.

Growing up here, I was immune to the spectacle of it all. To me, it was simply a part of the year's celebrations, like Christmas or the Fourth of July. It wasn't until I met you that I realized how truly special it is. You helped me see it from an outsider's perspective.

Thank you for that.

Tonight the Krewe of Iris was on parade. You know I love the bedazzled sunglasses they throw. I caught two pair! They're sitting on my bookshelf next to the ones you caught for me last year.

Now I have three sets of sparkly, garish sunglasses. If you and Luc ever come back, we'll have to wear them to the parades.

Oh, and I forgot to tell you in yesterday's letter that I laughed for the first time since you left. At least I think it was the first time. It surprised me when it came out of me, and it sounded kind of rusty.

I went to the animal shelter to walk the dogs, but someone had dropped off a box of puppies. The staff vet said they were probably around eight weeks old, and the folks at the shelter had them in a pen set up in the lobby.

I climbed inside to play with them, and they were so wiggly and fluffy. They scrambled all over me and licked my face and... Just like that, I was laughing.

It felt good.

I'm feeling good. Or at least I'm feeling better.

And that gives me hope that maybe, someday, I'll be able to put what's happened behind me and laugh all the time.

Do you think that's possible? Do you think it's possible to have a good life with something awful weighing on your conscience?

Are YOU laughing wherever you are? I hope so. I hope so with all my heart.

I want you to be happy, Cash.

Love, Maggie

I once heard someone say that we should all be like postage stamps—we should stick to one thing until we get there.

Good advice.

I repeat it to myself when I have the urge to throw a comforting arm around Maggie's shoulders. She's not herself today. She's tense. Brittle. If I flicked her with a finger, she'd break.

I hate not being able to comfort her. But sticking to *The Plan* means I have to mind my Ps and Qs. Can't do anything to give her the wrong idea about my intentions, including, but not limited to, keeping my comforting arm to myself.

"I can't believe I've never been here," she says as we push through the door to the Voodoo Museum. "I guess I always thought it was a tourist trap."

"It is." Luc unzips his jacket. "And good God! What's with the heat?"

The museum *is* uncomfortably warm, and I use the term *museum* lightly.

We make our way toward the cramped rooms and narrow hallways that are crammed full of artifacts. Dried chicken feet hang from the walls alongside little dolls made of Spanish moss. There are human skulls and skeletons, horse-jaw rattles and statues of the Virgin Mary. But the pride and joy of the museum seems to be an altar used by New Orleans's own Marie Laveau—or so the plaque claims. The entire place smells old and musty, and everything is covered in a fine layer of dust that tickles my nose and makes the back of my throat itch.

"Gotta keep it warm on account of Bebelle." A man wearing a worn top hat and sporting a walking stick carved to look like an alligator materializes from nowhere. Coiled around his neck is a big-ass python. The snake flicks its long tongue at the man's beard while keeping a beady black eye on the rest us. "Snakes are cherished in the Voodoo religion, doncha know?"

Maggie shakes the hand the man offers her. "Hi, I'm Maggie."

"Voodoo Vinnie is the name." His dark eyes dance with mischief.

"Pleased to meet you," she sparkles at him. I can't tell if she's truly coming out of her funk, or if she's putting on a show for Voodoo Vinnie—pause for laughter, because *Voodoo Vinnie*? He sounds like a poorly written Marvel villain.

"Damballa, the serpent god, is the oldest in the Voodoo pantheon," Vinnie explains, stroking his snake lovingly. "He's the one who created the world, and it's his job to transport the souls of the dead into the afterlife. Those of us who practice use snake skins in our rituals to commune with Damballa. If you've a mind to, you can buy some of Bebelle's shed skins on your way out. I keep bags by the register up front."

Of course he does.

"Are you a Voodoo priest?" Maggie asks as we make our way deeper into the museum, Vinnie following close behind.

"I am." His chest swells with pride.

All I can think is, *What a load of shit*. Vinnie's got a round belly and cherub-red cheeks. He looks more like a drunk uncle than a Voodoo priest. Although, to give credit where credit is due, he *does* carry a certain energy with him, seeming to brim with life-force.

"And do you do spells?" Maggie asks.

"You got somethin' in mind?" Vinnie slides Luc a knowing glance. "A love potion perhaps?"

Maggie laughs, and it's all golden and light. Okay, I don't think she's faking. I think she's actually enjoying herself.

Score one for me and my brilliant idea to come here.

"There's no lack of love in this room," she tells Vinnie. "Save your potions for those who need them."

"Then how about a healin' spell?"

Is it my imagination, or do Vinnie's black eyes dart my way?

Nah. Just the dim light playing tricks on me. Still, I figure…*why not?* We could all use some laughs, right?

"Sure," I say before Maggie can turn him down again. "I'll take some healing. How much will it cost me?"

"Depends on what's wrong with you." Vinnie eyes me up and down.

"Head trauma." I point to the scar above my temple. "Accompanied by terrible headaches, wonky vision, and nausea."

"You've never said anything about wonky vision." Luc frowns at me.

"New symptom," I admit. "So?" I turn back to Vinnie. "How much?"

"You lookin' for relief of symptoms or a full-on healin'? Because a potion for the relief of symptoms is cheap and easy. It'll run you twenty bucks and probably last a week or two. But a full on healin'? That takes a lot more time and energy on my part."

I grew up with a con man, so I recognize the game. Still, Maggie's enjoying herself, and if I'm being honest, I'm having fun too.

"How much?" I ask again and watch Vinnie's eyes spark. He thinks I'm a sucker. Looking at Maggie's bright smile, I admit he's probably right.

"Ninety dollars for the ceremony," he says. "Ten dollars for the doll."

Luc's eyebrows climb up his forehead. He jerks his chin side to side, his eyes saying, *Not worth it*. But I'm already digging in my pocket for my wallet.

After counting out five Andrew Jacksons, I slap the bills in Vinnie's outstretched palm. They immediately disappear into the front pocket of his raggedy black trousers. No muss, no fuss, done deal.

"Come with me." He motions me through a curtain of beads into a room not much bigger than a walk-in closet. Dozens of candles burn on variously sized shelves. A side table with a bunch of clay jars is nestled into one corner. And tacked to the walls are more chicken feet, snake skins, clutches of herbs, and crosses that have been fashioned out of the long, bleached bones of animals.

At least I *hope* they're animal bones.

The beaded curtain crackles and hisses as Luc and Maggie step into the room behind us. Maggie looks around with wonder. Luc looks around with skepticism.

Funny, he used to be like Maggie, open to the mystery and thrill of the unknown. But the army hardened his mystic's heart.

As if to prove my point, when Vinnie turns away to gather supplies, Luc whispers, "This hell-born idea is your worst yet."

"Where's your sense of adventure?" I wiggle my eyebrows.

As I'd hoped, it's enough to make his lips quirk. "Fine. Suit yourself. But if you come outta here covered in chicken blood and feathers, don't say I didn't warn you."

Maggie's made her way over to the table in the corner. "What are these?" She runs a finger along a clay jar.

"Govi jars," Vinnie explains, plucking a doll from a tray. "They're for storin' the souls of the dead."

Maggie jerks her hand away and anxiously clutches her locket. "Whose souls are in these?" she asks dubiously.

"Those are empty." Vinnie walks over to me with a pair of scissors.

My chin angles back when he reaches toward my face. Maybe Luc's right. Maybe this is a bad idea.

"I need a lock of your hair," Vinnie explains.

"Right." I swallow, trying not to wince when he snips a fringe.

Bebelle takes advantage of her proximity to me by flicking her tongue to taste my shoulder. Is it my imagination, or is she looking at me in a new light? In a *hungry* light?

"Why would you want to store the souls of the dead?" Maggie asks, still examining the red clay pots...from a safe distance of three feet.

"'Cause the livin' can call on the souls in the jars to solicit advice and guidance. Those who've moved on are wise beyond measure. They know what lies on the other side." He grabs the hem of my flannel shirt and quirks an eyebrow. "I need a piece of your shirt too."

"Have at it," I tell him. "It's not like I don't have ten more like it in my closet back home."

He cuts off a little square of material, then goes over to a small altar. He uses glue to attach my hair to the head of the doll and a pin to fasten the patch of flannel to the thing's chest.

"Now." He turns to me. "We need to animate it with your life force. What's your first and last name? No nicknames, please."

"Cassius Armstrong," I tell him.

Nodding, he holds the doll in front of him and stares deep into its black eyes—which look like they've been drawn on with a Sharpie. "Cassius Armstrong. *Cassius* Armstrong. Cassius *Armstrong*," he chants, and damned if the hairs on my arms don't lift.

He hands me the doll. "Blow into its nose and mouth, please."

Maggie's expression is transfixed. Luc crosses his arms, looking bulky and brooding and slightly bored.

Feeling foolish, I take the doll from Vinnie, cover its fabric face with my mouth, and blow. It smells of glue and old cloth and tastes of dust.

"Good." Vinnie nods. "Now we must baptize it." I hand the doll back to him and he dunks it into the bowl of water sitting on the altar.

"Here comes the hard part." He clutches the dripping doll to his chest. His eyes roll back in his head, and for a good two minutes he sways and chants and sings under his breath.

Bebelle seems mesmerized. She tucks her scaly face under Vinnie's beard and goes completely still. Even her tongue stops its constant flickering.

A gust of air blows through the room, rattling the curtain of beads and bending the candle flames on their wicks. Maggie glances apprehensively at Luc. He motions for her to come stand next to him. When she does, he tucks her close to his side with an arm around her shoulders.

Dark, oily jealousy tries to seep into my brain. *He* can do for her what I can't, hold her close, comfort her. But then I remind myself that's exactly as it should be.

Vinnie's chanting and singing gets louder, his swaying faster. Then, with a great cry of "Ayibobo!"—which I've heard is the Voodoo word for "amen"—he stabs a rusty nail through the doll's soft head.

Sympathetic pain slices through my skull.

When he finally opens his eyes, his shoulders slump as if he's been drained of energy. I stifle the urge to applaud. It's been one hell of a show.

"Is it done?" I ask.

"Not yet." He hands me the doll. Bebelle is back to her old self, sinuous body slithering slightly, tongue darting. "You have to bury it in your backyard or toss it into flowin' water. *Then* it'll be done."

"Awesome. Thanks, Voodoo Vinnie."

"My pleasure." He pats his pocket full of money and gives me a wink.

Chuckling, I motion for Luc and Maggie to precede me out of the museum. Once we're standing on the curb beside Smurf, Luc says, "So what'll it be? You gonna bury that thing in your backyard, or you wanna toss it into the Mississippi?"

"The river," Maggie declares. "If you bury it, someone might accidentally dig it up one day. It'll give them nightmares for life."

"You heard the lady." I open the truck's passenger-side door. "To the river!"

As the three of us head in that direction, I roll down the window and let the clean air hit me in the face. Maggie is humming along to the radio, her fingers tapping out the rhythm on her knee. My head still hurts as much as ever, the doll is leaving a wet spot on my jeans, and I'm down a hundred bones. But she's smiling, and her mood seems to have lifted, so it was well worth it.

Chapter Forty-two

Luc

Dear Luc,

I helped Auntie June bake half a dozen king cakes this morning. She put me in charge of the icing and the plastic babies, which reminded me of the king cake you and I shared with Cash last year.

We sat on the riverbank, remember? The Mississippi was running high because of all the snowmelt up North, and we watched the barges dodge the dead trees zooming by on the current.

You were the one to get the baby. But that's no surprise since you ate more than your fair share of the cake.

And speaking of eating more than your fair share... Are they feeding you enough in the army? I think about that a lot, whether you're eating enough, sleeping enough, being kept warm enough.

I tried visiting your mother this evening, hoping she could tell me how you're doing and maybe give me your address so I could send you a care package. I've been too ashamed to see her before, knowing I'm the reason you followed Cash into the army in the first place. But I finally bit the bullet and made the trip to the mayor's house.

But when I got there, the new housekeeper said your mom moved to Shreveport. I called information for her number, but she's unlisted.

So...that's that, I guess. She's not on MySpace or Facebook. I have no way of contacting her, which means I've officially run out of ways to contact YOU.

I still don't agree that we should forget the past and move on in life without each other. But what else can I do? You haven't left me a choice in the matter.

Some days, that makes me unaccountably mad at you. Then I remember all you did for me. I remember how much your friendship changed me and shaped me into the person I am today, a person who CAN move on in life without you, and all I feel is grateful.

Grateful to have known you and had you there with me, even if it was only for a little while.

Forever and always, Maggie May

Memory is an odd thing, a capricious creature. You can't trust it. Not completely.

Take that night in the swamp when I saw Maggie struggling beneath Dean. Did I say anything to her before I told her to run? And how long did the encounter with Dean last after she took off? Did I do enough? Was there anything I *could* have done?

"You're in love with her, aren't ya?"

A rusty-sounding voice draws me from my reverie. I've been standing outside Bon Temps Rouler, staring through the front window at Maggie, for some time now. I like watching her behind the bar. Not only is she quick on the taps, but she has a way of listening to folks that makes them feel heard. She seems to chew up and swallow every word spoken to her.

"That obvious, is it?" I ask, watching Chrissy, one of Maggie's regular bartenders, blow a smoke ring into the evening air.

"Only to anyone with eyes," she tells me, smiling with her mouth closed. "Does she know?"

"I reckon she must, since I told her."

When Chrissy isn't slinging beer or pouring bourbon, she comes outside to chain-smoke Parliaments. She's got to be closing in on fifty, has frizzy, bottle-blond hair that she wears in a ponytail, and is the owner of a pair of keen, no-bullshit eyes.

She strikes me as one of those folks capable of truly *seeing* others.

"And yet she isn't shacked up with ya 24/7?" She looks me up and down. "Considering you're a triple threat, that must mean there's something wrong with ya. So what is it? Some incurable STD? Micro-penis?" Her face contorts around an expression of disgust. "Don't tell me you're one of them guys who likes to dress up in fuzzy animal costumes."

I laugh. "First of all, what's a triple threat?"

"Tall, dark, and handsome," she explains, taking another drag on her cigarette. The cherry on the end burns bright orange.

"Right." I nod. "So then second of all, no STDs. Third of all, I've never had any complaints size-wise. And last but not least, I think you're talking about Furries. And while I don't like to criticize anyone's particular tastes, I guarantee you I find nothing sexy about folks dressing up like foxes and rabbits and boning each other."

"So then what's the holdup?" she challenges. "Why aren't you running in there and sweeping her off her feet?"

Why indeed? The story of my life. "'Cause she's in love with my best friend," I say.

"Ouch." Chrissy winces. "Tough break."

I shrug. "Life's full of 'em. Now, if you'll excuse me, I needa go have a quick chat with the lady herself."

"Luc!" Maggie waves me over to a stool at the end of the bar after I shove inside. "What are you doing here?"

Her voice is more chipper than it needs to be, and I can tell by the pinched look on her face it's all a show. Yesterday Cash may've been able to take her mind off what we had planned for today with that crazy trip to the Voodoo Museum and the subsequent tossing-of-the-Voodoo-doll-into-the-river ceremony. But I'd bet my bottom dollar she's been a bundle of nerves since she woke up this morning.

She pulls an Abita from the cooler and lifts a brow. When I nod, she pops the top and slides the bottle my way.

The place is sparsely populated. A few locals are keeping Earl Greene company down at the other end of the bar. And there's a group of four men (who I assume hail from Ohio seeing as how one of them is wearing a Cincinnati Reds hat and another is sporting a Buckeyes shirt) occupying a table near the back. They're sharing a pitcher of beer, playing some dice game I don't recognize, and listening to Dr. John on the jukebox singing "Iko Iko" in his scratchy voice.

Glancing at the clock above the bar, I see it's almost seventeen hundred. The regulars are probably just now getting off work. And it's too early for the tourists, who are still out taking carriage rides or touring the cemeteries.

Maggie waits until I suck down a neck's worth of beer before leaning her elbows on the bar top. In a low voice, she asks, "How'd it go?"

"He's sick," I say.

Her brow wrinkles with concern. "Who? Cash?"

"Nope." I shake my head, then reconsider. "Well, yes. Him too. But I'm talking 'bout Rick. We staked out his house, but we never saw him come out. And the only person who went in was his assistant. She was delivering a bag from the pharmacy."

"What's wrong with him?"

"Hell if I know." I shrug. "But considering he looked fit as a fiddle not long ago, I reckon it's a bug. Cold maybe? Flu?"

"That's not good news for us." She tries to keep her voice steady, but a muscle ticks near her right eye.

"Just a setback," I assure her. "He'll be up and around soon enough, and then Cash and I will spend some time learning his schedule. Once we know when he's least likely to turn up at home, we'll sneak in and try for the safe."

"Hey, Maggie!" Earl hollers. "I'm so dry I'm spitting cotton over here!" He holds up his empty beer bottle.

"Don't you yell at me like I'm one of your racing dogs, Earl Greene!" she scolds, hands on hips. "I'll snatch you bald-headed and then go after your mustache!"

Earl protects his 'stache with a knobby-knuckled hand. "You're meaner than a wet panther today. What's gotten into you?" He pins me with an accusing look.

"Hey!" I lift my hands. "Don't blame me."

Maggie pops the top on a beer and slides it Earl's way. Then she turns to the table of Midwesterners. "Y'all good? Need another pitcher?"

"One more!" the one in the Reds hat calls as he rolls the dice.

After Maggie pulls a fresh pitcher and sets it on the end of the bar for someone in the group to pick up, she turns back to me. I recognize her expression. Something's giving her fits.

When she's quiet for too long, I reach across the bar and chuck her under the chin. "Out with it. You'll feel better once it's off your chest."

She frowns at me. "*Stop* being so insightful, dang it!"

I pretend offense. "My, my. Earl's right. You *are* in fine form today."

She worries her bottom lip with her teeth, then sullenly admits, "I owe you an apology."

"You do?" I blink in confusion. "For what?"

"For bringing up Sally Renee yesterday when you were flirting with Eva. It's just that…" She twists her lips. "The thought of you and Eva starting something terrifies me."

I go still, my silly heart ever hopeful that someday she'll look at me and see something more than the goofy kid she used to know. (Which makes me feel completely disloyal to Cash. But there you have it.) Then a thought occurs that has my silly, ever-hopeful heart caving in on itself. "Why? You think I'm not good enough for her?"

Maggie clasps her throat in surprise. "Of *course* you're good enough for her. You and Eva are two of my favorite people in the world. But that's the whole dadgummed problem."

97

"Sorry." I shake my head. "Not following."

"What happens when you have your fun and then you're done with her, huh? Eva might look fierce, but she's got a heart like whipped cream. You could hurt her, and then where would I be? I'd have to choose sides."

And that, ladies and gents, marks the last time I get my hopes up.

"Eva is a beautiful woman," I admit. "There's no denying that. But I've never looked at her as anything more than *your* friend."

"But…you two were *flirting*."

"Yeah. And you as well as anyone should know flirting doesn't mean a damned thing."

She narrows her eyes. "Me as well as anyone? What is *that* supposed to mean? Do you think I've flirted with you? Do you think I've led you on or—"

"Oh, for the love of living, Maggie May." I toss up my hands. "I'm talking about Cash and how *he* flirts with everyone and everything."

"Oh." She makes a face. "Sorry, I…" She shakes her head. "Sorry."

"Is it okay if I change the subject now?" Irritation makes the skin across my shoulders feel tight.

Her smile is lopsided. "Please."

"Mom said she'd love to come to Thanksgiving dinner at your aunts' house next week. Since Cash was aiming to spend the evening with us, that means he's coming too. Tell Miss Bea and Miss June they'll have three more at their table."

"Oh good." All the tension leaves her face. I wish I could say it leaves mine too, but this entire conversation has been an exercise in exasperation. "They'll be so happy," she adds.

I take a fortifying swig of beer, hoping it'll help sweeten my suddenly sour mood.

"I can't wait to see your mom again." She plucks a beer mug from the drying rack and uses a towel to polish it. "It's been too long. Has she changed much over the years?"

"She's cut her hair shorter, but that's about it," I admit.

"She always looked dark and mysterious in her peasant skirts and bangles. I totally get why the mayor fell for her so hard he was willing to risk his career."

As soon as the words are out of her mouth, I can see she wants to reel them back in.

"Sorry." She shakes her head. "I don't know why I said that. I know you…" She trails off and looks at her feet. "I know it's a touchy subject."

"Not so much anymore." I shrug. "With age comes wisdom. Mom did what she thought she had to do to keep us clothed and fed. I respect her for that, and for what she's made of herself since."

Maggie slides the dried mug onto a shelf and reaches for another from the rack, watching me curiously, as if she has more she wants to say but isn't sure she should.

When I lift a questioning eyebrow, she stammers, "You, uh…you never told me how all that…came to be."

When I was younger, I was careful not to broach this subject. For one thing, I was tall and gangly and pimply, and that made me stand out from the crowd at a time when I'd have given *anything* to blend in. For another thing, the last thing I wanted to talk about with *anyone*, even Maggie, was the high-profile affair my mother was having with the mayor of New Orleans. And finally, I was ashamed. Not so much of Mom, but of the scandal. I thought if I ignored it, if I acted like it wasn't happening, people would stop staring at me, stop calling me names, and leave me well enough alone.

Wishful thinking on my part, of course.

"We were poor even before Dad died," I say. "But we had what we needed. 'And not an inch more,' Dad would always say." I smile at the memory of him. Even though I was young when he died, barely thirteen, I can still remember the laugh lines around his eyes and how gentle his big, work-worn hands could be when I was scared or hurt.

"After he was gone, things got bad fast. There were taxes due, not to mention the mortgage on the land. Even though it was what most folks would consider pennies, it was more than Mom could handle on her own. Not that she didn't try. She took up cleaning houses during the day and quilting during the evenings to bring in a little extra. It wasn't enough though. When the bank threatened to foreclose, Mayor Gibson stepped in."

Maggie's brow wrinkles. "But how did he know?"

"She'd been cleaning his house for about three months by then. She musta confided in him."

"And he magnanimously agreed to help her out of the kindness of his heart?" Maggie makes a face. "I'm sure it had nothing to do with your mom being shaped like Sofia Vergara."

"I'm not gonna blow smoke up your ass and say it started out innocent. But it wasn't as salacious as *The Times-Picayune* made it sound." I grimace at the memory of the newspaper headlines that reported on the affair. None of them painted my mother in a pretty light.

"Gibson hired her to work for him full time and gave her an advance on her salary so she could keep the bank at bay. When that money ran out, he agreed to up her pay if she joined him for dinners every evening. I reckon it went on from there. Eventually, he installed us in his guest house, I was enrolled at Braxton Academy, and Mom became his full-time mistress. She says it's not something she's proud of, but she claims to have come to care for Gibson over time. And he was nice, from what I can recall. Sorta tragic and lonely. I reckon he was looking for company more than anything else."

"His wife had been bedridden for years, hadn't she? Something about an accident?"

I nod. "Her car was hit by a drunk driver out on Highway 10. By the time my mom came into the picture, Mrs. Gibson had been in a vegetative state for nearly five years."

Maggie shakes her head sorrowfully. "That must've been hell on the mayor. To have a wife, but *not* have a wife."

I spread my hands. "I don't aim to judge the situation. Not anymore."

"So what happened between them? Your mom and Mayor Gibson, I mean. Not long after you left, your mom up and moved to Shreveport, and the mayor announced he wouldn't be running for another term."

"I think the scandal was too much for 'em. They were both good people at heart, *ethical* people. Some folks might've been able to weather the storm of an entire city pointing fingers and judging, but they couldn't."

I realize I've been tearing at a cocktail napkin. It lies in shreds atop the bar. "You know," I confide, "it all came out 'cause of George Sullivan."

"Wait." She blinks. "*What?*"

"Yep." I nod. "Mayor Gibson got wise to the rumors about Sullivan encouraging police brutality and went after Sullivan's job. He didn't budge even after Sullivan pressured some of the city's movers and shakers into attempting to persuade him into keeping Sullivan on. Feeling the noose closing around his neck, Sullivan hired a private investigator to dig up dirt on the mayor, and it didn't take long for the snoop to come up with my mom. Sullivan gave the story to the papers. And the rest, as they say, is history. Gibson finished the remaining years of his term, but he never ran for public office again. Last I heard, he moved to Little Rock."

"And he never got enough on Sullivan to bring him down?"

I shake my head. "Mom tells me he tried, but too many of the rank and file refused to testify against their superintendent. Even the clean ones probably reckoned if Sullivan could air the mayor's dirty secrets, then he could certainly air *theirs*."

She sighs. "What an unholy mess."

"And we're still dealing with the fallout. Dean took to harassing me 'cause of my mom. Then he probably took to harassing you 'cause you were friends with me. Then Cash beat the stuffing outta him for harassing you. Then he followed us into that swamp and attacked you probably 'cause he was thinking that'd be a way to get back at me or Cash, and now…" I spread my hands.

"Links in a horrible, twisted chain," she mutters, her expression cloudier than a thunderstorm.

Purpose fills my chest. "It's a chain I aim to break," I assure her.

CHAPTER FORTY-THREE

Maggie

Good news is never unwelcome, and sometimes it comes your way right when you need it.

When I pull my cell phone from my hip pocket after a loud ding alerts me to a new email, I expect to see an invoice from my liquor supplier or a link from Eva to a funny cat video—the woman *lives* for funny cat videos. Goat videos too. She thinks the ones with the fainting goats are especially hysterical. But *I'm* the one ready to keel over when I see who it's from.

He responded! I can't believe he actually responded!

With shaky fingers, I tap open the email.

> **From:** Dr. Sean Stevens, Neurology, Johns Hopkins
>
> **To:** Magnolia May Carter
>
> **Subject:** RE: Traumatic Brain Injury Consult for Green Beret
>
> Dear Miss Carter,
>
> I'm honored you reached out to me regarding a second opinion for your friend. From the information you've given me, his case sounds interesting. I would be pleased to review his medical records and supply you with my professional opinion regarding his prognosis,

pain management, and any potential surgical solutions. Please send any and all relevant documentation to me at drstevens@johnshopkins.com.

No payment is necessary at this time. If, after reviewing his records, I agree to take on his case, we'll work out the details with his insurance and the VA.

Kind regards,

Dr. Sean Stevens, MS, MRCS, ABNS

I have no idea what all those letters after his name stand for, but they look important and impressive and *Oh! My! Lord!* For the first time in weeks, I feel a sense of hope. It's like I'm taking a deep breath after having my head underwater.

I haven't seen Cash or Luc in days. They've been alternating between renovating Cash's house and surveilling Cash's *dad's* house. Apparently, Rick Armstrong, that sorry sonofagun, contracted one heck of a nasty virus. He's yet to emerge from his sickbed.

Any other time, I'd be jumping for joy. After the way I saw him lay into Cash—and after what I now know he did to Cash for years—it's safe to say I wouldn't be the least bit sorry if he came down with a bad case of necrotizing fasciitis. But as it stands, his timing couldn't be worse, and I've been falling victim to despair.

I mean, how much can go wrong before a person begins to wonder if the Fates have lined up against them?

Then this email comes in and changes *everything*. The tides are turning in our favor, right? *Right?*

"Charlie," I call to my barback. "You think you can mind the store for fifteen minutes until Gus shows up for his shift? I need to take off early."

This news is too good not to share immediately.

"'Course he can," Earl answers for Charlie. "He can mind the store better than you."

I scowl at Earl. "You only say that because he lets you badger him into pouring double shots while only charging you for one."

"Not every time," Charlie argues, pink sneaking into his cheeks.

I pull the dish towel off my shoulder and toss it onto the bar. "Don't worry about it," I tell Charlie, slipping from behind the bar. "Sometimes it's easier to give him what he wants and avoid his petulance."

"Who you calling petulant?" Earl's mustache is cocked at an angle that can be described as...well...*petulant*.

I blow each of them a kiss before pushing through the front door and out into the cool fall evening. If I could eat the air, I would. It's thick and rich with Cajun spices. With a skip in my step, I set off in the direction of Cash's house.

It's not quite seven p.m., but the buskers on Royal are in full swing. On the corner, a girl with a fiddle sits atop an overturned crate, sawing away on the strings until the instrument's full, throaty sounds fill the world around her. I drop a few dollars into her open case. She bobs her head in thanks, never once breaking stride.

Farther down, a Dixieland band, complete with a washboard, stand-up bass, and banjo, has set up in the middle of the street. A girl in a frilly skirt tap-dances on a piece of plywood that's been tossed onto the ground. I drop a few more bills into an upturned hat and get a wink and an air-kiss for my efforts.

The beauty of the Vieux Carré is that on any given day of the week, you can wander the streets and hear some of the most talented musicians on the planet.

In other cities you see the guys who drum the bottoms of five-gallon paint buckets. And not to discount their talent, but as Earl would say, "That mess don't fly here." If you want to make a buck on the streets of the Big Easy, you better be able to make an instrument sing like nobody's business.

I turn onto Orleans Avenue and see Cash and Luc exit Cash's place. They head in my direction, but they don't see me. Which affords me the rare opportunity to study them at length.

Where Cash is lean and sinewy, Luc is sturdy and muscled. Where Cash is light and golden, Luc is dark and enigmatic. Where Cash is messy and disheveled, Luc is clean-cut and freshly shaved.

A study in opposites.

And yet, in all the ways that count, they're exactly alike. Both brave. Both gallant. But loyal to a fault.

Warmth spreads through me when I think how lucky I am to have these two amazing men in my life. And when Cash glances up and sees me, the corners of his eyes crinkling, I want to run to him. I want to throw my arms around his neck and whisper my good news into his ear. But his insistence on keeping things platonic between us works like glue on my feet.

"We were headed your way!" he calls from more than a block away. "We thought we'd surprise you and take you to dinner!"

Hearing his strident voice reminds me of his reaction on the streetcar when I told him about contacting the neurosurgeon. For the first time, it occurs to me that he might not view this email from Dr. Stevens in the same light I do.

Shoot.

Maybe I should've stopped to give this plan of mine more thought.

"I was hoping to see how y'all were coming along on your house!" I holler back, ungluing my feet and forcing myself to continue in their direction.

It's not a lie. I *have* been itching to check out the progress they've made.

When we meet at the corner of Orleans and Bourbon, Luc bends to kiss my cheek. His lips are warm and the whorl of hair flopped over his brow tickles my forehead. Cash, I notice, only continues to smile at me.

"Cut out of work early, did you?" He turns up the sidewalk and heads back toward his place.

"It was slow." I shrug. "Charlie will be fine until Gus shows up."

Once we've climbed the stoop, Cash puts his hand on the doorknob and cautions, "Remember. It's a work in progress." Then he opens the door and hits the switch on the wall.

The single bare bulb dangling from the center of the room shines over newly sanded floors, bare trim, and a crap-ton of brand-new drywall and plaster.

They've stripped years of paint from the fireplace. In its place is a whitewash that softens the color of the brickwork, turning it a delicate gray. They've installed a reclaimed barn door between the living room and the hallway leading to the bedrooms. Its detailed ironwork and thick, shiny wood stands out as artwork among the drop cloths and sawdust. And they've added to the crown molding until it's nearly a foot thick, a massive architectural statement that runs through the open living room, dining room, and kitchen.

I whistle. "How can a guy who has such questionable taste in clothes, books, and television shows build something that looks like this?" I indicate the three expansive rooms.

"The design choices are mostly Luc's," Cash admits. "I sand what he tells me to sand and paint what he tells me to paint."

"Horseshit," Luc grunts. "Don't fall for his hang-dog humble act, Maggie May. The man has a vision. All I'm doing is helping him realize it."

"What about the bedrooms? The bathrooms?" I ask.

"Work zones you want no part of," Cash assures me. "Besides, since you're here, I want to get your take on paint colors." He walks over to one of the folding chairs and picks up a thick binder filled with paint swatches.

A trill of pleasure skips up my spine.

He wants *my* take on paint colors?

I try to act casual when he hands me the binder, but my insides are throwing a dance party complete with keg stands and body shots. Flipping through the swatches, I take my time walking from the living room to the dining room to the kitchen and back again.

"This one." I finally point to a dreamy blueish gray. "It's soft enough not to overpower whatever color scheme you decide to go with, and yet it still makes a statement."

He looks down at the swatch, then up at me. "What statement would that be?"

"Home."

When his mouth curls up at the corners, my toes curl inside my boots.

"Silver Mist it is." He folds the swatch to mark its place. "Now"—he takes the binder from me and sets it back on the chair—"about dinner."

"What do y'all say we grab hot dogs from a Lucky Dogs vendor and head to Fritzel's?" I propose. "The band will be starting soon, and I'd like to tell Eva I made an effort to go listen to her cousin."

Lord forgive me, but I think I'll have better luck bringing up the issue of Dr. Stevens if I can get Cash into a party atmosphere. He's always been more receptive to things when he's in a festive mood.

"I'm game," Luc agrees easily.

"Cash?" I turn to him. "Do you think it'd be too loud at Fritzel's? Would it hurt your head?"

He shrugs. "Let's give it a shot and find out."

Twenty minutes later, I'm sitting at one of the long, wooden picnic tables inside the jazz club.

Most locals wouldn't be caught dead on Bourbon Street. The famous thoroughfare is strictly for tourists. But Fritzel's is the exception. It boasts enough authentic New Orleans flare to put the pepper in *everyone's* gumbo.

We've finished our hot dogs when the band stops tuning their instruments and jumps into the first song of the night. Not long after, the waitress arrives with our drinks.

I lean over and whisper in Cash's ear, "How's the volume?"

He gives me a thumbs-up. It's all the encouragement I need to bide my time and enjoy the show.

Eva's cousin proves to be a savant on the piano. He doesn't tickle the ivories, he *thrills* them. In fact, all the musicians at Fritzel's are at the top of their game. The trumpeter wails. The bass player thumps. And the saxophonist delights.

With the whole bar clapping and stomping and singing along to songs like "Sweet Georgia Brown" and "Muskrat Ramble," an hour passes in the blink of an eye. By the time the band takes its first break, the room is stuffy from the press of too many bodies, Cash is two drinks in and smiling lazily, and I figure there's no better time than the present.

"Let's get some fresh air!" I holler above the noise of conversation and ice clinking in glasses. When Luc and Cash follow me out the back door into the small courtyard, I try to calm the butterflies in my stomach by covertly taking deep breaths.

The smell of the climbing nightshade vine growing along the back wall sweetens the air. The sounds of Bourbon Street echo in the background. And above our heads, the sky is an expanse of black silk shot through with pinholes of silver starlight.

It's a gorgeous Southern night. The kind that happens only in early spring or late fall when it's not too cold and not too hot. The kind that makes you grateful to be alive.

"I forgot how great this place is." Luc's grin stretches from ear to ear, making those dastardly dimples wink.

"I know, right?" I happily agree. "I don't come here often enough."

"Maybe we should add it to our regularly scheduled get-togethers," he suggests. "Every other Sunday morning at Café Du Monde and every Thursday night at Fritzel's."

"Except I can't make promises when it comes to working the evening shifts at Bon Temps Rouler. I never know when Gus or Chrissy will want a night off."

"Right." He gifts me with a pitying look. "Tough being a working stiff, huh?"

I stick my tongue in my cheek. "On that note...y'all haven't said a thing about your plans for opening your security business."

"'Cause we don't have any plans. Every time I bring it up, this one"—Luc points at Cash—"cuts me off and tells me, 'One thing at a time.'"

"House first," Cash insists. "Business later. Besides, right now our hands are full with those *other* things that need taken care of."

The mere allusion to Rick Armstrong and George Sullivan is enough to make my heart skip a beat. And just that easy, this perfect Southern night is wrecked.

Since that's the case, *here goes nothing*…

"I received an email from that neurosurgeon I wrote to about your head."

I don't know what I expected, but what I get is crickets. Nothing. Nada. It turns into one of those never-ending moments that stretches into eternity, and even though folks are usually scared by loud noises, it's silence that's truly terrifying. The hairs on the back of my neck lift as Cash continues to stand there and stare at me.

Swallowing convulsively, I place an unsteady hand on his shoulder. "Cash?"

"I told you to leave it alone." The words barely make it past his clenched teeth.

I carefully remove my hand and curl it into a fist. "I know. And I understand. But if you'll think about it for a minute, you'll see—"

"Think about it?" His eyes cut into me like daggers. "*Think about it?* You think I don't think about how my fucking head is fucking broken every fucking minute of every fucking day?"

I wince as his voice rises with each word. Groups of people who've come outside to cool off turn in our direction.

"Cash, come on now." There's a warning in Luc's tone. "Maggie May only wants to help."

Cash turns on Luc. "Well, she can *help* by butting the fuck out!"

"I know you're trying to be strong about this." I keep my tone soft and modulated, like I'm talking to a spooked horse. "But you don't have to be strong. You don't have to deal with this on your own. You have me and Luc to—"

"*Trying* to be strong about this? Woman, I'm not *trying* to be strong about this. I *am* being strong about this. You have no fucking clue how—"

"Lower your voice," Luc interrupts, his words a quiet counterpoint to Cash's fury.

"She's questioning my strength." Cash stabs a finger in my direction.

I open my mouth to object, but Luc beats me to it. "No, she's not, you dumbass. She's saying you don't *gotta* be strong all the time. We're here to help you. And besides, you're not being strong, you're being *hard*. There's a difference."

"I'm sure you're going to tell me what the fuck that is."

Every time Cash says *fuck*, I feel its percussive effects inside my chest. Not because of my delicate sensibilities, but because it shows he's growing more livid with each passing second.

This was a mistake. This was a *huge* mistake.

"Strength bends." Luc maintains his steady tone. "Hardness breaks. So, how about you bend a little, huh?"

"Hardness breaks? You think I'm broken?" Cash swings back to me. "You think I need to be fixed? Well, I hate to tell you, but this is *me* now!"

His lips are curved into the kind of sneer I've only ever seen directed toward school bullies. It's a steel arrow straight to the tender center of my heart.

"This is as good as it gets!" he yells, uncaring of the audience we've attracted. "And I'm not asking you to take it or leave it! I'm telling you to fucking leave it! Leave it alone! Leave *me* alone!"

"That's enough!" Luc bellows, finally losing his cool. "Don't talk to her that way. You need to adjust your attitude for gratitude, man."

"Fuck you!" A big vein snakes up the center of Cash's forehead. In this moment, I can see some of his dad in him, and it makes me ill. "And fuck you too, Maggie, for making me feel worse about myself than I already do!"

He spins on his heels and slams through the door back into the bar.

I want to go after him, to explain or cajole or somehow make things right, but my world tilts off its axis and my knees go unsteady. Luc keeps me upright with a hand under my elbow.

"Easy," he says.

"We need to—" I realize I'm crying when my voice catches.

"Give him some space."

"But—"

That's all I manage before he pulls me into his arms. "Show's over!" he calls to the people milling around the courtyard. "Go about your business!"

I hear the scuffle of feet over brick as the crowd quietly shuffles back into the bar. Luc can be pretty darn imposing when he puts his mind to it. And even though I can't see his face with my cheek pressed against his chest, I know his expression brooks no argument.

Wiping the wetness from my eyes, I whisper, "I sh-shouldn't have done that. He said he didn't want my help. I should've listened."

"Don't." He holds me at arm's length to point a finger at my nose. "Don't blame yourself 'cause he's a horse's ass. You love him. You're scared for him. And instead of sitting on your hands and crying, 'woe is me,' you had the gumption to do something to help him. He should be *thanking* you, not screaming at you in a courtyard full of folks."

"He won't forgive me for this." Even as I say the words, I pray they're not true.

"Hell yes, he will. He won't have any choice."

I search his face in confusion. "Why's that?"

"'Cause y'all are meant to be. I mean, you gotta be, right? You both held a flame for each other for ten years. If that's not destiny, I don't know what is."

Five minutes ago, I would have agreed with him. Now?

"You truly believe that? You truly believe *anyone* is meant to be? Or is it simply life and circumstances and peculiarities and timing that bring people together? And then pigheadedness that *keeps* them together?"

"Who cares?" He shrugs. "The point is, if ever two pigheaded people deserved each other, it's you and Cash."

I'm startled to find myself smiling through my tears. "You're the only one who can do that, you know."

"What?"

"When I'm suffocating, you make me able to breathe again."

CHAPTER FORTY-FOUR

Cash

Dear Cash,

It's nearly Valentine's Day, so this afternoon I took the streetcar from the Garden District to The Quarter and stood for a while in front of the Faerie Playhouse. That little Creole cottage is so sweet with its pink paint and big wooden hearts.

It reminds me of the times you talked about owning a place exactly like it. "Not pink," you'd say. "And no hearts. But everything else is perfect."

You know what I think? I think you LIKED the paint and the hearts. I think you liked the story of the guy who lives there having decorated it in tribute to his lifelong partner who adored Valentine's Day.

You try to hide it, but you're a romantic when it comes right down to it.

Anyway, by the time I got home, my throat was KILLING me. Auntie June got out the flashlight and looked inside my mouth. She's diagnosed me with strep throat, and I have an appointment to see the doctor first thing tomorrow morning. But tonight, I'm lying in bed, feeling wretched, and thinking of the gummy bears you brought me the last time I was sick.

That was over a year ago. Can you believe it? In one way, it feels like it was only yesterday. In another way, it feels like I've lived a lifetime since then.

So much has changed.

But that brings me to my point. Which is that despite all the changes, I'm still a romantic too. It doesn't matter how many days go by, or how many miles separate us, you'll always be my valentine. My one and only.

Love, Maggie

"Love is the truly great manifesto; the urge to be, to count for something, and, if death must come, to die valiantly, with acclimation—in short, to remain a memory."

I'm not much for foreign writers, but a long time ago, Luc gave me a book by some Italian guy named Cesare Pavese and that one quote has stuck with me.

Love *is* the great manifesto. The end-all, the be-all. The answer to the big question, *Why are we here?*

If we do it right—love, I mean—then our lives count for something.

Which means…yeah… I need to fix things with Maggie.

Been an ass to her in the week since Fritzel's, ignoring her texts, not answering the door when she came to drop off a bag of groceries, and generally keeping to myself like an ill-tempered ogre in a cave. Been an ass to Luc, too, telling him to stick to surveilling Rick's house and staying the hell away from me.

My only excuse? Pride. Plain and simple.

And maybe too much booze.

Okay, *definitely* too much booze.

I *hate* what I've become. What I'm *becoming*. But I hate it more when I see the shadow of my former self reflected in the eyes of the only two people I love.

With them, it's impossible to ignore that I'm so much less than I was. And the fucking *unfairness* of it all makes me want to scream. But when I scream, my head splits in two. And when my head splits in two, I reach for my flask. Then pop goes the weasel!

Love is truly the great manifesto. As I climb the steps to Miss Bea's front porch, I remind myself it's the only thing that matters.

Once I'm standing in front of the massive wooden door, I bask in a hundred memories of the times I came here to pick Maggie up for a date. Back when things were easier, sweeter. Back before life and death and love got so tangled and twisted up.

I press the doorbell with a shaky finger. A hollow-sounding gong echoes inside the big house and inside my head. On a scale of one to ten, my headache is sitting at about an eleven. But the second the door swings open, I forget about the pain because…

Maggie.

My breath hitches.

"Cash?" Her voice is tentative.

"Happy Thanksgiving." Feel like scuffing my toe against the ground like a conscience-stricken kid.

"I didn't know if you'd come. I thought—" She stops and steps into me, going up on tiptoe so she can wrap her arms around my neck.

I close my eyes at the feel of her, the smell of her.

"I'm glad you're here," she whispers in my ear. Always so ready to welcome me back. Always so quick to forgive.

"Come in. Come in." She motions through the open doorway once she releases me.

"Mind if we sit out here for a bit?" I hitch my chin toward the porch swing.

Her brow wrinkles, but she quietly closes the door behind her. When we're seated, I set the swing rocking, listening to the delicate creak of the chains and breathing deeply of the soft autumnal smells of mums and sweet, wet leaves.

We had a rain shower last night, a short burst of precipitation, but the drumming of fat drops on the roof was enough to wake me. After lying there for hours, staring into the darkness and feeling the loneliness of the empty house seeping into me, I finally made the decision to get over myself and come today.

"I'm sorry," we blurt in unison.

I laugh, then insist, "No. *I'm* sorry. Never should've said those things to you at Fritzel's. And I definitely never should've wasted a week ignoring you. I'm a fucking idiot."

Before I finish speaking, she's shaking her head. "You *told* me to let it go. But I didn't listen. I went crashing around and breaking things between us."

"Nothing you do could ever break things between us, Maggie."

"No?" She searches my face.

I shake my head, and her angel eyes are so relieved, so optimistic I have to look away.

My gaze lands on the two live oak trees. They're huge and ancient looking. If they could talk, what stories would they tell of the lives that have passed beneath their branches? What births have they seen? What deaths? What promises of never-ending love have they heard? What words of hate and heartlessness?

Compared to theirs, the span of my own life seems wispy and insubstantial, like the Spanish moss that hangs from the them.

"Give me the information for that doctor." I make the decision in that moment. "I'll have my records sent to him."

"You will? Oh, Cash! That's fantastic news!" She has her cell phone in hand before I can blink. My phone buzzes in my pocket barely five seconds later.

"I forwarded his email to you," she says excitedly. "And I know you think you've come to the end of the road where your head injury is concerned, and you want to be left well enough alone to deal with it as you see fit, but maybe Dr. Stevens can help. That's his name, by the way. Dr. Stevens at Johns Hopkins. He's the best neurosurgeon in the country. If anyone can find some answers, or come up with some solutions, he can and—"

She cuts herself off. "Sorry. I'm babbling." Her smile is brighter than the noonday sun. It sets my heart on fire. "But I can't help it. I'm so *happy* you're going to let him try to help you. And I know you're going to be—"

She laughs and shakes her head. "Sorry. Babbling again."

Her hopefulness threatens to become contagious, so I jump up and offer her a hand. "We better go inside before Miss Bea comes out and scolds us for ignoring her."

She makes a face and motions toward Smurf. The ancient blue pickup truck is sandwiched between a long line of cars parked at the curb. "Luc's here. You're not his favorite person at the moment, just FYI."

"So I'll give him an apology too." I sigh. "Weird. For someone who's pretty much the antithesis of AA, I'm getting good at whichever step it is that's all about making amends."

It's a bad joke. I'm not surprised she doesn't laugh.

Once we're inside, she leads me to the library. Luc is sitting on a long, upholstered sofa. Helene, his mother, perches next to him in a leather wingback chair. The room is something out of a fairy tale. Parquet floors, Persian rugs, and floor-to-ceiling shelves of books—no doubt some first editions.

Always thought this house was intimidating. But this room skews into the category of *formidable*.

"Cash!" Helene sees me standing in the doorway with Maggie, and her brown eyes—so much like Luc's—light up. "We didn't know if you'd come!"

Making her way over, she plants a kiss on my cheek. She smells like warm spices and her flowing skirt and soft sweater showcase the figure of a woman half her age. If not for the web of fine lines around her eyes and lips, she could pass for Luc's older sister instead of his mother.

"Helene." I squeeze her shoulder affectionately and give her a once-over before wiggling my eyebrows. "As always, you take my breath away. You sure I can't change your mind about trying a younger man on for size?"

She pinches my cheek. "You're a terrible flirt. It's going to get you into trouble someday."

"What makes you think it hasn't already?"

"Mmm." She glances over her shoulder at her son, who has

yet to rise from the sofa. "Well, your charm's wasted on me. But I know someone who could use a dose of it. In case you didn't know, he's not very happy with you at the moment."

At first, Helene wasn't too stoked about me striking up a friendship with Luc. She thought I was a rabble-rouser. And I was; there's no denying it. But over the years, she's mellowed toward me. Maybe she knows how much I needed Luc back then. Maybe she knows how much I still need him now.

"We better go help Miss June with the food," she says to Maggie, herding her in the direction of the wafting smells of roasting turkey, baked ham, and dense, rich biscuits.

"Smooth," I tell her back. "Very smooth."

She glances over her shoulder and winks.

Chuckling, I turn to find Luc eyeing me narrowly. My grin falls from my face. "Right. Okay. So I'm an asshole."

He slowly stands from the sofa. "Also, you suck at apologies."

"What can I say?" I spread my hands.

"I think the traditionally accepted phrase is, 'I'm sorry.'"

"You know I am."

"Yeah. I do." He motions me over, his expression softening. "Come here then. Gotta hug it out."

I meet him in the center of the room, and we do that bro-hug thing complete with awkward angles and hard back slaps. Like Maggie, Luc can't hold a grudge for more than a minute. It's one of the many things they share and one of the many things I love about each of them.

After we pull apart, he keeps a hand on my shoulder. "You squared things away with Maggie May?"

Of course his first concern is for her.

"I agreed to send that doctor my records like she wants me to, if that's what you mean."

He nods. "And who knows? Maybe the old sawbones *can* help you."

"I'm tired of getting my hopes up," I sigh.

"But you'll do it for Maggie May."

"Yeah. I will."

"Good man." He squeezes my shoulder.

"Aw. Isn't bromance sweet?" At the sound of an annoyingly familiar voice, I turn to find Violet leaning against the doorjamb. If the sight of Maggie is enough to calm the relentless throbbing inside my skull, then the sight of her sister is enough to set my scrambled brain pounding again.

"Looking for your witch's spell book?" I ask. "I know the library seems the obvious choice, but I think you should check the cellar next to your cauldron."

"Ha-ha." She advances into the room. "You're funny. You should take your act on the road and become a stand-up comedian. And in case you missed it, the important part of that suggestion is the bit about going *on the road*. As in, be gone. Take a hike. Shoo."

"Think I'll go see how the turkey's coming along." Luc heads toward the sound of voices coming from the back of the house so quickly I feel the breeze of his departure.

Maggie told me Miss June's kids would be here, along with their spouses and *their* kids. And who knows how many of Miss Bea's lofty friends have come to partake of June's famous cooking? But it sounds like there's a houseful.

I use that as an excuse to follow in Luc's footsteps. "Should probably go say my hellos."

Before I can make my escape, however, Violet stops me with, "I have something to say to you."

It's strange. She and Maggie share so many of the same features. And yet, on Violet that small, upturned nose and that cupid's-bow mouth don't look fairylike and charming. They look small and pinched.

"Okay." I stop at the door and cross my arms. "So say it."

"You hurt Maggie. *Again.*"

Hearing the words aloud ties my stomach into hard knots. It also puts me on the defensive. Which, in my case, generally provokes an attack. "What do you care? You've always had it out for her anyway."

"You have no idea what my relationship is with my sister." Her dislike of me drips from her lips like venom.

"Maybe not. But I know what your relationship is with me. You took one look at me and decided to hate my guts. Why is that? Did you think I wasn't good enough for Maggie?" Before she can answer, I add, "Not that I think I'm good enough for her. I've always known I'm not. But man, you sure were quick to judge, weren't you?"

For a while, she says nothing, searching my face. Then she shakes her head and laughs. "You don't remember, do you?"

"Remember what?"

"Your first day of school when you sat beside me in biology class."

Don't know if it's the head injury or the booze or if I simply have a terrible memory, but I have no idea what she's talking about.

She reads the truth in my face. "Wow. You truly *don't* remember."

"So tell me," I challenge.

"Never mind." She waves a hand through the air. "Forget it."

"No." When she starts to brush by me, I touch her arm. "What did I do? What did I say?"

"It doesn't matter." She shakes off my fingers. "What matters is I'm sick and tired of you hurting my little sister. Do it again, and I'll cut off your balls and fry them up for breakfast. I know where you sleep."

Turning on her heel, she exits the room, leaving me with that rather unpleasant imagery.

Huh. Violet taking up for Maggie? That's new.

Or maybe it's not. Maybe Maggie's been right all along, and none of us has ever truly known Violet Carter the way we think we do.

Before I can delve too deeply into that possibility, or rack my aching, broke-ass brain for some sliver of a memory of biology class, Miss June hollers from the dining room, "Dinner's ready! Y'all come eat!"

I frown when I catch myself automatically reaching for the flask in my back pocket. Left it at home. Didn't want to inadvertently overindulge and embarrass Maggie or her aunts. But, man, I sure do miss it.

More than that, I *need* it.

Chapter Forty-five

Maggie

Denial is like paint. You slather on enough layers, and you forget what's underneath.

For the last week, my worry for Cash has overshadowed my other concerns. And all afternoon long, while I've enjoyed a true New Orleans-style Thanksgiving filled with family and friends, Cajun-spiced turkey, crawfish gravy, and cream biscuits, I haven't let my mind touch on anything but the pleasure of the moment and the conversations at hand.

But with the last bite of dessert eaten, and folks pushing away from the table to take their dirty dishes to the kitchen and then go in search of a soft spot to unzip and nap, I can't escape Luc's pointed expression. It says, *We need to talk.*

Just like that, my thick coating of denial is stripped away and I'm forced to remember that, *yes*, we're in serious trouble.

Hello, reality, you sorry sonofagun.

"Y'all headed into the living room with the others?" Auntie June asks from one end of the long dining room table where she's covering what's left of the Creole okra with plastic wrap. Her cheeks are rosy from a day spent standing over a hot stove, and her eyes sparkle with pleasure. With the house full of her kids and grandkids, and everyone's bellies stuffed with her amazing cooking, she's in hog heaven.

"Think we'll mosey on out to the veranda," I tell her, motioning through the front window to a sky alive with vibrant splashes of pink and orange. "It looks like it's turned into a gorgeous evening. But I'll come back in a bit to help you finish putting away the leftovers."

"Never mind that." Helene grabs a couple of empty pie dishes. "You three go on out and enjoy the sunset. I'll help Miss June and Miss Bea tidy up." The expression on her face tells me she's wise to the look Luc sent me.

I nod my thanks before following Luc and Cash outside. The fall breeze is cool and fresh. The sun is glorious in its descent. And the day birds are singing their final chorus before making way for the creatures of the night.

Without a word, the three of us head for the porch swing, squeezing in side by side. Luc rests an arm against the back of the swing and sets it rocking with a gentle push of his booted toe. I'm struck by the thought that many of my life's big moments have happened while I've been sitting in this very spot.

It was here a police officer doffed his hat and informed me the bodies of my parents had been located inside a stranger's attic. It was here Cash first told me he loved me. And it was here Luc held me as I read that Dear Jane letter and felt my young heart shatter.

This porch swing seems to be the fulcrum upon which my life pivots. Glancing at Luc, knowing he has something important to share, I'm nervous about which way my world will turn next.

"I can say this for Richard Armstrong." His voice is soft and low, but his words are crystal clear. "He keeps to a schedule. Outta the house at zero eight hundred. Home by eighteen hundred. That being the case, I reckon we should go in first thing Monday morning."

"What's my role?" I ask anxiously. "Wait outside with my cell phone at the ready in case someone shows up and I need to call y'all and tell you to skedaddle?"

Luc is shaking his head before I'm finished speaking. "I want you to stay outta this."

My hackles rise. Luc isn't the Me-Tarzan-You-Jane type, but that sounded pretty darn close. "I'm not a little girl anymore, Luc. You don't need to protect me."

"That's like asking my heart to stop beating."

His words make my cheeks heat. Trying to hide my unease, I turn to Cash. But before I ask him to back me up and let me help out, I notice the tightness of the skin around his eyes and the pinched look of his mouth.

Running through the events of the afternoon, I realize he had wine with dinner, but not once did he reach for his flask. It shows in the shaky hand he pushes through his shaggy hair.

"How bad is it?" I ask. In the face of his pain, all other concerns and arguments are forgotten.

"Bad enough," he admits.

It's anathema, but I offer, "Aunt Bea keeps a bottle of bourbon in the study. You want me to run and fetch it?"

The difference between Cash's quick smile and the shattered look in his eyes is heartbreaking. "Nah. But would you be offended if I took off? My pillow back home is calling my name."

"Of course I won't be offended." I battle the urge to pull him into my arms and soothe the pained wrinkles from his brow.

"I'll drive you," Luc offers.

Cash shakes his head. "You should stay and enjoy the rest of the evening. I'll call a cab to—"

"I'll drive you." Luc's tone leaves no room for debate. "Tell Mom I'll be back in a bit," he says to me as he stands and offers Cash a hand up.

"I'll come with y'all," I offer.

"No," they say in unison.

I peer up at them through narrowed eyes. Do they want time alone to talk more about breaking into Cash's dad's place? Or are they trying to spare me the true scope of Cash's condition?

Neither reason sits well, but I don't argue since, with each passing second, Cash looks greener around the gills.

"Okay, then." I nod and watch them make their way down the steps and across the walk. Cash is a bit unsteady on his feet. Luc is ready to lend him a hand should he need it.

He's not getting better. In fact, he's getting worse.

The thought blazes through me, as swift and terrifying as wildfire.

They're pulling away from the curb when Helene ventures onto the veranda, a cup of coffee in hand.

"Luc's running Cash home," I explain as Smurf disappears around the corner.

"I noticed he was looking like he got pulled through a knothole backward." She takes a seat beside me, arranging her flowing skirt with an unstudied grace. "They stayed with me for a couple weeks after getting out of the army and before coming back here. Did you know that?" When I shake my head, she continues. "Cash was in a lot of pain then, but he was managing it. Doesn't much seem like he's managing it now. He's lost a good fifteen pounds since I saw him."

Realizing he's getting worse is bad enough. Hearing it confirmed makes every bite of my Thanksgiving meal congeal into a hard stone in the bottom of my stomach. I tell her about the Johns Hopkins neurosurgeon, then add, "I pray to God he'll be able to help."

"And if he can't?" She watches me closely.

I shrug, my mind refusing to accept delivery on that possibility. *Nope. Return to sender immediately.* "Guess we'll cross that bridge when we get there," I tell her.

We fall into silence then. Because, really, what more is there to say?

Eventually, she remarks, "You know, I always wondered why you never asked me for their information."

I frown at her. "What do you mean?"

"I mean, when I first got your friend request on Facebook, I reckoned you were contacting me because you wanted to know how to get in touch with them."

I twist my lips. "By that point, it'd been four years since they joined the army. I thought that was plenty of time for them to answer my emails or give me a call if they wanted to."

Her gaze is intent as she takes a sip of coffee. "Luc never told me what happened between you three. All he ever said was that he and Cash were called to duty, and you were so young they didn't want to burden you with their decision to join. He said they didn't want you wasting your last couple of high school years worrying over them."

"Well, if that's what Luc said, then I'm sure it's the truth." Although, it's not the whole truth, and I wish I could tell her. I wish I could come clean to *someone*.

She sighs and says, "But I reckon they failed, huh?"

"What do you mean?"

"I mean, Luc said it didn't matter how much time passed. He said the minute they showed up at your door, he knew you'd never stopped worrying over them. And that you'd never stopped loving Cash."

Even though Luc and I were friends for nearly two years before he left, I never spent much time around Helene. Certainly not enough to encourage such personal dialogue now. Then again, Luc got his in-your-face honesty from someone, so…

"I guess it's true what they say." I lift my hands and let them fall. "First love never dies."

"Let's hope it does in some cases." She takes another sip of her coffee, staring out at a sky that's deepened to soft lavender and shadowy purple.

"What?" My scalp prickles. "Why?"

"If first love never dies, that means my boy will never get over you."

Wow. There's in-your-face honesty, and then there's in-your-face *honesty*.

"I..." I trail off. How the heck am I supposed to respond to *that*? Finally, I manage, "I had no idea Luc felt that way about me until recently. And I swear to you, I never once led him on. Luc's my hero. The absolute best human being on the face of the planet. The last thing I'd ever want is to hurt him."

She turns to me then, her gaze steady on mine. "Luc is a tenderhearted man. And with you, he's given love without the hope of having it returned." Her pride for her son is evident in the soft smile that plays with her lips. Then her smiles falters. "But I worry how much he can withstand before his tender heart grows hard."

Once again, I'm left speechless.

Chapter Forty-six

Cash

Dear Cash,

Last night I had a nightmare.

That's not all that unusual. Most nights, I relive the hours after you left, my unconscious mind replaying them again and again as if looking for a way to change things. To undo things. To make things right.

But last night was different. Last night it was the OLD nightmare that made me sit up in bed.

I told you about it, remember?

In it, I'm floating in the water outside the house where my parents died. I can hear them inside that attic, screaming for help. But no matter how hard I hit the window, the glass won't break. And the water keeps rising higher and higher until I can't fight the current anymore, and I'm dragged away having failed to save them. Again.

As I sat there in bed, trying to claw my way out from under all the guilt and remorse, I was reminded of something I read in Mrs. Tannahill's English class. We were studying folks who've won the Pulitzer Prize in Literature, and there was this one guy, a Frenchman, who wrote, "When the soul suffers too much, it develops a taste for misfortune."

Could that be true?

I shudder to consider it, since it would mean that for some folks, the only way to feel good is to feel bad.

I don't want to feel bad, Cash. I don't want to live a life of pain and sorrow, of shame and regret. I want to live a GOOD life, a HAPPY life.

So my hope is that Frenchman got it all wrong. My hope is it doesn't matter how much a soul suffers; there's always room for joy.

Love, Maggie

The pages of history are hard and sharp. They'll cut your fingers if you're not careful.

As I stand outside the all-too-familiar green door of my sperm donor's house, remembered torture and terror accost me. Zombies, vampires, and witches are said to walk among this city's citizens, especially in The Quarter where tradition and folklore run deep. But the only true monsters I've ever seen in this whole wide world are men like Rick.

It's zero eight thirty, and the residential street he lives on is quiet. The neighborhood kids have gone to school. The adults have left for work. The only sounds of life are coming from the wind chimes hung on the porch next door, their wistful, tinkling tune ringing slightly discordant.

Luc pulls out a small case with the tools necessary for picking a lock. But before he can go to work, I brandish a key from my pocket. "What are the chances?" I ask him.

His eyebrow arches. "I can't believe you kept that."

"A souvenir to mark the time I spent here and a reminder that I got the fuck out."

"Guess this'll be the first test to see if you're right about him. If he hasn't changed the locks, then it's a pretty safe bet he hasn't changed the safe or the combination either."

I insert the key into the lock. It sticks, but it always stuck. With a flick of my wrist, the lock clicks open and the door swings wide.

"Well, I'll be damned," Luc murmurs as we slip into the house.

The warning *beep-beep-beep* of the security system has me hurrying over to the wall panel. I punch in the four-digit code and turn to wiggle my eyebrows when a high-sounding chirp tells me the alarm has disengaged.

"Never thought I'd say this"—the wire clippers Luc has out and at the ready get tucked into his hip pocket—"but thank the good Lord for Rick and his blind arrogance." He glances around and frowns. "Damn. Would you look at this place? It hasn't changed a bit."

With a jaundiced eye, I take in the entryway and adjoining living room.

"The television is new," I say contrarily. Then I admit, "But you're right. There's the umbrella stand he bashed me over the head with when I didn't clean the gutters the way he wanted me to. And there's the armchair I nearly broke when I fell over it after he punched me for leaving a load of clothes in the dryer for too long. Oh, and let's not forget the landing where I stood with a gun in my hand, ready to blow his fucking head off."

Luc's lips thin as he silently watches me.

"Stop giving me that look. I'm fine. In fact, cheers to you, Rick, you fat, pompous prick." I salute the silent house with the flask I pull from my back pocket.

"I don't get it." Luc's brow is wrinkled.

"Don't get what?"

"If he's extorting a bunch of rich folks for boatloads of cash, where's he putting the money?" He makes a circular motion with his hand. "Not in this house."

The Uptown neighborhood where Rick lives is decidedly upper middle class. No one in their right mind would call this place a dump. But Luc's right. It *is* outdated.

"Rick's always been a beady-eyed squirrel, hoarding his scratch for who the fuck knows what. Maybe he plans to buy a private island or a big-ass yacht and retire early." I turn toward the back of the house. "Keep an eye out," I call over my shoulder unnecessarily.

Like the rest of the place, Rick's office is a blast from the past. I avoid looking at the photo of my mother sitting on his desk. Don't want to see the haunted expression in her eyes.

Truth is, I've often wondered why he keeps that picture. It's not like he loved her any more than he loves me. He certainly never spared her the hard kiss of his knuckles when the mood struck. If the cancer hadn't killed her, I'd bet my left nut he would have. Eventually.

Maybe *that's* why he keeps her picture. To gloat over the fact that she's dead and he isn't.

"There you are, you sweet thing." I pat the knee-high safe tucked between two filing cabinets. It's matte black, sitting on four wheels, and proudly boasting the name of a safe company out of Buffalo, New York.

Same locks. Same security code. Same safe. I'm not the praying sort, but recently I've taken to invoking Saint Roch.

Come on, man, I silently implore him. *Don't let this be the one thing that bastard changed.*

Squatting, I blow out a breath and spin the combination dial. Twelve, twenty-five, sixty-five, zero. Rick's birthday plus a zero tacked onto the end. Yes, he's the kind of jackass to choose his own birthday as a combination. Also, yes, he was born on Christmas Day. Which I find supremely ironic considering there are few men *less* Christ-like than Richard Bartholomew Armstrong.

An ice pick of unease slips up my spine when the door handle remains stubbornly stuck horizontal. Patting the safe like a lover, I say quietly, "Come on, ol' girl. You don't want to let me down, do you?"

Never underestimate the power of charm, even on inanimate objects.

I try the combination again. This time I'm careful to make sure the hash mark at the top of the dial precisely lines up with the four numbers. And then...hooah! The silver handle clicks downward, and the heavy door swings open.

Money has a specific scent. Not sure if it's the paper it's printed on, the ink the treasury department uses, or what. But you know it when you smell it.

I definitely smell it. No wonder since the safe is packed top to bottom with dead presidents. Grabbing a small stack, I flip through the bills.

Hundreds. All of them.

"Fuck me." I sit back on my heels, staring at what's got to be close to a quarter million dollars.

Did I give Rick too much credit? I mean, it's not like his business successes have come from an overabundance of brainpower. More like from running backroom deals, taking advantage of lack of government oversight, and strong-arming anyone who dares come up against him. Still…this? If it isn't Mason jars buried in the backyard, it's the next closest thing.

Taking out my cell phone, I snap a few pictures—never know what evidence might come in handy. Then I slide the blue, leather-bound ledger from the top of the neatly stacked cash and open it.

There are pages and pages going back years. Some of what's written might as well be in Mandarin for all I can make heads or tails of it. But other things, like transactions listed next to routing numbers, are far more clear. As are the dollar amounts printed next to the names of some of the small businesses Rick owns in and around the city—places like family diners and car washes are perfect for laundering a little moola.

I carefully photograph each page even though none of what I'm seeing seems to have anything to do with the people Rick is extorting. Then…pay dirt.

A list of initials with dates and dollar amounts scribbled next to them comprise the last three pages of the ledger. If I compare some of these initials with the names of the people Miss Bea gave to Luc, dollars to doughnuts I'll find matches.

"Got you now, you miserable prick," I mutter.

Stuffing the ledger back into the safe, I pull out my flask to toast to my success. I also need to administer some liquid medication. Used to be I had good days and bad days. Recently, the bad days have come to stay.

And yet, despite that, I still have the capacity to feel complete and utter joy at the prospect of putting my old man behind bars. I want to spin in circles atop a mountain, arms outstretched *Sound of Music*-style.

"So?" Luc turns away from his lookout spot near the front door when he hears my footsteps.

I pat my cell phone inside my hip pocket. "Let's go talk to Maggie."

Over the weekend, Luc convinced her to leave this part to us by promising her we would stop by Bon Temps Rouler and fill her in on what we found the *second* we found it. True to his word, twenty minutes later, we're bellied up to the bar as Maggie gets ready to open for the day.

She pours each of us a cup of coffee. When I add a generous double shot of Gentleman Jack to mine, I catch the worried look in her eye. I know what she's going to say before she says it.

"Have you sent along your medical records to Dr. Stevens?"

"Thursday and Friday were holidays. Then it was the weekend. And this morning, I was busy breaking into Rick's house to gather evidence that'll hopefully keep your pretty neck out of Sullivan's noose. So when were you thinking I was supposed to contact the VA to pass along my stuff?"

I wince at her stricken expression and mutter, "Sorry. My head's fucking killing me today."

It isn't a lie.

Then again, it's not why I lit into her either. I blame *that* on the hug she gave me when I came through the door.

It was soft and warm and lingering. She let me feel every inch of her. Made me remember what it was like to hold her and know she was mine. Which, in turn, left me unaccountably angry.

Not at her. At *life*.

"I plan to call my docs at the VA today and set things in motion," I assure her, careful to modulate my tone.

"I'm not trying to burden you with more stuff," she says. If I was capable of hating anything about Maggie, it would be the look on her face right now. It verges on pitying. "I swear I'm not. I just think before you—"

"I said I'll take care of it, Maggie," I interrupt her. "Now, can we talk about more important things?"

Pulling my cell phone from my hip pocket, I explain about the cash hoard in the safe as I thumb through the photos of the ledger pages until I come to the first one with the list of initials and amounts. Setting my phone on the bar, I point.

"See that one there? BJS? It's got to be that Billy Joe Summerset guy, don't you think?"

"Could be coincidence," Luc says, then starts reciting some of the other names Miss Bea gave him. A sixty-second comparison tells us that each of them matches a set of initials inside Rick's ledger.

"You said you thought there was probably a quarter of a million in the safe?" Maggie asks.

"Yeah." I nod. "Why?"

"Well, I don't need a calculator to see that if these figures are true dollar amounts, then Rick has extorted these people for way more than that over the years."

"So then, what's with the stockpile in the safe?" Luc wonders aloud.

I scratch my chin. "No way to know for sure. My guess would be this is the money he hasn't yet been able to funnel through his system of foreign bank transfers and small businesses."

"Good Lord," Maggie breathes, her eyes wide and blinking. "This is it, isn't it? This is the proof we need."

Hate to temper her excitement, but… "It's a start," I say cautiously. "We need to talk to your cop friend and see where we go from here.

Even if this is enough to begin an investigation into Rick, who knows if it's enough to bring Sullivan down with him? Or if it can even be *tied* to Sullivan. As much as it tickles my pickle to think of Rick rotting away inside a prison cell, it's not actually *him* we're after."

"Okay, Mr. Glass Half Empty." Maggie's hands go to her hips. "Where's your optimism?"

It got flushed down the toilet the day the doctors handed me my prognosis.

"Set up a time and place we can talk to your cop friend," I urge.

"I'll text him now." She takes out her phone and types a message. Before she's finished, the front door opens, and Earl finds his way to his spot.

He scowls at Luc and me, muttering, "This place is getting too crowded in the mornings for my tastes."

Maggie rolls her eyes before grabbing the coffee carafe and heading toward him. As she pours him a cup and tops it off with a generous portion of cream, she assures him, "You're still my favorite. Always and forever."

He harrumphs, but I see his mustache wiggle—an indication it's hiding a smile.

"And to prove it," she continues, "I'll let you choose what we play on the jukebox this morning. Although, I swear, if you pick Ray Stevens, I won't speak to you for a week."

"What's wrong with Ray Stevens?" he demands in affront. "The man's got a good voice. He's funny. And he sure as shit knows how to tell a story."

"Yeah, if the kind of story you enjoy involves a squirrel going berserk in church."

Earl chuckles. "Like I said, funny."

"No Ray Stevens." Maggie puts her foot down.

"Fine. Put on "Do-Wacka-Do" by Roger Miller."

She groans, but thirty seconds later, she's got the song cued up. The sound of snappy guitar strumming softly echoes through the overhead speakers.

"Happy?" she asks Earl.

This time his mustache can't hide his grin. "Now this is the way to start the day." He salutes her with this steaming coffee mug.

She chuckles, but it's cut short when her phone chirps. Slipping it from her pocket, she frowns at the screen and makes her way back to me and Luc.

"Bad news. Rory Ketchum took his family on vacation to Key West. They won't be home until Thursday."

"Damn." Luc rubs a hand over his face.

"Nothing to be done about it." I sigh in exasperation. "But ask him if he'd be willing to meet us as soon as he gets back into town."

Maggie shoots off another text and receives a reply almost immediately. She looks up from her screen. "Will seven o'clock on Thursday evening work?"

"Got nothing else on my calendar," Luc says.

I simply give her a thumbs-up and she types in a final message before sliding her cell phone back into her pocket.

For a while, none of us speaks, each lost in our own thoughts. Then Maggie asks Luc, "Your mom left for Shreveport yesterday, didn't she?"

He nods. "She called 'round seventeen hundred to tell me she'd made it home and was snug as a bug in a rug." His eyes narrow. "She also asked me to tell you that she enjoyed your talk and she hopes you won't hold anything against her. She said, and I quote, 'Tell Maggie I'm only a momma bear looking out for her cub.' Since I reckon I'm the cub in question, you wanna fill me in on what y'all discussed?"

Maggie looks uncomfortable. But she plays it off with a smile and then mimes zipping her lips. "What's talked about on Aunt Bea's front porch swing stays on Aunt Bea's front porch swing."

I can't put my finger on it, but there's something in her face when she looks at Luc that wasn't there before.

CHAPTER FORTY-SEVEN

Maggie

What you don't see with your eyes, don't witness with your mouth.
I heard that from a young man who used to stop into Bon Temps Rouler for a drink while he studied the Torah.

Unfortunately, folks around here don't seem to cotton to that particular piece of wisdom. No telephone, no internet, no cable news station is as blisteringly quick at spreading information as the denizens of New Orleans.

That being the case, I should've known the visits Luc and I paid to Sullivan's blackmail victims would reach his ears. I should've known he would react by barging into my apartment first thing in the morning with two police officers in tow. And I *definitely* should've known he'd drag me downtown for questioning despite Jean-Pierre's objections and Yard's feral-sounding growls.

"What do you think you're doing going around town trying to make people tell lies on me?" His expression hasn't changed in the hour he's been interrogating me. It looks like he's caught a whiff of something fetid.

"I don't know what you're talking about." I've repeated that phrase—that *lie*, heaven help me—at least two dozen times. With each passing second, and with each repetition, my fear grows like the yeasted dough Auntie June uses for her homemade bread. "Now, I want a lawyer," I add.

In case you didn't know, let me be the first to tell you that television gets lots of stuff wrong. I mean, have you ever seen a character have to wait for change after buying something at a store? No. They simply pay and leave. And have you ever watched an actor drive around a parking lot for thirty minutes looking for a spot? No. There's always a space available right in front. And yet every police procedural or court drama I've ever watched has nailed it when it comes to an interrogation room.

Small space. White walls. Creepy mirror that everyone knows is two-way. And a camera with an evil red eye blinking in the corner.

That's where I am. A room that might as well have graced the set of *Law & Order*.

I realize now that what I've missed while watching those shows is the *feel* of the place. It's hot. Literally. This room is made to make a person sweat. And it smells bad. Like the body odor and terror of hundreds of "perps" or "persons of interest."

Sullivan ignores my request for a lawyer, *again*, and instead walks around the table toward me, the heels of his cowboy boots clapping against the tile. My heart pounds in time to each approaching step, and I now know how those wild pigs who live in the swamp feel when they have to go to the water's edge to grab a drink despite knowing an alligator is lurking in the depths below.

It's a crapshoot. And the stakes are life and death.

"What are you up to, little missy?" he demands, his eyes shining hot beneath the shadow of his cowboy hat's brim.

"Nothing," I say, hating that my voice sounds as thin and as brittle as a twig. "I want a lawyer."

He props one hip on the table in front of me. His thigh brushes my forearm. Since my hand is cuffed to a steel bar in the middle of the table, I can't move away.

I think he can see how uncomfortable his touch makes me. I think he likes it.

His leg swings slightly. The scales on his shiny alligator-skin boot catch the fluorescent light overhead and wink as if to mock me.

"You're trying to get something on me because you know I'll never stop coming after you for killing my boy," he asserts matter-of-factly, and I swallow because he's right.

For a split second, I'm tempted to let the truth bleed out of me like a mortal wound. I'm not cut out for keeping secrets, and this one's been a cancer in me for ten long years.

If I confessed, maybe I could keep Luc out of it. I could say I hit Dean with that rock while Luc was back at the truck, that Luc never saw what happened, and then…what? How could I, a sixteen-year-old girl who barely weighed a buck ten soaking wet, have gotten rid of Dean's two-hundred-pound body?

Plus, Luc would never let me go it alone. If I confessed, *he'd* confess. And I can't… I *can't* let him suffer for something *I* did.

Glancing at the blinking red light on the camera, I lift my chin and refuse to speak.

Sullivan's lips press into a line so thin they're completely covered by his mustache. Then he leans forward, his mouth close to my ear, his words too low for the camera to record. "Go on and keep quiet. It won't matter none. In the end, by fair means or foul, I always get my man. Or *woman*."

A bead of perspiration drips down the groove of my spine. If I look down, I know I'll see the armpits of my pajamas dark with sweat stains—he didn't wait for me to change out of my Harry Potter jammies before frog-marching me to the police station.

"Now…" he continues, sitting back and allowing me space to drag in a shaky breath. "I'll ask you again, why are you going around trying to make folks tell lies about me?"

I'm ready to let loose with the same old song and dance, but I'm stopped by a commotion outside the door. Raised voices sound alongside a scuffling noise that's immediately followed by a loud bang when the door bursts open.

"—can't go in there!" One of the officers who came to my apartment with Sullivan is blocking the door.

"I can. And I will." A man I don't recognize pushes past the policeman. He's wearing a three-piece suit and shiny brown Oxfords. An expensive-looking satchel is slung over one shoulder, and a pair of stylish glasses magnifies the sharpness of his gaze when he looks at me. "Miss Carter?"

"Y-yes?" Dang it. There it is again. That brittle, weak-sounding edge to my voice.

"I'm David Abelman. Your lawyer."

I blink dumbly. "My lawyer?" Is it possible I conjured one from thin air?

"Are you arresting her?" a familiar voice demands. I turn to see Luc standing in the doorway. With his muscled arms crossed and righteous indignation shining in his dark eyes, he looks like an avenging angel.

I didn't realize how tightly my insides were wound until I feel them unravel so fast I get dizzy.

He came.

"Well?" Abelman asks Sullivan, checking his watch. His salt-and-pepper hair is neatly parted on one side, and his face is pleasant without being particularly handsome. It's impossible to guess his age. "*Are* you arresting her?"

Sullivan jumped from the table when the door burst open. Now he's standing behind my shoulder. When I turn to look up at him, I can see he's livid. His face is so red it's nearly purple. Instinct has me scooting forward in my chair, putting as much distance between us as possible.

"If you're not arresting her," Abelman goes on, "then I'll kindly ask you to uncuff her."

Sullivan glances down at me, his left eyelid twitching. "I'm not done with you," he hisses.

"Mr. Sullivan" — Abelman's tone borders on boredom — "I'll thank you not to threaten my client unless you want me to file a formal complaint with the district attorney's office."

Sullivan doesn't respond. Instead, he stomps from the room, shoulder-checking Luc on the way out.

Luc looks like he'd like nothing better than to smash Sullivan's face in. But rather than attacking a man of the law inside a police station, he turns toward the officer still standing in the doorway and says, "Uncuff her, please."

His request would sound perfectly cordial if I didn't know him so well. It takes a learned ear to hear the latent threat in his voice.

Reluctantly, the policeman shuffles over to me, unlocking my cuffs under the watchful eyes of Luc and Abelman.

As soon as I'm free, I run to Luc. He catches me against him, holding me tight when all my courage deserts me. Tears clog the back of my throat. Every muscle in my body shakes.

"Shhh, Maggie May." He runs a hand down the back of my hair. "It's okay. I gotcha."

CHAPTER FORTY-EIGHT

Cash

Dear Cash,

Vee came home for the weekend. Besides a basket full of dirty clothes, she brought with her tons of stories of college life. She actually came into my room, sat on my bed, and TALKED to me.

I can't remember the last time she did that. And it made me think that maybe she's forgiven me.

Yeah, yeah. I know you and Luc and Eva and everyone else say there's nothing to forgive. That it's not my fault my folks are gone. But whether that's true or not, the fact of the matter is their deaths drove a wedge between me and Vee that I thought could never be removed.

Now I have some hope.

Anyway, to celebrate her homecoming, the aunts took us to the Napoleon House for dinner. Auntie June loves their grilled alligator sausage sandwich. And it's weird. I've eaten there dozens of times, but I never thought to ask where the place got its name.

Turns out, it was actually supposed to BE Napoleon's house. As in THE Napoleon.

Apparently, Jean Lafitte hatched a plan to spring Napoleon from his exile on Saint Helena. Lafitte was going to bring the Little Corsican back to the Big Easy, and the house on the corner of Chartres and St. Louis was set up to be his residence. But Napoleon died before Lafitte could set sail.

Isn't that fascinating? To think I've lived here all my life and that's the first time I've heard that story. It makes me wonder, are places like people? Do you ever truly know them?

Did I ever truly know you? The more time that goes by without hearing from you, the more I wonder...

Love, Maggie

The narratives we tell about ourselves are always filled with misrepresentations, blind spots, and partial truths.

It's rare to be completely clear when indulging in self-reflection. But one thing I can't deny or discount is that my anger tends to spark easy. Probably because I was born with more fuses than the average person.

I blame that on the man who sired me.

"Why the hell didn't you call me?" The volume of my voice sends a meat cleaver into my cerebral cortex. I hastily remove my flask to take a sip of Gentleman Jack.

"There wasn't time," Luc insists.

He's sitting in one folding chair, while Maggie, still in her pajamas, slumps listlessly in the other. She looks like a wet dishcloth that's been hastily wrung out and left crumpled on the kitchen counter. As for me? I'm pacing the length of the living room, too outraged to sit or to appreciate the beauty of the wood floors, which are finally ready for stain and varnish.

Can't believe Sullivan had the nerve to barge into Maggie's apartment at the butt crack of dawn and drag her down to the police station.

Oh, wait. Yes, I can. The man's a total dickbag.

"When Jean-Pierre called to tell me what happened, I was already fifteen minutes from the swamp house," Luc adds. "I spent the rest of the drive into town frantically calling everyone I know who might be able to put me in touch with a good lawyer. I reckoned springing Maggie May from the clink was more important than taking the time to fill you in on what was going on."

"Saying I was in the clink makes me sound like a convicted felon," Maggie mutters. "I wasn't in the *clink*. I was in an interrogation room."

Yeah. An *interrogation room*. The thought of Sullivan handcuffing her to a table and grilling her for even one second is enough to make a sick sensation swirl in the bottom of my belly. Or maybe that's the whiskey. Skipped breakfast, so there's nothing in my gut to cut its strength.

"You were in an interrogation room without a lawyer. Without having been granted a phone call. Without having been read your rights. What happened will not stand." I stop pacing to point a finger at Luc. "Get that lawyer to press fucking charges."

He pats the air. "Look, what Sullivan did sticks in my craw too. But that doesn't mean I'm ready to go off with my pistol half-cocked. We gotta play this thing smart. Let's talk with Maggie May's cop friend, see where we stand on bringing Rick *and* Sullivan down before we go 'round pressing charges that may or may not hold water."

"He illegally detained her." My back molars might explode if I grind my teeth any harder.

"Yeah. But that'll get him what? A slap on the wrist? A suspension? Are we or are we not looking to bring the bastard down for good?"

I hate to admit when Luc's right, but... "You're right." I take a deep breath, hoping it'll tamp down my rage.

"Maybe we *should* press charges," Maggie says. "If we press charges, then Sullivan will be too busy fighting those to come after us."

Luc cocks his head. "Did he tell you something about what he's cooking up? Did he give anything away that might give us—"

"No." She cuts him off. "But there was a look in his eye and a tone in his voice. I think he's close to setting something in motion."

That disconcerting announcement fills the room like a noxious gas, making each of us grimace.

Eventually, Luc shakes his head. "We can't start playing defense. We gotta stick with our plan."

"I agree." I nod emphatically. "Once we're knocked back on your heels, it'll be tough as hell to gain the upper hand."

"Exactly. And if Sullivan *does* make a move before we're further along in the process"—Luc's jaw sets at a hard angle—"*then* we'll bring Abelman in to throw as many wrenches in the works as he can."

"Right," I agree. Then I frown when an unsettling notion occurs. "Did you…" I pin him with a look. "Did you tell him why Sullivan detained Maggie? Did you tell him what happened in the bayou?"

"I told him the same story we've been telling everyone else," Luc says. "The only folks who know the true scope of what happened that night are here in this room."

"Right." I nod. Then a memory surges, and I turn to Maggie. "Wait a minute. That first evening we met Jean-Pierre, he thanked Luc for saving you. If he wasn't talking about the bayou, what *was* he talking about?"

Luc and Maggie exchange a look. Is it my imagination, or does color climb into her cheeks? "What?" I demand. "Why are you two sending each other coded eye messages?"

She starts picking at a hangnail. "Jean-Pierre was…uh… talking about Luc befriending me and giving me a reason to live when I'd lost all hope," she admits quietly.

I blink, too stunned to speak.

She glances up at me, and this time there's no mistaking the two red flags of color flying in her cheeks. "Don't look at me like that, Cash. I was a teenage girl with dead parents, clinical depression, oppressive guilt, and raging hormones."

I finally find my voice. "Why didn't you ever *say* anything?"

She hitches a shoulder. "By the time you arrived on the scene, the impulse had passed, and I was ashamed I'd ever had it in the first place." Her chin firms as she looks at me pointedly. "You understand how shame can make someone keep secrets, don't you?"

Touché. I run a hand through my hair. "Damn, Maggie. I wish I'd known."

"Would it have changed anything? Would it have made you stay?"

I clench my jaw, not knowing how to put into words that my leaving didn't have a thing to do with her. On the contrary, it was a question of survival. The survival of my soul.

"Exactly." She nods, accurately reading my expression. Then her chin wobbles, evidence that even though she's trying to be brave, this conversation is getting to her.

It's a mistake to touch her, but I can't stop myself from pulling her from the chair and into a hug. The guilt and shame I feel at being the one to have set this awful chain of events into motion, coupled with the knowledge that she'd once been so lost she'd thought death was her only option, are too much to bear. A world without Magnolia May Carter would be a dark and hopeless place, indeed.

Her arms are around me in an instant, squeezing me tight.

"I'm sorry," I whisper into her hair. "I'm sorry for everything." The whiskey on my breath mixes with the wildflower smell of her shampoo. I hate that I'm tainting her in that way. In *any* way.

Her muscles seem to uncoil until she's soft and pliable in my arms. "It's okay. I'm okay." She pats my back as if it's *me* who needs reassuring.

I hold her at arm's length and force a smile. "Thank goodness Jean-Pierre was at your place this morning, or we'd never have known that dickmunch Sullivan grabbed you."

She makes a face. "Jean-Pierre's at my house *every* morning. He claims to like going on walks with me and Yard, but the truth is he's too cheap to buy the good coffee. So he drinks mine."

"Bullshit," Luc says, making Maggie turn to frown at him. "Jean-Pierre told me he comes over for coffee every morning because you leave out a mug for him with a sticky note attached, and on it you've written an inspirational quote. He says he can't think of a better way to start his day."

"He did?" A tremulous smile flirts with her lips. Then she waves off the gesture as if it's nothing. "Well, I just share whichever quote is on my calendar for that day."

Oh, Maggie. Always acting as if her thoughtfulness amounts to nothing.

"Well, I don't care why he was there," I declare. "Next time I see him, I plan to kiss him on the mouth."

Her smile widens. "He'll like that. And speaking of Jean-Pierre... Luc, would you let him know I'm all right?" She glances down at her pajamas—even though I don't get the whole Harry Potter thing, I can admit she looks ridiculously cute. "I don't have my cell phone on me."

"Already done," he assures her. "I texted him as we were leaving the police station."

"Good. Thank you." She brushes a hand over her forehead and blows out a windy breath.

This day has already taken its toll. There are bags beneath her eyes and a chalkiness in her lips.

I'm struck by an idea... "What's your work schedule like today?"

"I have the evening shift." She frowns up at me. "Why?"

"What do you say to getting the hell out of Dodge? Let's put this city and that asshat Sullivan behind us for a few hours."

Her eyebrows twitch, indicating her intrigue. "What'd you have in mind?"

"We could knock off another excursion. Fort St. Philip?"

I don't add that we need to get a move on if we're going to hit everything on our list. If things keep going the way they have been, time could be running out.

CHAPTER FORTY-NINE

Luc

Dear Luc,

I took a drive to the swamp house today.

I don't know why. Maybe the bayou was calling to me in its mystical and magical way. Maybe I was missing you. Or maybe I simply needed to get away.

Peering in through the back window, I saw all your stuff is still there. I guess your mom is going to keep the place. I'm not surprised considering your father's mausoleum is there.

Anyway, I hope you don't mind, but I took your pirogue out. It's spring, and the dragonflies are flittering through the cattails, connected to each other in that age-old dance of procreation.

Wow. That sounded poetic, huh?

I just impressed myself.

Or maybe you rubbed off on me.

That's a nice thought, isn't it? That I'm keeping a little of you with me and maybe you're keeping a little of me with you?

In any case, I tied up to a tree with red lichen clinging to its side. Then I lay in the bottom of the boat and closed my eyes so I could listen to the chorus of bugs and bullfrogs.

I must've dozed off. The next time I opened my eyes, the sun was setting and the air around me had turned cool.

On the drive home, I realized I felt closer to you today than I have since you left. Maybe I'll go back again soon.

Forever and always, Maggie May

When you spend most of your life outdoors, you can smell a storm brewing. It's like it's written in the air with invisible ink that your nose somehow knows how to decipher.

"We're in for some weather," I say as I pole my pirogue past a clump of knobby cypress knees.

"What?" Maggie glances up through the canopy to the clear blue sky. She's sitting in the middle of the pirogue, Yard perched in her lap. Her brow wrinkles. "Are you sure?"

"Storm won't hit today." I squint toward the south. "But she's out there somewhere. And she's building."

Before heading out on our excursion, we stopped by Maggie's apartment so she could change into a pair of jeans and a lightweight waterproof jacket. She didn't bother with makeup, simply brushed her hair back into a ponytail and clipped Yard's leash to his collar. (I think, after the morning she had, she needed the comfort of her faithful canine companion.) Then it was a quick stop by the swamp house to load up my pirogue.

The remains of Fort St. Philip sit on a small spit of land in Buras-Triumph, an unincorporated community in Plaquemines Parish. It's about as close to the end of the Mississippi River Delta as you can get without floating into the gulf.

As we approach the grounds of the fort, Cash's eyebrows bob upward. "Guess I didn't realize how difficult it'd be to get here."

"Why *did* you put this place on the list?" I ask.

He shrugs. "Read somewhere it'll probably disappear after the next big storm. Most of it has already been reclaimed by the water and the sediment. Suppose I wanted to see what was left before it goes. Plus, I like the idea that if the three of us see it, then even if it *does* disappear, it won't actually be gone. It'll live on in our memories."

"That's pretty introspective for you, isn't it?"

"What can I say?" He spreads his arms wide. "I've become an introspective guy."

Positioning the nose of the pirogue at a ninety-degree angle with the bank, I dig my pole into the soft sediment below the water until it finds purchase. The muscles in my shoulders rejoice at the familiar exercise as I push off and the canoe darts up the bank, wedging itself atop the spongy soil.

"Touchdown," I announce. "Everyone outta the boat."

After clambering from the pirogue, Maggie sets Yard on the ground. The mutt immediately plants his nose in the dirt, filling his snout with new and exciting smells, his back end swinging side to side in doggy elation.

I grab my jacket from the bottom of the canoe. It's a cool day, and as the damp air mixes with the smell of muddy water, the three of us set off to see what we can see.

The first thing we stumble upon are the rusting and rotting remains of an old tractor. All that's left are its metal parts. And the weeds are threatening to overtake those.

"Who'd need a tractor way out here?" Maggie wrinkles her nose.

"Probably those cult people." Cash walks over to inspect the steel carcass.

"Who?" Maggie and I ask in unison after sharing a concerned glance.

"Yeah." He nods. "From what I read, the fort had been abandoned for years when a spiritual community called Vela-Ashby set up a commune here." He gestures around at the high grass, cattails, and kudzu. (The latter, a non-native species from Asia, is the South's greatest lament.) "But no one really knows anything about who they were or what they were doing. And after their leader committed suicide, the group scattered to the four winds."

Maggie looks around the overgrown area with wide, unblinking eyes. "He committed suicide *here*?" She points to the ground beneath her feet.

Cash nods, a devilish glint entering his eyes. "Some say his ghost still walks these ruins."

She glances behind her when there's a rustling in the underbrush that causes Yard to stop sniffing and stand at cock-eared attention. All the color drains from her face.

"I'm pulling your leg." Cash chuckles. "About the ghost, I mean. All the other stuff is true."

She scowls at him. But then her expression turns contemplative. "I wonder what happened to drive him to it?"

"Who knows?" Cash shrugs. "Maybe he didn't care for the position of cult leader. Maybe he got tired of people worshiping him, and the only way he saw to end it all was to end himself. Or maybe he had a terminal illness and wanted to snuff out his own light before pain and disease could do it for him."

"Why is it that lately our conversations have started taking these god-awful dark turns?" I demand.

He only stares at me, and I'm aware of the fevered look in his eyes as he takes a quick drink from his flask.

A muscle ticks in my jaw as I remind him, "You're not terminally ill."

Maggie swallows as realization dawns. "The pain in your head isn't making you think about—"

"For the love of Saint Roch." He waves her off. "*No.*"

I narrow my eyes. "I notice you've been invoking him a lot recently."

"Invoking who?"

"Saint Roch."

He rolls his eyes. "That's just me goofing around."

It's obvious Maggie isn't buying his explanation when she clears her throat and hesitantly asks, "Were you able to get your records to Dr. Stevens on Monday?"

He lets his head fall back on his neck. "*Yes.* I had the VA forward them along."

CHAPTER FIFTY

Cash

Dear Cash,

Aunt Bea took me on a campus tour of Tulane today.

My favorite thing was the Mardi Gras Bead Tree on the Gibson Quad. It's absolutely DRIPPING in colors. So the story goes, if a student throws a set of beads into the tree and they stick in the branches, the student is guaranteed to pass all their classes.

Aunt Bea says she'd love for me to choose her alma mater, like Vee did. But I think the real reason she wants me to go there is because she'd like me to stick close to home.

Honestly? I'd like that too.

Does that mean something's wrong with me? Most kids DREAM of going far away to college. It's a rite of passage, the first step toward independence and adulthood.

Why don't I want that?

I tell myself it's because I already live in the coolest place on the planet. But truly, I think part of the reason I want to stay is because if I leave, I won't be here if you come back.

How pathetic does that make me? I feel like such a fool. Especially since going away to school would be the smart thing to do. For one thing, I wouldn't have to turn a corner or walk down a street and run into something that reminds me of all the people I've lost here. For another thing, maybe if I was a thousand miles away, Sullivan would leave me well enough alone.

157

But every time I think of going, I get a sick feeling in my stomach. So, I suppose I'll stay. I'll stay and try not to live on the hope that someday I'll see you again.

Love, Maggie

We all have character defects; we are all works in progress.

One of *my* character defects is the urge to shake Maggie's cop friend, Rory Ketchum, until his teeth rattle inside his head. Especially when he tells us, "I don't know of a single detective who'd open an investigation based on this evidence alone." He points to my phone, open to the photos of Rick's ledger.

We're sitting at his kitchen table, surrounded by the smells of Pledge furniture polish, Tide laundry detergent, and Crayola crayons. The fridge is covered in dozens of stick-figure drawings, and a case of unopened juice boxes sits on the counter. His wife and twin girls made themselves scarce after we arrived, taking a walk around the sleepy Bywater neighborhood. But their presence is still everywhere I look.

A home. A wife. Cute kids. It's enough to make me ache.

"Why not?" I demand. "He's extorting these people for money, and they're *important* people. People who dictate policy for this city. Does anyone want them compromised by a sleazy businessman from Jersey?"

"No. But every cop in the department knows Richard Armstrong and George Sullivan are as thick as hair on a dog. None of them will be willing to suffer the superintendent's wrath or risk their careers by going after your dad."

My lips curl in disgust. "I prefer the term sperm donor."

Rory's expression is sympathetic.

"What if I told you our ultimate goal is to bring down Sullivan himself?" Maggie says.

Rory's eyes widen. "Seriously? Why?"

"Because it's time someone took out the trash in this city's police department," she declares.

Rory cocks his head, studying her. I can tell he wants to ask more questions, but isn't sure he should—ignorance is bliss, after all. He probably wonders if Miss Bea is one of Sullivan's victims and that's why Maggie is going after the superintendent.

"We figure if we can get someone to start an investigation into Rick and the blackmail," she continues, "they'll find evidence Sullivan is involved in the schemes too."

"I'm telling you," Rory insists, "you won't find any joy with the NOLA Police Department."

When I grumble my displeasure, he lifts a finger. "*But*, you could go to the district attorney. He'd be *very* interested in any proof that the bigwigs of this city are being blackmailed to keep the police superintendent in a position of power."

I exchange a glance first with Luc, then with Maggie.

Could it be that simple?

"Please tell me you know the DA and will vouch for us," Luc says. "If we walk in off the street and start spouting these kinds of accusations, he's liable to think the three of us are nuts."

"I'd say I know Leon Broussard pretty well." Rory smiles. "He's been my father's best friend since sixth grade and has been like an honorary uncle to me my whole life. He's at a fund-raiser for Children's Hospital tonight, but I'd be happy to give him a call first thing tomorrow morning and set something up."

"Oh, Rory!" Maggie grabs his hand. "If Jackie wouldn't skin me alive for it, I'd kiss you smack on your face."

He leans her way. "My wife doesn't need to know."

She giggles and plants a loud kiss on his cheek.

After straightening, he winks at her. Then his expression contorts into a grimace. "Fair warning, Leon's busier than a cat covering crap on a marble floor these days. It'll likely be next week before he'll have time to see y'all."

Luc blows out a breath. "Probably for the best anyway. By then we should know what's what with this storm."

Luc has this weird sixth sense when it comes to Mother Nature. At Fort St. Philip, he said we were in for bad weather. Sure enough, we turned on the radio on the ride home to hear the National Weather Service announce that a tropical depression had formed off the island of Cuba and was heading west into the Gulf. By this morning, meteorologists were predicting it would strengthen into a tropical storm.

"I heard it'll probably make landfall in north Texas," Rory says. "And I hate to wish ill on our neighbors to the west, but I can't help thinking better them than us."

For a couple of seconds, no one says anything. And then, in typical Southern fashion, Maggie dons her mask of congeniality and asks to see pictures of Rory's vacation. By the time he gets out his phone, his wife and daughters have returned, and for the next hour, I'm surrounded by the affable chitchat of people who've mastered the art of separating work from pleasure.

Under normal circumstances, I'd appreciate the easy topics and the high, sweet giggles of the two adorable girls. But I'm preoccupied by two things. One, the pain in my head has reached epic proportions since I left my flask at home—figured it wasn't the thing to bring to a police officer's house. And two, Maggie's hand is on my knee beneath the table.

CHAPTER FIFTY-ONE

Maggie

Nothing grows without a little rain.

That's what Auntie June says when a storm blows through. It's her way of putting a pretty face on the precariousness of our position here so close to the Gulf of Mexico.

The meteorologists' predictions turned out to be correct—the gale never strengthened into a full-force hurricane, but it *is* officially a tropical storm. They've named him Nestor.

For four days, Nestor made his sluggish way toward the mainland, turning north at the last minute to slam into southeast Louisiana.

I wonder if anything will remain of Fort St. Philip once the storm passes. Was it fate or simply good timing that made Cash insist we go see it?

We're told we're not in any real danger of losing life or limb here in New Orleans. Even still, the mayor issued a voluntary evacuation order since it's possible with all the rain—and all the street flooding that will follow—electricity in parts of the city could go down for the duration. Lots of folks loaded up their cars or packed into buses to head north.

But the Vieux Carré is notorious for "holding up." Considering a lot of the buildings in the French Quarter have been standing since the early 1800s, hold up it has.

When Nestor turned our way yesterday evening, I put out a call to employees, friends, family—and a few of my most loyal customers—to say I'd be hosting a hurricane party. Where? The bar. When? From the moment it starts coming down until the storm blows over. Why? Because why the heck not?

Laissez les bon temps rouler!

"Where do you want me to set up the grill, Maggie?" Gus, my second full-time bartender besides Chrissy, calls from the sidewalk outside.

The wind is already picking up and blowing his hair around his face. Although he was born and raised just up the road in Lafayette, Gus claims to be a Scotsman by blood. With his red hair and a build like a stevedore, I can totally see him sporting a kilt and carrying a broadsword.

His wife and two nearly grown teenage boys push into the bar ahead of him, setting their gear by the front window.

"Set it up inside the back door! It should be protected from the wind and rain there!" I yell above the noise of people arriving and choosing which corner they'll call home for the next twenty-four to forty-eight hours.

Everyone who got a call from me knows the drill. They also know what essentials to bring to a hurricane party, and the place is filling with sleeping bags, cases of water, food, and flashlights.

"Hey, everyone!" I clap my hands together. "Gus has arrived with the grill!" A cheer goes up. One of the staples of a hurricane party is the meat from everyone's freezers and refrigerators. "All you carnivores take your perishables to the back and put them inside one of the three big coolers I've stocked with ice!"

Chrissy walks up to me with a plastic grocery bag in hand. "I didn't have any steaks or chops in my fridge. Only four packages of hot dogs."

"Perfect," I tell her. "Gus's boys will love those." I look past her shoulder. "Where's Harry?"

"He'll be here in a bit. He had to finish a few things at the lot first."

Chrissy's husband, Harry, owns a used-car dealership north of town off Highway 90. But he's about as far from the typical used-car salesman as you can imagine. He's soft-spoken and shy, and I'm not sure I've heard him say more than twenty words in all the years I've known him.

Before Chrissy turns away, I ask, "On your way to dropping off the hot dogs, would you mind looking in on my cats in the storage room? I've been so busy, I haven't checked to see if they still have water in their bowls."

She frowns. "Last time I stopped by your apartment, Sheldon hid under the couch and then jumped out and bit me on the ankle when I walked by him. I'm telling you right now, you don't pay me enough to stick my hand inside his crate."

I laugh. "You can tip a water bottle through the crate holes to fill his bowl and not come anywhere near his teeth."

"Fine." She narrows her eyes. "But if he hisses at me, I'm squirting him with that water bottle instead of using it to fill his bowl."

I shrug. "Seems fair."

With an evil grin of anticipation, she sets off toward the back room.

I smile as I look around the bar. It's not unheard of, but it's incredibly rare to have a storm this late in the season. Given that, this hurricane party looks particularly festive, thanks to the Christmas decorations Charlie and Gus helped me string up over the weekend.

Twinkle lights zigzag across the ceiling. Silver and red garland frames the windows and the bar back. A small tabletop tree sits on a shelf in the corner by the jukebox, sporting the ornaments patrons have given me over the years. And two huge jars of candy canes stand like happy holiday sentinels at the corners of the bar.

I love this time of year, when the world comes alive with lights and laurels and wreaths, pink cheeks and pretty packages and songs about Santa. Which reminds me... I need to go shopping. Particularly since I have two more people to buy for this year.

A soft snore interrupts my musings and has me glancing at Yard. He's curled next to the beer cooler, nose to tail. For the first few hours, he ran around like crazy, sniffing everything and everyone. It wore him plumb out. Now, despite all the noise and commotion, he's sawing doggy logs.

"Earl Green is here! Let the party begin!"

Standing at the front door with the straps of a large backpack pulling at his shoulders, is my most loyal customer.

"I saved your usual spot for you!" I motion toward his stool and the corner he occupied the last time I held a hurricane party.

"Better make it a double!" He steps aside to reveal a fifty-ish woman wearing a polo shirt with the Omni Royal hotel emblem on the breast. She has a backpack and bedroll with her. "This here's Stella," Earl says. "She's my plus-one."

I welcome Stella in with a wave and a smile and make my way toward Earl's end of the bar.

After he deposits his backpack in the corner, he leans over and plants a kiss on my cheek. His handlebar mustache tickles my nose.

"Lord, Earl." I curl my upper lip and whisper, "You smell like a Las Vegas strip club. I can't separate the booze from the perfume."

He wiggles his wiry eyebrows. "Me and Stella started partying early. If ya know what I mean."

I point to Stella's shirt. "Hasn't anyone ever told you you're not supposed to get your nookie where you get your cookie?"

"Psshh." He bats the notion away. "Nothing wrong with some workplace romance now and again."

I shake my head even as I grin. "Well, make yourselves at home. The coolers for perishables are out back."

He lifts a brown paper grocery sack above the bar. "Got me five pounds of hamburger meat in here and the buns to boot. Let's get this party started."

"Argh!" An affronted bellow draws my attention to the front door and I see the sky has opened up. Eva darts inside too late, and her head and shoulders shimmer with plump, sparkling raindrops. "I thought I was going to make it before the wet stuff started!" she complains, brushing away the moisture.

I scurry around the bar to give her a hug. "You're sweet, but you're not made of sugar. You won't melt."

She points to her crowning glory of tight, springy curls. "No matter how many times I've tried to school you on black hair, you still don't get it."

"Your hair is beautiful," I tell her truthfully. "Everything about you is beautiful, and you know it. Now do me a huge favor and put your stuff away so you can come help me stack these cases of water. Last time we put them by the bathrooms, but that meant everyone had to go to the back of the bar if they wanted a bottle. I'm thinking maybe we should set up three separate stations. It'll be more convenient."

"Mmm." She nods. "Sounds good to me. Has anyone claimed the storage room yet?"

I grin. "You think I'd let someone steal your favorite piece of real estate?"

"It's not my favorite piece of real estate. I'd much rather be out here with the rest of y'all. But remember what happened during the last storm?"

I try to hide my smile by curling my lips around my teeth. "Yes. You woke up with Earl spooning you."

She narrows her eyes and points to my face. "It's not funny. I still have nightmares."

A chuckle escapes me, but I cut it off so it sounds more like a snort. Clearing my throat, I gesture toward Stella. "If it's any consolation, you should be safe this time. He's brought a spooning companion with him."

Eva eyes Earl's date before turning back to me. "He strikes me as the type who could somehow find a way to spoon two women at once." Taking hold of her duffel bag and backpack, she disappears through the door to the storage room.

"Toilet paper in da house!"

I laugh as Jean-Pierre stumbles inside, shaking off the rainwater slicking his face and hair. He has two huge sixteen-roll packages of toilet paper under each arm.

"Hallelujah!" I applaud as he shuffles around people on his way to the bathrooms.

When he comes out empty-handed, he joins me behind the bar.

"I appreciate all your help today," I tell him. He's been with me since early this morning, readying the bar for the party. "And as a thank-you, I got you this." From beneath the bar I whip out the brown felt fedora he's been eyeing every time he walks by the posh little clothing boutique three doors down from our building.

"Maggie!" He reverently reaches for the hat, running his fingers along the blue-and-white-striped band. "No! Dis is too expensive!"

I lift one shoulder. "I was able to negotiate Donny down a bit on the price."

Jean-Pierre gives me the side-eye. "You used your feminine wiles on him. Admit it."

"There may have been some light flirting involved," I concede.

It's no secret in our neighborhood that Donald P. Seitz, owner of D.S. Haberdashery, has a weakness for a wink and a smile. Considering he's nearly ninety, sports fun bow ties and the most amazingly architectural comb-over, offering him winks and smiles isn't any hardship.

"Thank you." Jean-Pierre pulls me in to press a kiss to the top of my head.

"You're more than welcome," I tell him, picking a corner of toilet paper from where it's stuck on his sleeve. Holding it up, I quirk an eyebrow. "You think we have enough this time?"

He grimaces. "We better. My ass still hasn't recovered from da last hurricane party when we ran out and had to use paper towels and cocktail napkins."

I chuckle in memory, watching the activity around the bar as folks settle in with card games and board games and battery-powered radios for if and when we lose the juice. Which reminds me... "Did you make that playlist I asked for?"

"Everything from "Rock You Like a Hurricane" by da Scorpions to "Ridin' the Storm Out" by REO Speedwagon. I even included "Hurricane Betsy" 'cause I know Miss June likes Lightnin' Hopkins. Speakin' of...your aunts comin'?"

I shake my head. "They took Vee and went up to the cabin. Auntie June says her bones are too old for sleeping on the floor, and you know my aunt Bea likes her creature comforts."

Jean-Pierre nods. "So who we left waitin' on?"

I look around, comparing the faces I see with the folks who RSVP'd. "Lauren and her sister. Chrissy's husband Harry. And Cash and Luc, of course."

Jean-Pierre twists his lips.

"What?" I demand.

"Luc and Lauren, dat didn't work out, no?"

I shrug. It seems like a long time ago that I tried to play Cupid for Luc and set him up with my spinning instructor. "Guess I need to hang up my matchmaking credentials."

"Don't do dat." He gives my arm a squeeze. "Me, I'm dependin' on you to find my first husband."

"Ha!" I sock his shoulder. "My good conscience won't let me if you keep referring to him *that* way. The only way I can agree to set you up with someone is if I believe he could be *the one*. The forever and ever, amen, one."

He shakes his head sorrowfully. "You're such a sentimentalist, *cher*. And on dat note…" He hitches his chin toward the front door.

Luc is standing inside the threshold, his dark hair damp with rainwater. An army-green duffel bag is casually tossed over one shoulder.

I'm so happy to see him, my stomach somersaults.

"Holy Mary, mother of God," Gus's wife, Debra, breathes from the table near the front window where she and her sons are playing gin rummy. She's staring at Luc like he's the next coming of Christ.

"Momma." Her eldest son elbows her.

She shakes her head and pretends to refocus on the game. But she continues to shoot Luc furtive glances as he saunters over to the bar. In fact, *everyone* sporting double-X chromosomes is watching Luc. But, bless him, he's completely oblivious as he hops atop a barstool.

"You made it." I squeeze his hand. "I'm so glad."

Luc and Jean-Pierre exchange handshakes. Then Yard wakes up, yawns, stretches, and whines that whine that all dog owners recognize.

"I'll take him," Jean-Pierre says.

"No. I'll do it," I protest, but he waves me off.

"No reason for you to get wet when I'm already halfway there." He carefully stows his new fedora on a shelf beneath the bar and grabs Yard's leash.

I go up on tiptoe to kiss his cheek. "I love you, you know."

He sighs dramatically. "Join da crowd."

After he clips on Yard's leash, the two of them disappear through the front door and I notice the wind is picking up and the rain is now coming down in sheets. It smells like the sea, salty and fishy and slightly sweet. So different from the storms that blow in overland from the north.

"Did you talk to Cash?" I ask Luc.

The look on his face makes my heart sink.

"He's not coming." I don't pose it as a question.

"He said he'd rather ride things out at home. After all the work we've put into the place, he wants to hang 'round and make sure the wind and rain don't do any damage."

I frown. "And you believe that?"

"Nope." He shakes his head.

I nod, my heart dropping further. "You think it's because of his drinking? Because he doesn't want a captive audience for the next couple of days?"

"Yep."

"Dang it." I glance out the window, foolishly hoping that, despite Luc's words, I'll see Cash on the street headed this way.

"I tried wheedling and begging and talking reason to him, but…" Luc spreads his hands. "He was having none of it."

I hate what this injury is doing to Cash. Of the three of us, he was *always* the social one. He used to love a good party. Now he'll spend the storm alone, locked away in an unfinished house with only a few sticks of furniture.

"Look who I found!" Jean-Pierre barges back through the door with a sopping-wet Lauren and her bedraggled younger sister in tow.

Chrissy's husband saunters in behind the group, touching one finger to the brim of his dripping baseball cap when his eyes meet mine. That'll probably be the extent of our interaction over the next couple of days.

Okay, so that's it. All the guests have arrived.

"Welcome one and all!" I paste on a smile that no longer feels natural. Cash's absence has cast a dark gloom over the entire affair. "Make yourselves at home!"

Jean-Pierre unleashes Yard to run over for belly scratches from Gus's oldest son, and then he heads toward the bar. After claiming a stool beside Luc, he asks, "Cash?"

I shake my head.

He nods, but doesn't say anything else. He doesn't have to. I know what he's thinking. It's what we're *all* thinking.

A large gust of wind whips through the front door, blowing things off tables. Folks cry out as cards and game pieces go flying.

"Batten down the hatches, everyone!" I yell.

"Wait for me!"

I close my eyes. Relief and joy and a hundred other emotions swirl through me as surely as the wind swirls outside. When I open them, I find Cash rushing through the front door before Debra can kick aside the river rock I use as a doorstop and haul it shut. He stands on the threshold, dripping and grinning that devil-may-care grin that stole my heart all those years ago.

"*Now* you can batten down the hatches," he says with a firm jerk of his chin.

When I think about the long string of hours that stretch out before me like precious pearls, whole *days* when I can be with him, be *near* him, I can't help but smile.

"Okay, folks." I clap my hands, my festive mood instantly restored. With the doors and window shut, the inside of Bon Temps Rouler is strangely quiet. That won't last for long. "We're in it for the long haul. So let's get this party started!"

Another cheer goes up. Bob Seger's "Against the Wind" croons from the speakers when Jean-Pierre cues up his playlist. And Chrissy steps behind the bar to help me start pouring drinks.

Some lessons in life you learn when things are calm and quiet. Others come your way during a storm.

Little do I know, but I'm about to be taught one of those stormy life lessons. And afterward, things will start to change...

CHAPTER FIFTY-TWO

Luc

Dear Luc,

Today I took my guitar out to the swamp house—told you I'd go back. I poled your pirogue into the middle of nowhere and practiced playing "When the Saints Go Marching In" until I could get through it without one mistake.

You were teaching it to me before you left, remember? Now, anytime I pick up my guitar and play that song, I think of you and all the fun we had. Which inevitably brings me back to the first time we met. And THAT makes me remember all those hours we spent together in the library, sitting side by side, not saying anything, just reading.

I think I'll start the Harry Potter series again soon. I miss Dumbledore.

I mean, who WOULDN'T miss a guy who says things like, "Happiness can be found, even in the darkest of times, if one only remembers to turn on the light."

You were MY light back then. You saved me from the darkness. You're my light even now, because anytime I get too low or too lonely, I can come out here and feel close to you.

I'm sure Eva appreciates that. The poor girl has been forced to take up the slack you and Cash left behind. I call her too much. Text her too much. But I can't help myself. She's the only true friend I have left.

Although... I hope that's not true. I hope, despite your silence, that you're still my friend.

I know I'll never stop thinking of you as such. Not even if I live to be a hundred years old.

Forever and always, Maggie May

Who we are, deep down, the person we are on the *inside*, is simply a collection of choices. All our good and bad decisions are what ultimately makes us *us*.

I don't reckon most folks think of it that way. Listen to any momma talk about a baby boy who's gone to prison. *I know he's made mistakes,* she'll say, *but on the inside he's a good boy.*

Horseshit.

You can't separate a person from their choices. There's no two ways about it.

I've been falling into that "prisoner's momma" trap when it comes to Cash for quite some time now. Despite the crap he's said, and the hell he's put Maggie through (including but not limited to flaking out on her the night of the Halloween ball and bachelor auction and getting caught behind a barn with another woman), I've been saying to myself that deep down, on the inside, he's a good guy.

But I think the truer statement might be that he *was* a good guy. Before the bombing. Before the head injury. Before all the drinking and self-pity.

Part of the problem is he hasn't done anything huge and horrible. But he's done lots of little things. Drip, drip, drip. Each new lie or missed date or unseemly assignation erodes away more of the man I knew and replaces him with someone I don't recognize.

"For fuck's sake," he says from Smurf's passenger seat. "You want to tell me what's got steam pouring out of your ears, or should I just sit over here and watch it billow?"

That's all the opening I need.

"Does the pain in your head blind you to the pain you're causing others?" I snarl, checking my rearview mirror before changing lanes to avoid a pothole that's filled to the brim with rainwater.

The storm blew its way out of the city yesterday, but the streets are still awash. Despite that, the locals who heeded the voluntary evacuation are returning to town. Canal Street is bustling with traffic and pedestrians out enjoying clear, chilly skies after two full days of stinging wind and rain.

We're due to meet Leon Broussard, district attorney for Orleans Parish. But when I called Maggie earlier, telling her I'd pick her up after swinging by to get Cash, she made up some poppycock excuse about needing to do chores at her apartment.

I'll meet y'all there, she said, and I didn't push.

The real reason she wants to drive herself is that she doesn't want to spend one minute sitting next to Cash. Not after the way he acted at the hurricane party.

"Who am I causing pain?" he has the nerve to ask.

"You *know* who. But if it helps, I can give you three guesses. Except the first two won't count."

He sucks on his teeth. "Sarcasm doesn't suit you, Luc. Stick to your usual earnest self."

"Fuck you, Cash."

"See? Earnest. Much better."

"You hurt Maggie May."

Something I don't recognize moves behind his eyes. "For her own good."

I frown at him, and that's when I notice how drawn he is, how pale. It looks like he lost weight overnight. When I feel a tug on my heartstrings, I take imaginary scissors and clip the bastards.

"How can hurting anyone be for their own good?" I demand.

"A little hurt now to save a lot of hurt later."

"You mean you spent the better part of two days flirting your ass off with Lauren's little sister—"

"Her name is Kelsey."

"Flirting your ass off with *Kelsey* 'cause you're aiming to save Maggie May a lotta hurt on down the road?"

"Exactly." He stretches his neck from side to side. Then he uncaps his flask and takes a healthy swig. "You've seen the way she hangs on me. Touches me. *Talks* to me."

"I'm sorry. Are we talking about Kelsey or Maggie May?"

He rolls his eyes. "Maggie. She's made up her mind she's going to wear me down until I give in to her."

"And so...what? You thought you'd prove to her that she should back off by throwing yourself at another woman?"

"I didn't *throw* myself at Kelsey. I just, you know..." He makes a rolling motion with his hand. "Didn't discourage her when she started coming on to me. And now Maggie knows I'm not playing around." He blinks, and one corner of his mouth twitches. "Or more like, now she knows I *am* playing around. You picking up what I'm laying down?"

I'm desperately battling the urge to punch him. If I grip the steering wheel any harder, my knuckles are likely to burst through the skin.

"Did you have a dartboard full of shitty ideas and take aim at the first one you saw?" I say in disbelief.

I see it in his eyes then. Pain and sadness. And more pain.

"I'm all used up where it counts, Luc." His voice is hoarse. *Shit!* Somehow my heartstrings reattached themselves and they're being tugged to high heaven. "On the inside." He touches his heart and then the scar on his head.

"Shut your soup hole," I grumble, feeling... I don't know. *Something.* Pissed off and sad and helpless and dammit! "You're not used up. You're *hurt*. And drunk most times. Both things are causing you to make dumbass decisions."

He doesn't say anything to that. Instead, he stares out the window at the blue hybrid SUV parked on the street in front of the modern architecture monstrosity that is the DA's office building. The place looks like a Borg cube made out of cinder block.

"She's already here." He hitches his chin in her direction when she steps from her vehicle to stand on the curb.

As I parallel park in front of her, I watch her in the rearview mirror. She's nervously clasping and unclasping her hands, and I wonder if she's agitated about seeing Cash after that debacle of a hurricane party, or if she's apprehensive about our meeting with the district attorney.

Throwing on the parking brake, I glance over at Cash. Now it's his turn to watch her in the rearview mirror.

"I keep trying to convince myself she's not as beautiful as I think she is," he murmurs.

I don't need to look back to know every detail of what she's wearing. Black pencil skirt. White blouse with a big, loopy bow at the neckline. Pumps that accentuate the small turns of her ankles.

She dressed for the occasion.

"And I keep trying to convince myself she's not as wonderful as I think she is," he adds.

"Oh yeah?" I make sure there's a healthy dose of sarcasm in my tone. "And how's that working out for ya?"

He frowns over at me, refusing to answer. Then he hastily climbs out of the truck.

After indulging in a big, windy sigh, I join him on the sidewalk. The storm left the air crunchy and crisp, like a fresh candy cane. I guess that's appropriate seeing as how the Christmas holiday is just about two weeks away.

"Y'all ready for this?" Maggie asks, rubbing her hands together. "Because I'm not sure I am. I'm nervous as all get-out. I can't help thinking we'll have hit a dead end if Broussard doesn't come through for us."

That's the way she's going to handle it? Act like nothing happened? Act like Cash wasn't a total asswipe? Not call him on anything?

Okay, then. "We'll find a way to convince him," I assure her, playing along.

When we turn up the walk, she takes Cash's arm. He extricates himself from her grasp and gives her shoulder a squeeze. "Luc's right," he tells her. "No worries. We got this." Then he quickens his step, forging ahead of us.

From the corner of my eye, I see her mouth pinch. She's no dummy. She knows he's avoiding her touch.

The asshole couldn't have picked a worse time to make his point. It's obvious she needs more than words for reassurance; she needs the comfort of human contact.

It sucks to always be her second choice, but when I feel her hand slip inside mine, I curl my fingers around hers and hold on tight.

CHAPTER FIFTY-THREE

Maggie

When you're going through hell, keep going.

I don't remember where I heard that or who supposedly said it. But whoever they were, they were right.

My question is, if you don't keep going, what's the alternative? Say to heck with it? Throw up your hands and quit like I almost did when I was fourteen?

No, thank you. Having danced with that devil once, I'm determined to never accept his invitation again. Like Dory in *Finding Nemo*, I keep on swimming. *And* I keep smiling despite dying a little inside every time I look at Cash.

Except for my parents' deaths, nothing has been more painful than watching him flirt with another woman *for two full days*. Not even his disappearance ten years ago. At least then I didn't have to *see* his rejection. It wasn't branded onto the backs of my eyelids like the scenes of him snuggling up to Lauren's kid sister—I use the term *kid* intentionally; Kelsey turned twenty-one two weeks ago.

Just keep swimming. Just keep swimming.

But as the seconds tick by like hours while the DA scrolls through the photos Cash took of Rick's ledger and then compares the initials in the ledger to the names Luc gives him, I'm not so much swimming as squirming in my seat. Broussard has the best poker face I've ever seen.

"Beatrix Chatelain gave you those names?" he asks. His thick white hair, high cheekbones, and discerning blue eyes make him look like Ted Danson. And his deep voice echoes around his humble office.

I thought the DA would have swankier digs.

Then again, this *is* New Orleans. Despite its grand homes and old Southern money, the city operates on a shoestring budget. You'd sooner convince folks to set their hair on fire than increase their taxes to fund things like, oh, streets that aren't filled with potholes, sidewalks that aren't crumbling to dust, and decent offices for their public servants.

Broussard's desk is nicked and scuffed. The whole room could use a fresh coat of paint. And besides the bookcase full of law books and family photos, there's not a stitch of decoration on the walls.

"Yes, sir." I nod. "She's my aunt. Do you know her?"

A hint of a smile plays at his mouth. "You probably don't remember. But a woman named Gloria Davis was caught embezzling money from the city. Your aunt helped me bring her down."

"I *do* remember that," I tell him. "It was what? Six years ago?"

"Seven," he corrects.

"Gloria worked for the claims department putting together the settlement packets to resolve property damage disputes with the city, right? But it turned out she was fraudulently submitting claims on behalf of her family and friends. If I remember correctly, she stole close to half a million before she was caught." Broussard nods, and I think I see a spark of respect in his eyes. "How did my aunt help?"

He touches the side of his nose and winks. "That's privileged information. But suffice it to say, Mrs. Chatelain is a woman to be reckoned with. And someone I've come to admire and respect. If she thinks these folks are being blackmailed and extorted by Richard Armstrong and George Sullivan, then I'd bet my right arm she's right. But what I don't understand is how the three of you have come to be involved."

"Well"—Luc clears his throat—"that's a long story." And then he launches into the same spiel we gave the aunts, only this time he adds that George Sullivan admitted to me in the interrogation room that, by fair means or foul, he means to see us hang for Dean's disappearance. "We reckoned bringing Sullivan's misconduct to light was our best bet for keeping our heads out of his noose," Luc says. "And when we started asking questions, we were led to Cash's dad. And the rest"—he points to the photo still lit up on Cash's phone—"is as you see here."

Broussard isn't afraid of silence, evidenced by the fact that he lets it drag on for so long that I begin to sweat. If he asks me about what happened out in that swamp, I'm not sure I'll be able to prevaricate. Like a priest behind a screen, there's something about him that makes me want to confess and clear my conscience once and for all.

Instead, he says, "This isn't the first time I've heard it said that Sullivan has used his power to sully the good name of an innocent."

"That girl from St. Bernard Parish." Luc nods.

Broussard grunts. "And I'll be honest with you, I've been looking for a reason to open up an investigation of the man. He plays fast and loose with his position."

"So you'll call in for questioning the folks he and Rick have been strong-arming?" Luc asks eagerly. "Get 'em to go on the record and admit to the blackmail?"

When Broussard shakes his head, Luc's expression remains unaffected. He has a pretty good poker face too. What he doesn't have are good poker shoulders. Those droop a full inch in disappointment.

I reach over and give his thigh a reassuring squeeze. The large, ropy muscles bunch in response, and I quickly remove my hand.

"I can't drag people in for interviews on hearsay," Broussard says.

"But what about the photos?" Cash gestures toward his phone, still lying faceup on the DA's desk. "What about all that money?"

"You mean the photos you illegally obtained? As for the money, there's no crime against keeping large sums of cash lying around."

Like Luc, Cash seems to deflate.

I *don't* give his thigh a reassuring squeeze. I'm upset with him. I know he said he wants only to be friends, but given what we mean to each other...*how* can he rub my nose in his pursuit of another woman? *How?*

But of course I know how. With deliberation and intent. He truly believes his head injury has made him a lost cause, and he's trying to scare me off by being...well, there's no other word for it, a *dick.*

"If you don't mind me saying"—Broussard pins Cash with a no-nonsense stare—"you don't seem too broken up by the thought that if I was to find a way to move forward with this, it would mean you'd be instrumental in putting your own father behind bars."

Cash's expression turns ugly. "The bastard beat me pretty much daily from the moment my mother died until I was old enough to leave his house for good."

I wince at the imagery that flashes through my head, and I'm reminded of all the times I naïvely brushed off a bruise or a black eye as simply the result of another schoolyard scrap.

And just that easy, I forgive him for the hurricane party. I can't hold Lauren's little sister against him. He was trying to make a point to save me...even if his ways and means leave much to be desired. And he's already been through so much in life that I refuse to pile on.

Broussard nods. "Okay. So here's the way I see this happening. One, we go in with a warrant, search Richard Armstrong's house, and find the money and the ledger. Two, based on that evidence, we arrest Armstrong on suspicion of money laundering and blackmail. Three, we offer Armstrong a reduced sentence if he agrees to testify against his accomplice, George Sullivan. And four, that allows us to get Sullivan out of a position he's got no business being in."

"Sounds great." Luc nods. "Let's make that happen."

"One tiny problem." Broussard sits forward.

"You need evidence of a crime before a judge will sign off on a warrant to search Rick's house," Cash says.

"Bingo." Broussard shoots a finger gun Cash's way. "And since none of the victims seem willing to come forward on their own, the only thing I can think to do is to get a recording of Armstrong admitting to the blackmail…or some other crime that will afford us the right to search his property."

"*That's* all it'll take?" Cash chuckles. It's a deep, satisfied sound. "Leave it to me."

CHAPTER FIFTY-FOUR

Cash

Dear Cash,

I spent spring break in Houston with Eva this year, and for the first time, her grandmother told me about the Gates of Guinee.

Have you heard of them?

According to Granny Mabel, they're the way to the Voodoo underworld. If a person knows the right combination for opening them, they can go take a visit.

I asked if SHE knows the combo, but she told me only the most powerful Voodoo priests and priestesses do. She DOES, however, remember the children chanting a rhyme when she was young. "Seven nights, seven moons, seven gates, seven tombs."

I shiver even as I write it.

I know you'd say it's a bunch of donkey shine, but it's hard to grow up here and NOT believe in something...more. And the thought of visiting the dead IS enticing. There are so many things I'd love to say to my folks, starting with an apology for asking them to go in search of Eva and Granny Mabel and ending with me telling them how much I love and miss them.

Then again, a trip to the underworld might mean I'd run into...

Never mind.

Wow. I was getting super dark there, wasn't I?

Back to happier things. It was a perfect spring break. Well...almost perfect. Eva and I got in a tiff when she told me it was time to let you go.

Is she right?

Love, Maggie

In life, you only get a few perfect days.

Hope today is one of those. Hope it's the day I look back on as the first step toward ending my father and George Sullivan and freeing Luc and Maggie from the chains of Sullivan's revenge.

"You ready for this?" Luc asks as we watch my sperm donor head inside a corner spot in the Uptown neighborhood.

Broussard agreed that a happenstance encounter with Rick would be far more likely to elicit the confession we need than if I showed up at his house or office and started asking leading questions. So for the last three days, Luc and I have been trailing the sorry bastard. And finally, today, an opportune time and place for a "run-in" presented itself.

Domilise's Po-Boy and Bar doesn't look like much from the outside. It's a squat clapboard house with a hand-painted sign that's draped with tinsel for the holiday. But the smells of fried shrimp and oysters fill the air, revealing the delicacies served up inside.

"I've been pushing that man's buttons since the minute I learned to talk," I assure Luc. "When his buttons are pushed, he forgets himself. I'll get what we need. Don't worry."

He nods, but I can see the hesitation in his eyes. He knows Rick and I are like nitro and glycerin. Put us together and *boom*!

"You can't come with me," I tell him for the third time. "Rick won't open up if you're there."

"I know. But I hate sending you in alone after what happened the last—" He cuts himself off.

"It's okay. You can say it. After what happened the *last time*. Wasn't ready for him then. I'm ready for him now."

Not that I ever want Luc worrying about me. But I'd much rather see this concern on his face than the condescension of three days ago. Thankfully, cooped up together inside Smurf for the last seventy-two hours, he's worked his way around to forgiving me for the hurricane party.

Then again, that probably has less to do with me and more to do with Maggie.

She decided not to hold it against me that I spent the entire time with Kelsey on my arm. Although I'm not sure if that means she's given up on her diabolical scheme to test the boundaries of our friendship by constantly touching me since I haven't seen her since our meeting with Broussard. And I've been too cowardly to bring up the subject during the few text conversations we've had in the interim because...well...if I'm being honest, while I absolutely, positively *must* convince her there's no future for us that involves a revisit of our teenage romance, her persistence and angel-eyed grit *are* flattering.

What? I like my ego stroked as much as the next guy. So sue me.

After I hop out of the truck, the cool December wind whips at the ends of my hair and tries to sneak inside my jacket.

"Brrrr," Luc complains. "Shut the damned door!"

I make a face. "Says the man who survived two winters in the Hindu Kush."

"That was different." He shakes his head.

"Yeah. It was forty degrees colder."

"And we were geared up in polypropylene drawers, fiber-pile bib overalls, balaclavas, and bunny boots."

"True." I slam the door and give him the point.

Taking out my flask, I jog across the street while quickly throwing back two quick slugs. Then, standing on the sidewalk outside Domilise's, I snag my phone and click open the voice recording app I downloaded this morning. After squaring my shoulders, I push inside the restaurant.

It's your typical Big Easy po' boy shop. Diner-style tables topped with napkin dispensers and squeeze bottles of ketchup, mayonnaise, and mustard. Acoustic ceiling tiles. And mouthwatering sandwiches served on paper plates.

Rick is easy to find in the sea of coveralls and Dickies. In his blue pinstripe suit, he stands out from the crowd like pants on a dog.

Pretending I don't see him at a table near the back, I make my way to the line forming at the register. The moment he spots me, I know. My hands go clammy and my mouth tastes like I'm sucking on a penny.

When he waddles up behind me, the hairs on the back of my neck lift as if in warning of lightning strike. Or the presence of the devil.

"Well, well, well." The sound of his voice is nails down a chalkboard. "If it ain't the rotten fruit of my loins."

Slowly, I turn to take in his ruddy face and flinty stare. I hate that we share the same eyes. If I wasn't so enamored of my eyesight, I'd pluck my eyeballs right out of my head.

"Next!" the woman working the register shouts.

"Sorry," I tell her, playing my part. "I've lost my appetite."

Pushing past Rick, I make my way toward the door. It's a gamble. Can't be certain he'll follow. But if this is going to work, I have to act natural.

And natural for me is trying to get as far away from him as humanly possible.

"Not so fast." He catches me on the sidewalk.

I fight a grin of victory. He's so predictable.

Turning to him, I plaster my face with derision. "What do you want?"

"What has you on this side of town?"

"Not that it's any of your business, but the guy who helped me replaster my ceiling medallions lives over here. Luc and I dropped off his check and we were going to grab some po' boys before heading back to The Quarter. But seeing you has my heartburn acting up."

When Rick's eyes alight on Luc behind Smurf's steering wheel, his fat lips peel back.

"You're still hanging around that swamp rat even after I warned you to steer clear?"

"So it would seem."

He shakes his head sorrowfully. "Thought I taught you better than that, boy."

"You didn't teach me shit, old man, except to hate your guts." Button one pushed.

I go to step off the curb, but to my relief he stops me again. "Hold up," he says. "I got something important to say."

I don't try to hide how much I despise him as I turn back. "With actual words this time? I mean, I know you love to talk with your fists. And as much as I'd like to answer back the same way, I don't have time to administer the ass-kicking you so richly deserve." Button two pushed.

His jowls bunch when he smiles, revealing those ridiculous veneers. "I seem to remember that it was *your* ass getting kicked the last time we met."

"You always did go in for sucker punches."

He pretends to pout. "Sour grapes because your old man can still wipe up the floor with you?"

I sigh heavily and motion him forward. "Fine. If it's a fight you want, go ahead and come at me. Let's get this over with once and for all."

"It wouldn't give me any satisfaction." His eyes travel over me from head to toe. "What's wrong with you, boy? You sick or something? You look like a bag of hammered shit."

"Takes one to know one."

His nostrils flare, and I know I've succeeded in pushing the third and final button.

He curls his meaty hands into fists and steps toward me.

I'm ready for him this time. My heart pounds with an ugly, hysterical sort of anticipation.

Even though I'm here on a specific mission—one that doesn't involve grinding his fat, florid face into the pavement—I can't deny that I've been waiting to give him a taste of his own medicine for years. For as long as I can remember, actually, because I can't recall a time when I felt anything but hatred for him.

Even when I was young, before he began kicking the shit out of me, I loathed him for what he did to my mother. For all the bruises that marred her pretty face. And for all the times she locked herself in the bathroom while I sat outside listening as her wrenching cries slipped out from under the door.

I adjust my stance, giving myself a good, steady base. Adrenaline spikes my bloodstream, an intoxicating high. My muscles twitch, ready for action.

These are all sensations I remember well from my years in the service. But just when Rick looks poised to go on the attack, he reconsiders. Reaching into his breast pocket, he pulls out a cigar and takes his time lighting it.

I recognize the hollow feeling reverberating through me as disappointment.

After blowing a thick cloud of smoke, he says, "George tells me your friends are going around looking for dirt on him."

"Not looking for." I shake my head. "*Found.*"

His chin—or, rather, *chins*—jerks back. "What the fuck is that supposed to mean?"

"It means the years of him bleeding the good people of this city dry are over. The canaries in the cage are singing." When he continues to stare at me dully, I sigh and spell it out for him. "His blackmail victims are talking."

"Bullshit they are," he scoffs.

"It's true. Luc and Maggie convinced a bunch of them to confess to what's been going on."

"They wouldn't dare. They've got too much to lose."

I wallpaper my face in disgust. "And you know this how? Oh, right. You're probably Sullivan's accomplice." I act like a thought has just occurred. "Or is Sullivan *your* accomplice?"

"You're damn right." Rick puffs up like a peacock. I hold my breath, waiting for him to start digging his own grave. "George always thinks too small. All he wanted was to use what he had on these people to ensure he kept his job. But I was quick to show him the error of his ways. These are fatheads with fat wallets. They can afford to share their wealth."

I try not to smile as I imagine shovelful after shovelful of dirt flying over his shoulder. "Share it with you?"

"Hell yes with me. And that's how I know you're lying. I know these people. They'll never talk."

I shake my head like the entire conversation has made me weary. Inside, I'm dancing a fast jig.

"One of these days, your arrogance will be the end of you, old man."

He laughs, then takes a deep puff of his cigar. He thinks he's called my bluff. "God wouldn't put suckers on the planet if he didn't mean for them to be taken for all they're worth."

I stare at him. "You know the truly sad thing? You actually believe that bullshit. You've been rationalizing the horror of your existence for so long that you no longer recognize the difference between right and wrong. Or is it possible you never knew to begin with? You think maybe you were born a vicious, self-serving psychopath?"

Rage mottles his face. "You think you're so much better than me? Well, I hate to tell you this, *boy*, but you're a pale shadow of the man I am."

Trying to get him to see himself for the monster he truly is, is like trying to get blood from a stone. I haven't the time or the energy. Besides, I have what I came for.

Stepping off the curb, I head in the direction of Smurf.

"And I always knew you would be!" he calls to my back. "From the moment the doctor pulled you out of your mother all scrawny and screaming and red!"

"Go eat a dick!" I throw a parting shot over my shoulder.

"No, thanks! Of the two of us, it's *you* who needs to eat something!"

I let him have the last word because, in the end, it'll be *me* enjoying a victory. Pulling open the passenger-side door, I duck under the doorframe and slide into the truck's bench seat.

"Well?" Luc frowns through the windshield, watching as Rick continues to smoke his cigar while glaring daggers at us.

"What's that catchphrase you like from *The Big Bang Theory*?"

His brow furrows. "Bazinga?"

"That's right." I pull my phone from my front pocket and wiggle it. "Bazinga."

CHAPTER FIFTY-FIVE

Maggie

We're all at the mercy of the universe.

It's a lesson I learned long ago. But recently, the truth of it has been hammered home with a baseball bat. A baseball bat wrapped in barbed wire like the one on *The Walking Dead*. Lucille. That dirty girl.

"So you're saying we have to wait?" I ask in disbelief. *"Again?"*

Luc nods. "Broussard wants to approach a particular judge with the recording and the request for the warrant, someone he reckons will be amenable to our cause. Unfortunately, this judge is in south Texas on a golfing trip and won't be back till Friday."

"What is with everyone taking vacations?" I raise my hands in helpless frustration. "Did I miss the memo? Christmas is almost here. Couldn't this judge have waited until *then* to hit the links?"

"It is what it is." He shrugs laconically.

Most times I appreciate his ability to keep calm and carry on. Today I could use some company in that little place I like to call Freaking the Eff Out.

"And I suppose we're just supposed to cross our fingers, hold our breath, and pray to sweet baby Jesus that Sullivan doesn't pull the trigger on his plan before then," I grumble irritably.

"Broussard thinks this four-day delay is a boon," Cash says.

I turn my frown from Luc to him. "How's he figure that?"

"It gives him time to put together a team of outside investigators. Since he can't be sure who Rick and George have their hooks into here in New Orleans, he wants to tap some resources outside the city.

"Smart." I nod grudgingly, some of the fight draining out of me. "I hadn't thought of that."

The DA's office was closed over the weekend, so even though Luc and Cash emailed the recording to Broussard as soon as they made it, they didn't hear back from him until this morning. Then they came straight to my apartment to share the news.

Now the three of us are sitting at my kitchen table holding holiday mugs of steaming coffee, and there's no denying the tired strain on their faces.

"Not to change the subject," I say, "but y'all look like you're both missing a wheel and have an axle dragging."

"That's what three days cooped up inside an old pickup truck will do to you," Cash laments, rubbing a hand over his face. His beard stubble is in serious need of a visit from a razor.

"I hear you," I say with commiseration. "I pulled two doubles this weekend, finally got around to putting up my Christmas tree"—I motion to the brightly lit Douglas fir in the corner of the living room—"and googled the crap out of New Orleans's most rich and famous. Seriously, my laptop is still smoking."

Cash's eyebrows slash. "What did that accomplish?"

I rub my hands together. "I'm glad you ask. So, as y'all know, Aunt Bea only gave us names for six of the potential blackmail victims, but there are fifteen different sets of initials in Rick's ledger. I tried to find out who those remaining nine mystery folks might be, and I can't be completely certain of anything, of course. Lots of people share the same initials. But that pool gets a lot smaller when we're talking about those around town who have the means to pay blackmail."

I grin with pride. "Anyway, I think these folks I've come up with might be worth talking to. Just in case they *are* some of Rick's and George's victims and find themselves of a mind to spill the beans. All this would be so much easier if someone came forward to point a finger."

Cash chuckles. "Look at you, Nancy Drew."

I pantomime a curtsy while remaining seated.

"The ball's in Broussard's court now," Luc insists. "We gotta keep our noses outta it and let him do his job."

"I'm not saying *we* should approach them. But maybe if Broussard gathers enough evidence, he'll feel comfortable calling in some of these folks for an interview. And I figure the bigger the supply of potential whistle-blowers he has to pull from, the better. I emailed him the list I came up with this morning."

"Nice work." Cash nods.

"Why, thank you, kind sir." I squeeze his forearm, enjoying the warmth of his skin and the crinkliness of his man hair.

The half grin he's wearing slides off his face. "You have to stop that."

"Stop what?" I cock my head at him.

"Touching me every chance you get. Making sure your fingers linger."

I pull my hand away and curl it into a fist in my lap. I didn't touch him with a mind toward persuasion. At least, not this time. It was just a natural thing.

Holding onto my composure by sheer dint of will, I clear my throat and ask, "Why?"

"You know why." He pins me with a hard look that turns the coffee in my stomach to acid. "And don't think I can't feel you sitting over there giving me a dirty look." He turns his scowl on Luc. "Your silent disapproval is like a blunt-force instrument to the back of my head."

"You should be careful," Luc says slowly, sitting perfectly still in that way of his that makes you think he's putting down roots.

"I've *tried* careful." Cash's mouth is flattened into an angry line. "Careful isn't getting the damned point across. So she and I are having this out here and now."

"Cash—" I try to interrupt him, knowing what he'll say next. Not wanting to hear it.

He stops me with a raised hand. "I know what you've been up to, Maggie, and it has to end. You're only making this harder on both of us."

"You love me," I insist around the lump that's forming in my throat. "You *said* you did."

"Yeah. And because I love you, I can't let you make a fool of yourself any longer."

The sting of his words makes my breath catch.

"All I want is to be your friend, get it?" he says. "F-R-I-E-N-D. Nothing more. Nothing less." He pulls out his flask and, not bothering to add the whiskey to his coffee, pours it straight down his throat. He looks at me defiantly and wipes a hand over his mouth.

"You know what I've been up to?" I challenge. *Lean in.* Isn't that the trending philosophy? I decide to lean *way* in. "Well, I know what you've been up to too. You've been doing everything you can to run me off. That woman behind the barn at the *fais do-do*? Lauren's little sister? Rubbing your drinking in my face? You think if you tomcat around and play the part of a gutter-diving drunk, I'll give up any hope—"

"That's exactly right!" he shouts, startling me with his vehemence. "Give up hope, Maggie! For fuck's sake!"

I slam my hands down on the table, and poor Yard scampers from beneath my chair to cower by the cabinets. My instinct is to comfort him, and I will, but first I have to settle this thing with Cash.

"Not until we've exhausted all the options!" I'm shouting now too. "Not until we hear back from Dr. Stevens, and—"

"Fuck Dr. Stevens! I don't care what he says. What you and I had is over. *Done.* It was wonderful and pure and *In. The. Past!*"

"You're only saying that because you're trying to be selfless! Because you don't believe you can be helped, and you don't want to saddle me with your injury and your pain and—"

He shoves away from the table, standing so quickly his chair tips over. Yard yelps and scurries from the kitchen to join the cats beneath the sofa in the living room.

"Stop it, Maggie." His voice has gone frighteningly soft. "By trying to force something now, you're ruining what we had."

That takes me aback. The idea is abhorrent, tunneling through my brain like a diseased worm.

"Cash, please." I grab his hand.

"Stop touching me!" He shakes me off.

A hard sob threatens, and I gulp past it so I have the breath to beg, "Don't do this. Don't push me away because you think it's better to be strong than vulnerable around people who love you."

"Cash," Luc says quietly. "Listen to Maggie May."

"Stay out of this," Cash hisses. "This is between me and her." He swings back to me. "It's over, Maggie. Even if this neurosurgeon can help me, it's over. Ours was the kind of love only possible between innocent and inexperienced hearts."

"You don't mean that." Lord, that might be the saddest, most pathetic thing I've ever said.

"I *do* mean it. I loved you then, and I love you now. But it's not the kind of love you're hoping for." When I shake my head, he glares at me. "You're going to make me come out and say it, aren't you?"

I can feel my chin wobbling. "I guess you have to."

"I don't want you. Not like that. Not anymore. And I'm sorry I didn't admit it earlier, but I was trying not to hurt your feelings."

"I don't believe you," I whisper, my heart clinging to denial like it's a life raft.

He throws his head back and yells, *"Fuck!"* at the ceiling. Then he grabs his jacket from the back of the chair and reaches for the door handle.

"Where are you going?" Luc stands.

"Home," Cash grits from between clenched teeth.

When the door clicks shut behind him, I try to stand and go after him, but I'm dizzy. I can't tell up from down.

Luc is quick to thread an arm around my waist, steadying me. "Come with me, Maggie May," he says.

I don't know what else to do, so I let him guide me into the living room where he settles onto the sofa and pats his lap in invitation. Even though I'd love nothing more than to be cradled and comforted, knowing what I know now about how he feels, that wouldn't be right. So instead of his lap, I choose the spot next to him and rest my head against his shoulder.

"Do you think love has an expiration date?" I ask, feeling unaccountably tired. "If you don't use it by a certain time, do you think it turns sour?"

Luc is quiet for a moment, considering my question. Eventually, he shakes his head. "No. I think true love is endless. Boundless. Eternal."

I laugh, but it's devoid of humor. "Then tell me what I'm supposed to do about Cash."

His tone is somber. "Keep on loving him, I reckon. Loving him and supporting him and rooting for him."

"Even when loving him hurts?"

"Especially then." Now, there's a hint of sadness in his voice. "It's like most things in life. If it's worth having, it's not gonna come easy."

I think on that for a while. Then I get up the courage to ask the question that's topmost on my mind. "Do you believe him when he says he doesn't want me like that anymore?"

He doesn't answer at first, causing me to look up at him. I find he's staring into the middle distance, and tugging on his ear.

Old habits have me reaching up to help him out, and he tilts his cheek into my palm, his beard stubble scratchy against my skin. I take comfort in the solidity of him for a brief moment before pulling my hand away.

I know he wants things to be normal between us. I know he wants me to act like nothing has changed. But I can't go back to touching him with such familiarity without feeling a niggle of discomfort.

"He's different," he finally admits. "Changing. I can't read him anymore. So truth to tell, I don't know what to believe. All I know is, no matter what happens between the two of you in the end, you'll wanna look back on this without regret."

He pauses so he can sigh deeply. "So my advice to you is to make your decision about whether you wanna continue to push him for more, or decide to accept the friendship he's offering based on how you're gonna feel about everything a year from now. Ten years from now. Act in a way that means you never hafta say 'I'm sorry.'"

I already *am* sorry, I realize. I've been pushing Cash, not listening to him. The look on his face when he jumped up from my kitchen table... Good *Lord*.

A guilty breath escapes me before a mournful howl reminds me that my poor dog has been traumatized. I go down on one knee beside the sofa and coax Yard out from under it. He belly-crawls to me, whining pitifully.

"It's okay, sweet pea," I croon, gathering him into my arms. "I wasn't mad at you. I'm sorry I yelled."

After settling myself into the corner of the sofa, he's quick to snuggle against me, his tail thumping the back cushions.

Dogs are wonderful in their capacity to forgive and forget. We humans could learn a thing or two.

"Thank you for staying, Luc." I try to firm up the trembling smile I give him. "But I know you probably want to go check on Cash."

"Eventually." He nods. "For now, there's no place I'd rather be than right here."

"How do you do that?"

"What?" He cocks his head.

"When you're with a person, you have this way of making them feel like they're the only thing that matters."

It's not really a smile he gives me, more a subtle deepening of his dimples. "One of my many, *many* talents, I reckon." He wiggles his eyebrows, attempting to lighten the mood.

"I'm serious. It's a gift, and to be on the receiving end of it is a heady rush."

"You think so?" His expression turns thoughtful.

He's a lot like the bayou. On the surface, he always looks placid and serene. But there are deep currents swirling beneath.

"Yes." I nod. Then, because I'm beginning to feel uncomfortable with the turn in the conversation, I clear my throat and glance at the guitar on the wall. An idea occurs. "If you're of a mind to stay, will you play something for me? Something soft and sweet? Yard's nerves are shot, and the cats—"

"Nerves are always shot," he interrupts, chuckling.

"Only Sheldon," I argue. "Leonard is much more easygoing."

As if on cue, the Roomba hums to life and disengages from its dock in the corner. It begins its daily job of attempting to stay on top of the pet hair that I've accepted as a part of life.

Leonard darts from beneath the sofa to climb aboard. He sits primly atop the device, curling his tail around his feet and closing his eyes until they're barely slits. This is his version of kitty heaven.

"*See?*" I thrust my chin in his direction. "Told you. He's like the California surfer dude of cats. You can't stop the waves, broham, but you can learn to surf." I flash the hand sign for *take it easy*.

Luc laughs. "It's the damnedest thing." Then he gets up to snag my guitar. Retaking his seat, he pulls the strap over his head. But before he plucks out a tune, he says, "How about a little quid pro quo? I play you something soft and sweet, and you play me 'When the Saints Go Marching In.'"

I narrow my eyes. "Someone's been reading my letters."

"They're a pleasure."

"A pleasure?" I lift an eyebrow.

"Every evening, when I'm home alone and sitting out on the front porch, I get to take a trip back in time and commune with teenage Maggie May."

I make a face. "I warned you I don't have your way with words."

"On the contrary, I think you're a beautiful writer. Your letters are sweet and funny, poignant and sad. They're *you* when you were that age. I'm loving every word."

I swallow, searching for something to fill the silence because…there it is again. That uncomfortable feeling in my chest because I know his words aren't just the words of a friend.

Thankfully, he takes pity on me. "So whatcha wanna hear?"

"You still remember how to play that Jason Mraz song I loved so much? "I'm Yours"?"

He immediately begins to strum, reciting the lyrics as smoothly and confidently as if he's sung them every day for the past ten years.

Hugging Yard close, I lose myself in the power of his playing and the hypnotic tenor of his voice. By the time the song is over, I've convinced myself that the discomfort I feel at being around him now—and especially the discomfort I feel when I *touch* him—is all one-sided.

I should just get over myself.

So he held a candle for me. So what? That doesn't change who he is. It doesn't change what we have. The only thing that's changed is that now I know.

Yard hops from my lap, curling into a doggy doughnut at my feet when Luc passes me the guitar.

"Whatever happened to you becoming a songwriter?" I ask as I pull the strap over my head.

"Life happened."

"Amen to that. But you're still young. There's still time."

"Maybe." He shrugs. "But I've heard too many folks say that once they turn their passion into profit, all the enthusiasm and joy go out of it."

"Oh, I don't know. I mean, owning Bon Temps Rouler is a lot of work. And there're certainly things about the gig I could do without. Replacing urinal cakes being one of them." I wrinkle my nose. "But most days I love going into work. Passion and profit *can* go hand in hand if you know what you're doing. If you're careful to remain true to yourself. Your dreams have been delayed, Luc, but you shouldn't give up on them."

I realize I'm doing it again. Trying to make someone do what *I* want instead of listening, truly listening to what *they* want.

"Sorry," I blurt, looking down at the guitar to position my fingers over the correct frets. "Don't listen to me. Just listen to your heart."

He's quiet for a while, but eventually he says, "I always do."

Something in his voice has my head snapping up. I search his eyes, but can't see anything worrisome. He's looking at me the way he's always looked at me.

Stop making things weird! I scold myself.

"I haven't practiced this song in years," I warn him.

"Don't worry," he assures me. "I'm a forgiving audience."

Finding the chords, I begin to strum. Slowly at first and then with growing confidence, until soon the melody is flowing from my fingers as easily as a memory.

When I'm finished, we pass the guitar back and forth a few times, taking turns sharing the songs we've learned. Then he returns the six-string to the wall and comes over to offer me a hand up from the sofa.

"Better go check on Cash now," he says, proving what a true and loyal friend he really is.

I'm a terrible person, because I've never stopped to consider how difficult it must be for him to love me *and* Cash in equal measure, and I'm reminded of the nightmare I had about him hooking up with Eva. All the hypothetical things I worried about, having to juggle loyalties, having to carefully straddle the line between both parties, sometimes being forced into choosing sides. All of those things are Luc's realities.

"Should I come with you?" I bite my lip. "I owe Cash an apology."

"Nah." He shakes his head. "Give him a day or two to cool off. Then go talk to him."

"Okay." I nod. "But will you do me a favor? Will you tell him that I get it now? Will you tell him that I..." I stop and search for the words. "That I understand?"

"Come here." He pulls me in for a hug. I welcome the reassuring thump of his heartbeat against my ear. "It's gonna be okay, Maggie May. *You're* gonna be okay."

"I know." I turn my face into him. Allowing myself to relish his comforting *Luc* smell. But as soon as I do, it's back. That uncomfortable feeling that makes me want to jerk out of his arms.

This time, however, I don't give in to the instinct. This time I make myself stay and study it. Picking it apart and turning it over in my head, I realize my blood is warm and rushing through my veins. My breaths are shallow, each one hard and fast. And my skin is sensitized. Everywhere we touch, I—

Oh, Lord have mercy.

Is it possible I *want* him?

No. *No!* That can't be right. He's *Luc.*

Obviously, I'm as lost as last year's Easter egg. This thing with Cash has discombobulated me until I'm mixing everything up. Until black is white and up is down and wrong is right.

Yeah. That's it. That has *to be it.*

Chapter Fifty-six

Luc

Dear Luc,

I drove across the causeway today.

Auntie June and Aunt Bea needed to attend the funeral of a friend who lived in Mandeville. Since the service was held in the evening, and since neither of them likes to drive after dark, I volunteered to take them.

It was weird to spend twenty minutes racing over a bridge spanning nothing but open water. It made me realize how HUGE Lake Pontchartrain really is. By comparison, I felt small. Which for some reason reminded me of the time you and I were talking about the meaning of it all.

Do you remember?

I said I didn't know why any of us are here, or what it's all supposed to be about. But you said you thought the answer to "What is the meaning of life?" could be found in the question itself.

You said that life IS the answer. To exist. To leave your mark on those around you knowing that, in turn, they will leave their mark on others.

"It's like tossing a bunch of pebbles into a pond," you said. "They start out as individuals, but they cause ripples to spread across the surface of the water. Eventually, those ripples mix and mesh until what you're left with is a lovely, chaotic resonance that screams, 'I was here even though you can't see me!'"

201

Anyway, I figured I'd write and tell you that I still feel your ripples, still hear your resonance. You're still with me even though I can't see you.

Forever and always, Maggie May

How do you know if you're at the end of the beginning or the beginning of the end?

As I sit beside Cash and Maggie inside DA Broussard's sparsely decorated office, that's the question that keeps spinning around inside my head.

Is this the beginning of the end of Rick Armstrong and George Sullivan? Or are we only at the end of the beginning with them? Is there still a long and treacherous road to travel before their malevolence and dirty dealing are done for good?

"I called you all in this afternoon," Broussard says, "to give you an update on my progress." He leans back in his chair, his intelligent blue eyes traveling over the three of us. The only nod in his office to the upcoming holiday is his red-and-green-striped tie.

"But don't become accustomed to the courtesy," he continues. "While I thank you for bringing this matter to my attention, the fact remains that it's in my hands now, and things will begin to move quickly. I won't have time to check in with you. Nor would it be my inclination to do so even if I *did* have the time."

He clears his throat. "Pardon my candor. But I work best when I work free of interference. So this is a one-time shot. Be sure you get all your questions answered here and now. Going forward, I'll refuse to field phone calls or oblige emails. Although, I do appreciate the list of folks you sent me." He looks at Maggie. "However, my advice to you is to let the professional sleuths do the rest of the sleuthing."

She jerks her chin up and down. "Yes, of course. I was only trying to help. I felt like Cash and Luc were doing all the heavy lifting what with trailing Rick around town and—" She cuts herself off when Broussard narrows his eyes. He has the bearing of a hound on the scent of a fox. He'd much rather be elbow-deep in evidence than sitting here talking to the three of us. That much is obvious.

"You're absolutely right." She holds up her three middle fingers. "On my word, I'm hanging up my Sherlock Holmes hat."

"Good." Broussard nods curtly. "Now here's where things stand. As you know, I was waiting for a like-minded friend to return from vacation before attempting to secure a warrant. But what I *didn't* mention was that I wasn't simply after a warrant for Richard Armstrong's residence. I was after warrants to search his businesses as well. As I'd hoped, after hearing the recording you made"—he points a finger at Cash—"I was able to obtain everything I asked for this morning."

My knuckles ache, and I realize I have death grips on the armrests of my chair. I didn't want to admit it to myself, but after all the delays (and considering the unwillingness of any of the blackmail victims to help us) part of me expected to walk into Broussard's office only to run face-first into another wall. But maybe, just maybe, the tide has turned our way.

"When do you present the warrants to my sperm donor?" Cash asks. His wanness is severe today. The skin beneath his eyes looks bruised, and his lips are dry and cracked. When he rubs a hand under his chin, I notice it's shaking.

Has he not had enough to drink? Or has he had way too much over the last few days? Ever since his blowup at Maggie's apartment, he's been downing the Gentleman Jack like it's going out of style. I've had to redo half of the work he's attempted on the house, because everything he's touched has been complete and utter dog shit.

"They've already been presented," Broussard says. "Every business Mr. Armstrong owns has been raided and his records seized. He was still home when I showed up on his doorstep with my team of investigators. And he wasn't too happy to open that safe for us even after reading the warrant that required him to do exactly that. But when I threatened to arrest him on the spot if he didn't comply, he worked his way around to being cooperative."

"You could've asked me for the combo," Cash says. "I'd have happily given it to you."

Broussard's left eyebrow quirks. "Don't you think he'd have guessed the information came from you, then?"

"I figure he assumes I started this whole thing anyway."

Broussard shakes his head. "I don't know about that. He kept asking, and I quote, 'Which one of those rich pricks put you up to this?' I think he believed you when you said the canaries are singing. He thinks it's one of them."

"You said you *threatened* to arrest him," Maggie says. "I take it that means you *didn't*?"

Broussard shakes his head. "Today was about gathering the evidence we'll need to bring him in."

"How long you reckon it's gonna take you to work your way 'round to doing that?" I ask.

For the first time ever, the DA smiles. "The forensic accountant I have working the case says he's already found evidence of tax evasion, wire fraud, and money laundering." He makes a face at Cash. "You're old man isn't exactly the Stephen Hawking of white-collar crime. He's been incredibly sloppy. I'm surprised the IRS hasn't come knocking on his door long before I have."

"It's not stupidity," Cash explains, "so much as a God complex. He's always thought of himself as above the fray, untouchable."

"Well, he'll feel the cool touch of a set of handcuffs soon enough. I'll have my team work over the weekend, and then, if everything goes as planned, we'll make the arrest on Monday. I can hold him without cause for twenty-four hours. After that, it'll be Christmas Eve, then Christmas, and the courts won't be open for him to enter his plea or to set his bail. If we're lucky, with the holidays and the system backlogged like it is, he won't be able to post bond until after the New Year. At which point, I'm hoping he'll be so sick and tired of life behind bars that he'll be only too happy to cut a deal and squeal on Sullivan."

"He'll squeal." Cash nods emphatically. "That bastard is loyal to one man and one man only. Himself."

Broussard allows a moment of silence before planting his hands on top of his desk. "Okay. Well, like I said, thanks for bringing this to my attention." He stands. "Hopefully, the next time we see each other will be at their trials."

A pinch on my thigh has me wincing. When I glance down, I see Maggie's nails digging into the denim of my jeans.

"Will we be required to testify?" she asks. Her voice is steady, but fear and alarm swirl around her like a noxious cloud.

I know what she's thinking. She's thinking that somehow that night in the swamp will come up, and she'll either have to lie under oath, or finally come clean about what actually happened.

Nonchalantly, I curl my hand around hers, giving her fingers a reassuring squeeze.

Broussard's brow wrinkles. "Why would you have to testify? I know this all got started because you three were trying to find a way to stop George Sullivan from harassing you over the disappearance of his son, but the fact of the matter is, I don't give a rat's ass about any of that. Unless you want to change your story and tell me *you* are one of the blackmail victims—" He cuts himself off when Maggie adamantly shakes her head. "Good. Great. So then I can't see any reason why I'd need you on the witness stand."

"Okay." She nods. "I was just…you know…wondering."

"Wonder no more." He raps his knuckles on his desk. "If you don't have any more questions, I need to get back to work."

He solicitously walks us to the door of his office. But that's as far as he goes. He lets us find our own way out of the building.

Instead of heading for her SUV, Maggie falls into step beside me and asks, "What do you think Sullivan will do once he hears

Rick's in jail? Do you think he'll redouble his efforts to come after us?"

I'm quick to reassure her. "I doubt it. If he's smart, he'll head for the nearest border. Barring that, I reckon he'll get down to the business of covering his ass by trying to erase ties to Rick. Either way, he'll be busy with his own shit, and that's a win for us."

She lets loose with a blustery breath. "Lord, I hope you're right."

She shoots Cash a quick look from beneath her lashes, and I know she's working her way around to addressing what's *truly* on her mind.

"I'll get the truck warmed up," I say, turning toward Smurf.

She stops me with a hand on my arm. "Wait. I wanted to ask y'all what your plans are for Christmas Eve."

"Packing for Shreveport probably," I tell her. "Cash and I are driving up to see Mom first thing Christmas morning. Why?"

She shrugs. "It's tradition that I host a Christmas Eve party at Bon Temps Rouler. I close the bar to everyone but friends and family and a few regulars. Jean-Pierre judges the Ugly Christmas Sweater contest, we do a white elephant gift exchange, and we have a big potluck réveillon dinner. I'd love it if y'all came, but I understand if you want to take a pass since you'll have an early morning the next day."

"I'll be there," I assure her.

"You will?" She beams at me. Who needs the sun when you have Maggie's smile?

"Of course," I tell her. "Wouldn't miss it for all the world."

She turns to Cash and ventures hesitantly, "Will you come too?"

"Depends." He takes out his flask, slowly unscrewing the cap as he narrowly watches her.

I'm overcome by the sudden urge to punch him in the neck. Doesn't he recognize an olive branch when it's extended his way?

She bites her lip. "I've been meaning to come see you to talk about what happened at my apartment."

His Adam's apple works over a deep swallow. He makes a show of smacking his lips and indulging in a loud *ahhhh*. "Don't see that there's much to talk about. Seems to me we've reached an impasse. You want what I'm not willing to give, and I'm tired of trying to be someone I'm not."

"I don't want you to be anyone you're not," she's quick to naysay him. "I swear it. And I promise I won't try to tempt you or...or..." She shakes her head, at a loss for words. "Or do anything that makes you uncomfortable. But you can't ask me to stop loving you."

She glances at the tattoo on her wrist, rubbing her thumb over the inky symbol. "I'll love you to infinity and back again. I'll be your friend to infinity and back again if that's what you want from me. And I'll continue to hope that things with your head will get better."

"Hope can be a dangerous thing," he warns. "It likes to build castles in the sky."

She lifts her chin. "You can't stop me from hoping, Cash."

Again, he stands there eyeing her. After what feels like forever, he finally nods. "I'll see you on Christmas Eve. Thanks for the invitation."

With that, he skirts Smurf's front bumper and climbs into the cab, leaving me and Maggie alone on the curb.

"The way he's been looking at me today makes me feel like I'm shrinking in front of his eyes," she whispers.

I reach for her hand. "If that's true, then it's his loss. Not yours."

"I don't know. I *feel* small all of a sudden."

"You're not," I assure her. "To allow yourself to be vulnerable, truly vulnerable like you are with him, well...to my mind, that's the biggest, bravest thing a person can do."

CHAPTER FIFTY-SEVEN

Cash

Dear Cash,

This year the National Honor Society teamed up with a local charity to rebuild a home in the Lower Ninth Ward. For the last week, I've been spending every day after school at the site, swinging a hammer and stapling insulation into place.

It's hard being back in Eva's old neighborhood, seeing what's become of Granny Mabel's house. It's falling apart and the weeds around it are taller than I am.

Also, they've torn down the house where my parents died. The only thing that remains is an outline of the old foundation.

I don't know how to feel about that.

On the one hand, I'm glad it's gone so I don't have to look at the X-code the search-and-rescue team spray-painted on the outside wall. I don't have to see that glaring number three at the bottom of the X and know that two of the dead they found inside were my mom and dad. On the other hand, it's like the memorial to their sacrifice is gone.

Anyway, I'm glad you took me there before you left. I'm glad you stood beside me, holding my hand as I cried and tried to make peace with what happened. I don't know if I'd ever be able to step foot in the Ninth Ward if you hadn't done that.

So thank you.

Love, Maggie

There are so many things we can't control in life. When we have the opportunity to make a choice about something, we should.

When Maggie said that thing about hoping, I made my choice. Clear-eyed and sober and knowing it was for the best. But even so, the idea is thrashing around inside my aching brain, making me hot and cold at the same time.

No more playing it safe. It's time to pull out all the stops on *The Plan*.

"He grew up too far from the town of High Intellect to figure that one out," Miss June says to Miss Bea, arching a thumb toward Earl, who is seated beside her atop his usual stool.

"Hey." Earl frowns. "I don't use ten-dollar words, but that don't mean I'm stupid." His voice is boozy and difficult to hear above the holiday music issuing from the bar's overhead speakers. Maggie's Christmas Eve party has been in full swing for the past two hours, but I've only just arrived.

Miss June chuckles and slaps her knee, spotting me when I wander up behind Earl and set a festively wrapped gift on the empty barstool beside him.

"Cassius!" she cries. A string of Christmas lights blinks around her neck. She's wearing a sweater stitched with the words Fruit Cake and a lopsided depiction of that much-maligned holiday treat. "I thought you were going to be a no-show!"

"Me too." I bend to kiss her cheek. Her skin is as soft as talcum powder and she smells like expensive champagne and cheap rose water. The overly bright twinkle in her eye lets me know the flute of bubbly sitting in front of her isn't her first. "Finding a plumber willing to come out on Christmas Eve was damn near impossible. I thought I would have to keep a hold on that pipe from now until the New Year."

During a routine toilet installation this evening, all hell broke loose in the guest bathroom. Luc wanted to stay and help me mop up the mess after the plumber left, but I forced him out the door.

Didn't want him missing Maggie's party. It's important he continue to come through for her, since I can't.

"Well, we're tickled you could make it." Miss Bea pats my shoulder when I move past June to peck her cheek. *She* smells like something slightly exotic and desperately overpriced. "But you'll be sorry to hear you missed the white elephant gift exchange."

Miss June giggles like a woman sixty years younger and unfolds the wadded-up bundle of flesh-toned fabric sitting on the bar beside her champagne flute. It's a T-shirt with Nicolas Cage's face stamped on the front. That's it. Nothing more. No words or explanation. Simply Nicolas Cage's grinning mug.

"Wow." I snort. "If that's any indication of the quality of gifts, then I *did* miss out." Turning to Miss Bea, I ask, "So what'd you end up with?"

Beatrix Chatelain, unusually attired in a ratty sweater dripping with a hundred red, green, and white poof balls, makes a face.

"Go on." Miss June nudges her. "Show him what ya got."

Sighing, Miss Bea pulls a green phallus-shaped…uh…*device* from the depths of her purse.

Despite my pounding head and the bitter choice I've decided to make, I'm overcome by a moment of clarion glee. "Please tell me that isn't what I think it is."

"It isn't what you think it is." She hits a button on the side of the device, and it emits a distinctive-sounding warble.

I blink. "What's happening?"

"It's a yodeling pickle." It's hard to tell with all the Botox, but I'm pretty sure Miss Bea is stifling a grin. "It'll go perfectly with the bacon-flavored toothpaste I got out of the white elephant gift exchange last year."

Laughing, I turn to Earl. "And you?"

He reaches beneath the bar, pulls out a NERF gun, and peppers me with soft foam bullets that bounce off my chest as gently as the wings of a butterfly.

"Careful, old man." I don my best Green Beret tone. "I could snap you like a matchstick."

"You'd have to catch me first," he challenges, his mustache twitching. "I'm faster than I look."

I clap a hand on his shoulder and retrieve the present. No one is manning the bar—Maggie's opened it up for everyone to help themselves—so I set the gift atop it and attempt to straighten the lopsided bow. But I stop midstraighten when a prickly feeling skims over the back of my neck.

Gaze detection is the ability to sense when someone or something is watching us. It's a skill we inherited from our ancestors, whose survival depended on knowing if a hidden enemy was about to strike.

Slowly, I glance around. Jean-Pierre is dancing with Eva up by the front window, spinning her in circles and dipping her low. In contrast, Chrissy and her husband are slow swaying beside them, lost in love and the holiday spirit. The tables are stuffed with more familiar faces, many of whom I met during the hurricane party. And Gus and his family are at the other end of the bar, playing an enthusiastic game of Monopoly, if his wife's declaration is anything to go by. "Don't you dare, Gus!" she squawks, hitting his arm. "If you do, you'll have to S your own D for the next year!"

"Ew!" their eldest son complains. "Y'all realize we're not four, right? We totally understand your code talk."

Gus's wife makes a face. "It's just as well you learn the lesson now that when it comes to life, we women hold all the power because you men have a bad habit of listening to the little head in your pants instead of the big one that sits on the end of your neck."

Gus salutes her with a frothy, sweating pint of beer. "As it ever was and ever shall be, darlin'!"

I smile and continue to let my gaze travel around the bar, doing my best to ignore the mixture of smells emanating from the food piled atop a table set in front of the stage. My stomach is threatening a revolt. Of course, the bellyache might have more to do with the jackhammer in my head than the aroma of fried foods turning soggy.

Today is one of those days where the pain is almost unbearable. It's so bad that before leaving the house I swallowed two of the high-dose opioids my doctor prescribed. The pills have yet to take effect, and the call of whiskey is strong. But I'm hesitant to mix the booze and the meds after what happened last time.

"If you're looking for Kelsey," Violet says, slipping up beside me, a highball glass in hand, "then you're out of luck. She and her sister went to visit their folks in Pascagoula for the holidays."

The prickly feeling at the back of my neck disappears. Proof positive I've come face-to-face with my watcher.

Maggie's sister is sporting a formfitting ice-blue top with silver snowflakes. It's a sweater. But it's definitely not *ugly*. Jean-Pierre won't be crowning her head in the contest.

"Merry Christmas to you too, Violet," I say, but there's no joy in my tone.

"I told you what I'd do if you hurt Maggie again." Her eyes narrow over the rim of her drink as she takes a delicate sip.

"Who told you about Kelsey?" I can't imagine Maggie saying anything.

She laughs, and it's a practiced sound, light and airy. Only a trained ear can hear it holds no hint of humor. "Word travels fast in this town."

"Especially between people who don't have anything better to do than gossip."

Her smile fades. "Gossip usually only pisses off the folks who're trying to hide something."

Man, I could use a drink. "You don't think people are entitled to their secrets?" I ask.

"I don't think people are entitled to anything but life, liberty, and the pursuit of happiness."

I snort. "That's oddly constitutional of you."

"That's from the Declaration of Independence, you idiot."

Unable to stand it a second longer, I round the bar. Finding the Gentleman Jack, I pour myself a single.

I'll have only the one. Enough to take the edge off until the pills kick in. And hopefully, the booze will distract me from saying or doing something to Violet that I'll later regret.

"As much as I'm enjoying our conversation," I say after a comforting swallow, "I need to find Maggie and wish her a merry Christmas."

Before I can turn away, Violet stops me with, "Hold up. We haven't finished talking about what happened at her hurricane party."

I grip my glass so hard I'm surprised it doesn't shatter in my hand. "Probably best if you mind your own business, don't you think?"

"Maggie *is* my business. She always has been. And you may have everyone else fooled with that smooth charm and that smile that never quits, but I knew from that first day you showed up at the academy that you were bad news."

I cock my head. "You mean in biology class?"

Something flickers in her eyes. She takes another drink. "No. Not then. But after school? Yeah. I saw everything as clear as day."

Okay, now I'm confused. "What did you see?"

"That you're a taker, not a giver."

My throat closes up around the whiskey I try to swallow. She's cut too close to the bone. I *have* taken more from Maggie—and from Luc, if I'm being honest—than I've given. It's my greatest regret in life. But dammit! I'm trying to fix that!

"What happened in biology class?" I ask. "Refresh my memory. You know you want to."

Her expression is one of distaste. "Nothing happened, per se. You just flirted with me something awful and then made plans to meet me at the diner after school."

A fleeting memory skips through my broken brain. A conversation with a dark-haired girl on my first day. Asking her what everyone did for fun after classes. Telling her I'd see her at the local hangout that afternoon.

Except…the minute I stepped through the door of that dingy diner, I spotted Luc. And, more important, *Maggie*. After that, everything and everyone else was forgotten. Including, apparently, Violet Carter.

Damn. Well, at least now I know she doesn't hate me because she thinks I'm not good enough for her baby sister. She hates me because of *me*.

"I was an ass back then," I admit. It's not a defense. It's merely the truth.

"You're an ass now," she counters.

In response, I salute her with my whiskey.

"Cash!" Maggie squeals, bursting through the door leading from the back. She has a bottle of champagne in one hand and a mug full of eggnog in the other. Her sweater is such a hideous monstrosity of garland and rhinestones and cheap plastic doodads that I don't know if it's the sight of it, or the high, excited pitch of her voice that sends a spike through my skull. "You made it!"

I can tell by her heightened color that she's had too much to drink. When she goes up on tiptoe to kiss my cheek, I close my eyes at the wildflower smell of her, feeling like a drowning man who's in love with the water.

She is the alpha and omega of my life. The beginning and the end and everything in between.

When I open my eyes again, Violet has wandered off in the direction of the back table where Luc and three others are playing Texas Hold'em. After Maggie delivers the champagne to her aunts, she comes to stand next to me, looking up at me with such unflagging understanding and acceptance.

She breaks my heart and makes me whole, and all I want is to fall into her arms. But I can't. I *can't*. For once in my life, I have to do what's right.

"Is everything okay?" Her eyes travel from me over to Violet and back again.

"Fine," I assure her, managing a smile that feels fake and makes my facial muscles ache. "In fact, everything is *better* than fine. Broussard arrested Rick yesterday. Did you hear?"

"I heard." Some of the holiday cheer slips from her face.

"So why aren't you jumping for joy? We did it! He's going down!" I do a quick move like I'm slam-dunking a basketball and say, "Booyah!"

One corner of her mouth hitches. But it's only one corner. "Yeah. I know. It's just…"

"Just what?" I prompt when she lets the sentence dangle.

"I can't shake this feeling that something bad is going to happen. That setting this thing into motion will have unintended consequences."

"Stop worrying. 'Tis the season to be jolly." I grab the gift from the top of the bar and thrust it into her arms. "Merry Christmas."

That does it. A slow grin stretches her lips until she's beaming and looking like the sparkly, shiny girl who first stole my heart.

"Hang on." She sets her eggnog aside. "I got you something too." She snags a gift bag striped like a candy cane from a shelf beneath the bar.

When she hands it to me, I wiggle my eyebrows. "Please tell me this is a Nicolas Cage T-shirt. Miss June and I can be twins."

She laughs, and for a moment, all that's wrong with the world is set right. "Open it and find out."

Reaching into the bag past the tissue paper, I pull out a heavy silver picture frame. It's one of those that has slots for six different photographs, and I instantly recognize the pictures she's included. They're the ones from the time capsule. The ones from that lazy summer day the three of us spent at the swamp house.

A lump forms in my throat. When I take a sip of whiskey, it gets stuck and sends me into a coughing fit that doesn't do my clamoring cranium any favors.

She whacks me on the back until I've cleared the Gentleman Jack from my airways. I must be wearing a terrible look, because her brow pinches. "You don't like it? But I thought you said that was your favorite memory and—"

"I love it, Maggie." My voice is hoarse. "It's perfect. Thank you."

Her expression softens. "I thought it could pull double duty. It's a Christmas gift *and* a housewarming gift."

Since I can't tell her how much it hurts to see the three of us as we were back then—so young and happy—especially considering how things have been going lately and how they're bound to turn out, I hitch my chin toward the gift she holds. "Your turn. Open it."

She squeals and tears into the paper, tossing it heedlessly aside. Using the edge of her thumbnail, she cuts through the tape securing the top flaps of the box. She's always had a childlike exuberance when it comes to presents.

Most people prefer either to be a giver or a receiver, but Maggie likes both equally. She loves the thrill of finding the perfect gift that will make someone smile. And she loves unwrapping a treasure that someone picked out especially for her.

When she pulls the shadow box from the bed of tissue paper and sees what's inside, she gasps and places a steadying hand on the bar. Her eyes instantly brim with tears.

"They told us these were lost." She shakes her head as if she's having trouble believing what her eyes are telling her. "How did you find them?"

I look down at the two gold wedding bands affixed to a bed of black felt. One is large, while the other is dainty. They're both inscribed with *David and Trina* followed by the date *6-24-1989.*

"I read somewhere that the morgues were crazy after the storm and that a lot of personal effects got misplaced. But after the chaos died down, the stuff was boxed up and sent to the police department. I asked Rory Ketchum if I could spend an afternoon going through the boxes." I point to the shadow box. "And there they were. Stuffed in an envelope in the fifth storage bin I tried."

"Oh, Cash! *Thank you.*"

She throws her arms around my neck, pressing her cheek next to mine so that I feel the heat of her tears. Despite my agony, my blood begins to race the instant she's flush against me.

It's always been this way for me. Immediate, overwhelming desire. Burning, overpowering need. Proof that I was a big, fat liar when I stood in her kitchen and told her I don't want her.

I blow out a relieved breath when she releases me to rush over to her aunts, calling to Violet, "Come see what Cash gave me for Christmas!"

Violet takes her sweet time getting there. But when she finally spies the rings, her throat works over a swallow. She turns to stare at me.

I try to read her expression, but it's incomprehensible.

When Miss Bea and Miss June gush over the gift, it feels like every person in the bar gets up to crowd around Maggie and that damned shadow box. And when Maggie looks up and catches my eye, her cheeks shiny with tears, I realize my mistake.

This gift is too intimate.

No wonder she's been holding on to hope. No wonder she thought she could gently sway me into coming back to her. Call me Mr. Mixed Signals.

Fuck! I should've given the rings to Luc to give to her.

My headache instantly jumps from a firm nine on the pain scale to a resounding ten. And there's an annoying ringing in my left ear.

I have to get out of here.

Now.

I stuff the picture frame back into the gift bag, set my empty rocks glass atop the bar, and quietly slip out from behind the long mahogany expanse. Rushing for the front door, I rake in a deep breath once I'm outside. Unfortunately, the cool breeze and the cheerfully decorated storefronts of The Quarter do nothing to soothe my head or my regret.

And now my left arm is tingling.

"You didn't tell me you were aiming to do that."

I turn to find Luc leaning against the doorjamb, his arms crossed, his eyes seeing...too much.

I clench my jaw. "Didn't think she'd make such a big deal about it."

Light glows around him in the open doorway, making him look bigger and bulkier than he already is. "It's her folks' wedding bands. If finding them isn't a big deal, I don't know what is."

"I wanted to give her something special. I wanted..."

I glance out into the street. Most people are tucked in with their families tonight, visions of sugarplums dancing in their heads. Consequently, the Vieux Carré is eerily quiet. So quiet that, even above the ringing in my ear and the dulcet sounds of Eartha Kitt echoing from the jukebox inside, I can hear the soft rumble of the Mississippi racing by more than two hundred yards away.

It's weird. Lately, I've been noticing the little things. Hearing and seeing and smelling details that I never did before. I don't know if I've become more cognizant of life's little minutiae, or if it's something else. If it's something to do with my brain.

When I'm quiet for too long, Luc prompts, "You want *what*, Cash? 'Cause damned if I can figure you lately. It's like you're beckoning Maggie May close with one hand and pushing her away with the other."

"I know." I stare at the cracked sidewalk beneath my work boots and try to think past the crushing sensation of a past that promises no future.

"You gotta make up your mind, man. This push and pull isn't fair to her."

"For fuck's sake! I *know*!" I glare at him. "I've worked out a plan to fix that."

He snorts. "There you go again. Talking up your plan. Well, I gotta tell you, from what I've seen of it so far, it's complete and utter pig shit."

Before I can respond, Maggie appears beside him in the doorway. Silhouetted as she is, the garland sticking out from her sweater makes her look furry. A pint-sized Sasquatch.

"Are you leaving already?" she asks.

"Sorry, Maggie. My head is killing me."

She rushes toward me, placing a hand on my arm. Then she immediately wrenches it away. "Sorry. Old habits."

I sigh. Why the fuck does it have to be so complicated?

"I don't mind you touching me, Maggie. As long as we both agree on what it means. As long as we both know the rules."

"I thought you always said rules are meant to be broken." The night is clear, and the stars shine in her angel eyes.

"I was young and dumb when I said that."

"Well, at least you're not young anymore." She mimes a three-beat drum solo.

As far as jokes go, it's pretty lame. But I play along. "Hardy-har-har. When's your next show? Midnight?"

She winks. "I'm here all week."

I reach up to rub the scar above my temple. Beneath it beats a vicious heart.

Her expression turns from teasing to concerned. "You should go home and get some rest so you can enjoy Christmas with Luc and Helene tomorrow. But thank you for coming. And thank you for the gift." She clasps her hands in front of her chest, making a few of the rhinestones on her sweater gleam in the streetlight. "It means the world to me. Truly."

"You're welcome." I allow myself to hold her gaze, knowing this will likely be one of the last times she looks at me with such unconditional love. "Merry Christmas, Maggie."

I give in to impulse and bend to kiss her cheek. Her skin is so warm and smooth. It entices me to linger. But I remind myself to feel grateful for what was and forget what will never be.

Then I turn away from her.

CHAPTER FIFTY-EIGHT

Maggie

The thing about tipping points is that you recognize them only in retrospect.

Today is a tipping point.

As I sit at a table inside Café Du Monde, eagerly waiting for Luc and Cash to arrive, I entertain myself by listening to the trio of college boys next to me. One is wearing a Tulane sweatshirt. Another is sporting a Tulane baseball cap. And the third has on a pair of Wayfarer sunglasses the color of a traffic cone.

All of them have that clean yet slightly debauched frat-boy look about them. And, of course, they're talking about their favorite subject—sex.

"I'm tellin' ya, man," the one in the baseball cap says around a monster bite of beignet. "She poured maple syrup all over me and then said she was in the mood for a tall stack."

Sweatshirt rolls his eyes. "Lord Stud Muffin strikes again."

Baseball Cap grins, his lips covered in powdered sugar. "That's *stud* spelled with two Ds on account of my talent for deep dicking."

"Jesus." Sunglasses shakes his head, taking a sip of coffee.

I try to hide my snicker behind my own mug, glad I'm well past the age of dealing with young men who still act and talk like adolescents. Then Luc and Cash push through the door, and the college boys are forgotten because...be still my heart.

It's bizarre. You can know a thing intellectually without ever *internalizing* its truth or its magnitude. Like, I know Cash and Luc are attractive men. But this morning, with the light pink and playful behind them, I'm struck by the sharp reality of them.

Even though Cash's condition and the heavy drinking are beginning to take their toll, even though he's lost weight and the skin beneath his eyes looks dark and crepey, he still seems to glow in golden glory. And then there's that smile that has unquestionably turned many women from Miss Look But Don't Touch into Miss Panties Drop Like Hot Potatoes.

In comparison, Luc has that whole darkly sensitive poet thing going for him. With his deep dimples, tanned skin, and thickly lashed eyes, one look at him and hearts melt. Broad-shouldered and lean-hipped, he's an archangel fallen to earth. Every woman's deepest, smuttiest fantasy and—

I blink. That crazy sensation is back. My skin feels hot and tight. My stomach dips and swirls. There's an unwelcome tugging low in my belly that I force myself to disregard as simple excitement over seeing them both again.

It's been five days since my Christmas Eve party. Ever since, I've been busy with family obligations and things at the bar. They've been busy with the house and trying to finish projects before all work grinds to a halt for New Year's.

We've exchanged a few text messages and tried to meet for a dinner that fell through because I had to cover Gus's shift when he came down with food poisoning—which he blamed on the Jell-O mold his ninety-year-old grandmother brought to Christmas. And I didn't realize how much I'd missed them until this moment, when they saunter toward me through the crowded café.

They take turns kissing my cheek, bringing the crisp smell of the outdoors inside with them, and I'm the envy of every woman in the place. But when Cash sits down heavily, grimacing and running an agitated hand through his hair, my frivolous pride at being the sole beneficiary of their affection is quickly replaced by concern.

Something more than the usual is wrong with him.

I've been trying to forget about Rick Armstrong and George Sullivan. I've been convincing myself that DA Broussard has everything well in hand. But now I can't help blurting, "What's up? Did your dad make bail or something?"

He frowns at me.

"Sorry." I'm quick to correct myself. "I mean your sperm donor."

"Not that I know of. Why?"

"You look like you sat on a porcupine."

His grin is lopsided. "That's just my face these days."

"He's not joking." Luc waves down the waitress and puts in an order for two coffees—one black, one café au lait—as well as requesting a plate of beignets.

After the waitress moves away, I study Cash. "Is it your head? Is it getting worse?"

"Actually, I've felt better the last few days." He grabs my coffee cup and takes a quick drink. Apparently, he's too thirsty to wait for his own. Then he makes a face. "Ugh. Chicory. I swear you can taste it more when you add the milk."

"Makes the taste buds sing, doesn't it?" I'm relieved he's feeling better. I want to ask about Dr. Stevens. See if he's heard anything from the neurosurgeon. But I don't dare bring up the subject. *Way* too touchy.

"You people are nuts." He wipes his hand over his mouth in an attempt to scrub away the flavor.

"By *you people*, I'm assuming you mean *we charming, intelligent, lovely Southern folks.*"

"Sure. Yeah. That's what I mean. You realize chicory was originally sold as a coffee substitute for people too poor to afford the real stuff, right? It's a dirty root that has absolutely no caffeine.

A *root* for fuck's sake. Drinking it is like drinking muddy potato water." He looks around at the bustling café. "And while we're on the topic of things that don't make any sense, why the hell do we always come here? It's a tourist trap. Too crowded and too expensive. Why don't we go to Morning Call instead?"

"He's in fine form this morning, if you haven't noticed," Luc observes.

"I've noticed." I nod. "And to answer your question, even if the taste of chicory wasn't a delight, it's humble origins are the whole point. You know people down this way love tradition. As for Morning Call, they serve their beignets naked. It's scandalous!"

"Exactly." Cash lifts a finger. "They let you add precisely the amount of powdered sugar you want. Far more democratic, if you ask me."

"Nobody asked you," Luc and I answer at the same time, smiling at each other.

Remembering what started us on this topic to begin with, I say, "Okay, so if it isn't your sperm donor and it isn't your head, what's got you wearing a face that looks like ugly on an ape?"

His mouth flattens, reminding me of Kermit the Frog. "I can't decide on cabinetry."

It's such a mundane, everyday, first world problem—and so completely *not* what I was expecting—that I blink. A snort escapes me. "Seriously?"

His chin juts out. "These are big decisions, Maggie. Cabinets aren't like paint color. You can't change them on a whim."

I force a serious expression. "Sorry. No. You're absolutely right. I mean, in a world of criminal fathers, corrupt police superintendents, and traumatic brain injuries, cabinet selection ranks right up there."

He gives me the evil eye. "Fine. Make fun. But now you don't get to flip through the catalogs and help me pick them out."

I sit up straighter.

Like when he asked me to look at paint swatches or approve the kitchen countertops, a trill skips up my spine. But I remind myself that I'm not supposed to read too much into it. Same as I've had to remind myself over and over again every time I see my parents' rings on the mantel that he doesn't want me attaching too much meaning to the gift.

"You want my help?" I ask hopefully.

"*Wanted*," he emphasizes. "Past tense."

"Aw, come on. " I stick out my bottom lip. "Don't be a bitter bear. I'd love to come flip through catalogs with you." *Whoa. Was that too eager?* "I'll swing by while I'm taking Yard for a walk tomorrow morning." *There. That sounded like it's simply another part of my day, right?*

The waitress arrives with their coffees and beignets, and our conversation turns to their trip to Shreveport. Luc has me enthralled with the story his mother told him about Santa's reindeer.

"She says they're all female."

"What?" I nibble on a fat pillow of fried heaven. For the record, it's topped with the perfect amount of powdered sugar.

He nods. "She read that both male and female reindeer grow antlers. But the males shed theirs in late fall, whereas the females keep theirs until after they've given birth in the spring."

I screw up my face, conjuring up every depiction of Santa and his reindeer that I can remember seeing. Yep. Antlers. One and all. From Dasher to Dancer to Prancer to Vixen.

"Mom says she's suspected it all along," Luc says.

"Really?" I lift an eyebrow. "How? Why?"

"She says only a group of women can drag a fat man around the world and not get lost."

I laugh, picturing Helene saying this in her earnest and forthright way, with a hint of a sparkle in her dark, dancing eyes.

"Speaking of the holidays." I lick the powdered sugar from my fingers. "What are your plans for New Year's Eve? I ask because Aunt Bea is throwing a big party. Something along the lines of the Halloween ball and bachelor auction, but without the ball and the bachelor auction part. No tuxes or gowns required. Just cocktail attire. There'll be a band and a dance floor and roaming waiters with trays of canapés. A champagne fountain—at Auntie June's request, natch—a balloon drop, and lots of party hats and horns. Y'all should come."

Luc cocks his head. "You're not hosting something at the bar?"

"Nope." Then I reconsider. "Well, there is a big bash planned, but every year I leave it to Gus and Chrissy to handle. The Quarter is so packed, and people are feeling so generous on account of the holiday season, that my employees can make a month's worth of tips in one night. I figure they've earned it. And the truth is, I *like* ringing in the New Year at Aunt Bea's. I don't know what it is. Maybe it's the end of the year and everyone feels like they can get as rowdy and as drunk as they want since the next day they can claim a fresh start. But of all the events Aunt Bea hosts, this one is where her high-class friends let their hair down. It's something to see."

"Sounds good to me." Luc shrugs.

I turn to Cash. "Lauren and Kelsey are coming too."

He narrows his eyes. "Is that supposed to be an enticement or a dissuasion?"

I study him closely. "You tell me."

"I have no plans to start anything with Kelsey. She was entertaining for a couple of days, but we haven't even texted each other since the hurricane party."

Relief slides through me, even though I tell myself it shouldn't. We're just friends, right?

"Fun for now but not forever?" I ask. "Watch out. You've been hanging around Luc too long. His bad habits are rubbing off on you."

He shrugs. "Considering *I've* been the bad influence for over a decade, I figure it's only fair. And since we're on the subject...

You take up the priesthood or what, Luc? Haven't heard you talk about a woman since Sally Renee ran off to find herself in Europe."

Luc stares down at the steaming liquid in his mug before finally lifting his chin. "Life's been busy. Or haven't you noticed?"

"Oh, I've noticed." Cash nods. "But a busy life has never stopped you from—"

"I'm sure Maggie May could do without the details," Luc interrupts.

"Thank you," I say. "Back to New Year's Eve." I pin Cash with a look. "You coming or not? I need to let Aunt Bea know."

"Sure." He lifts one shoulder. "Why not? Let's raise a glass and celebrate the fact that, come next year, life as we know it will look a whole lot different."

"What's that supposed to mean?" I frown. Then, "Oh, you mean you'll have a new house, and you and Luc will be starting your new business." I don't add, *And hopefully you'll be well on your way to figuring out something to help with your head that doesn't involve a daily bottle of Gentleman Jack.*

Something strange flashes across his face. Something that piques my curiosity, but before I can ask about it, I hear a familiar voice. My skin prickles and I'm reminded of that old saying about someone walking over my grave.

"Let's get outta here." Luc pulls some bills from his wallet and tosses them atop the table.

"Way ahead of you." I stand and grab my jacket from the back of the chair.

As the three of us race out of the café, I don't dare glance back over my shoulder. Afraid of what I might see. *Who* I might see.

We're about to step off the curb when I hear, "Tucking tail and running like scared rabbits, are ya?"

I cringe and slowly turn, thankful for the reassuring hand Luc closes around my elbow.

George Sullivan clomps toward us, his cowboy hat pulled low over his scowling brow.

"Shouldn't you be packing your bags and heading for a nonextradition country?" Cash dons a falsely curious tone.

That brings Sullivan up short. "What the hell is *that* supposed to mean?"

Cash rolls his eyes. "If you don't know, you're dumber than you look."

Beneath Sullivan's mustache, his lips curl into a snarl that reveals his tobacco-stained teeth. "What's happening with your dad don't got nothing to do with me. It's about his dirty business dealings."

"Is that what you've been telling yourself?" Cash's expression is the picture of naked disbelief with a smidge of disgust thrown in. "You don't think Rick will finger you for being his accomplice in this blackmail scheme faster than you can say 'traitor' if it means cutting a better deal for himself?"

The tendon in Sullivan's neck starts twitching like crazy. Something flickers in his eyes.

I reach over and pinch the back of Cash's arm. My intent is clear. *Stop poking the bear!*

His jaw clenches, and I can see he wants to say something more, but he heeds my warning and turns to me and Luc. "Let's go."

The three of us hasten across the street. It's only after we're on the opposite sidewalk that I chance a quick look over my shoulder. Sullivan is staring after us, hands on hips, his face the color of Auntie June's summer radishes.

"What the hell was that about?" Luc demands of Cash as we head deeper into The Quarter.

"I want him focusing on something besides you two," Cash explains. "Now"—he rubs his hands together—"how do you guys feel about knocking off another excursion? The Museum of Death is open today."

"The Museum of Death?" I ask dubiously. "Like our morning hasn't already been grim enough?"

"It's a good way to remind ourselves that some people have it worse than we do."

Chapter Fifty-nine

Cash

Dear Cash,

I don't know what possessed me, but I woke up this morning and climbed into Aunt Bea's attic to go through my parents' things.

I thought I knew every single thing we kept of theirs, but apparently not. Because I came across a bunch of letters tied up with red ribbons and stuffed inside shoeboxes. I've never seen them before.

Turns out, they're love letters.

Did I ever tell you that my folks were high school sweethearts? Then graduation—and colleges in two different states—forced them apart. But they kept in touch by writing to each other.

Some of the letters are boring, mostly filled with the details of their day-to-day lives. But some of them are unbelievably sweet. Two young lovers aching and yearning for each other across a great distance and through four long years.

I'm sure the letters don't tell the whole story of that part of their lives, but they told me enough to know that my folks' love for each other never wavered. Not once.

Even in death, they are still teaching me about the kind of person I want to be. The kind of person who doesn't give up when the going gets tough. The kind of person who can give her heart away *and then never ask for it back. The kind of person they would be proud to call daughter.*

Lord, I miss them. And I miss you.

Love always, Maggie

The world is full of injustice.

Butter is bad for you. The sun gives you skin cancer. Unprotected sex can result in unwanted pregnancy and STDs. And men like my sperm donor and George Sullivan can spend years terrorizing people and leaving carnage in their wake.

Standing outside the Museum of Death, this shrine to the end that all of us are barreling toward, I'm struck by the unfairness of it all.

"They say death is the great equalizer," I mutter. "I think that's lip service used to make dumb schmucks feel better about how fucking unfair *life* is."

"This is gonna be fun," Luc grumbles. "Remind me again why we're here?"

"Because it's on the list and it's a New Orleans institution."

Maggie makes a rude noise. "I don't know about *institution*. Preservation Hall is an institution. Commander's Palace is an institution. The Museum of Death is more of a curiosity, don't you think?"

"Whatever. We're here, so let's go in."

After paying our entry fees, we walk into a large room filled with everything death-themed. From body bags to skeletons to letters from serial killer Jeffrey Dahmer. There's hair from the OJ Simpson trial, a weird jar full of yellowed teeth—not sure how *that* relates to death—and one of Dr. Kevorkian's suicide machines.

It's damned macabre, especially the graphic crime scene photos. Don't know what I was expecting, but when I thought of a Museum of Death, I thought of stories of dying. When it happened. How it happened. *Why* it happened. What happened afterward. How the people left behind coped with the loss.

Something meaningful.

Looking around, however, I realize this is merely a place of shock and gore. There are no answers here. No insights into that great, lonesome journey into the beyond.

Pulling my flask from my back pocket, I throw back a long swig, trying to temper the terrible ache in my head and the slow, insidious slide of disappointment.

"Hey, buddy! There's no drinking in here!" the guy behind the counter calls.

He barely glanced up from his comic book when he took our money—with his Buddy Holly glasses, skinny jeans, and man bun, he's the epitome of the modern-day hipster and the picture of apathy—but take one nip of Gentleman Jack and he's Mr. Pays Attention.

"Right. Sorry, man." I salute him with my flask before shoving it back into my pocket.

I'd already made up my mind that I'd seen all I needed to see of this place, but that clenches it for me.

Spying Luc and Maggie by a glass display case, I amble over in time to hear Maggie ask, "What do you think it means?" She's clutching her locket in her fist.

Luc shrugs and throws an arm around her shoulders. I envy them their ease with each other. They've been that way since the beginning.

"Can't rightly say," he murmurs. "All her poems are ambiguous. I remember reading an article once that called her stuff 'a study in abstractions.'"

I peek over their shoulders to see what's caught their attention.

It's a human skull, carved with intricate and slightly crude black designs. In front of it is a placard that lists the name of the skull's curator along with a single line attributed to Emily

Life isn't one big party. It's a roller-coaster ride. And on nights like tonight, I'm reminded that the combination of ups and downs is what keeps things interesting.

Letting my gaze travel around Miss Bea's festively decorated ballroom, I soak in the atmosphere and the raucous music. The sight of the gold and silver balloons waiting patiently in a net above my head for the midnight hour when they'll be released to rain down on the crowd reminds me that, despite everything that's happened and is still happening, I'm unbelievably glad to be home. And Jean-Pierre's witty company makes me smile.

For the last fifteen minutes, he's been pointing out the debutantes in attendance and regaling me with salacious gossip about each of them. I doubt half the stories are true, but they're damn entertaining.

"She does not," I declare, glancing at the twentysomething in the blue sequined cocktail dress who's hanging on Cash's arm—not Kelsey, but some new bird he's taken a shine to tonight. The two of them are up by the stage where a jazz band keeps the party hopping with classics like Duke Ellington's "Take the A Train" and Thelonious Monk's "'Round Midnight."

"Swear on my mawmaw's grave." Jean-Pierre lifts a hand. He's wearing a sparkly black fedora with a hatband made of quarter-sized rhinestones. Jumping up from the table, he snags two canapés from the tray of a roving waiter, cradling them atop a napkin.

When he sits back down, I remind him, "You forget I *met* your mawmaw at the *fais-do-do*. I know she's alive and well. I still have the bruise on my ass where she pinched me to prove it."

He snorts. "Mawmaw's always had an eye for handsome men, *mais* yeah? But back to Scarlet." He gestures with one of the canapés toward Cash and his arm candy. She's a redhead with long legs and hair held in place by so much hairspray that it looks stiff. "I got dat information straight from da horse's mouth. She told me herself she goes over to a salon in da Tremé and pays a woman two hundred bucks to bleach her butthole."

I glance around furtively. The music isn't overly loud here at the back of the ballroom, but Jean-Pierre still has to raise his voice to be heard above it.

Thankfully, the couple at the table next to us is too busy trying to suck each other's faces off to pay attention to our conversation. (Maggie wasn't kidding when she said people let their hair down at this party. By Miss Bea's standards, it's a rager.)

I look toward the stage and spot Scarlet aka Miss Bleached Butthole reaching down to squeeze Cash's ass. Sitting up straighter, I dart a glance around the crowded room to see if Maggie caught the exchange. I don't see her anywhere, but when I turn back to Jean-Pierre, I can tell *he* didn't miss the move.

"You reckon he's drunk again?" he wonders aloud. "Or is he still tryin' to make a point?" When I lift an eyebrow, he nods. "I know he's your friend and all, but I think he's more confused than a fart in a fan factory."

"Maggie told you what he's been up to?"

He shrugs. "She didn't have to, *mon ami*. Me, I got eyes in my own damned head. And I was at da hurricane party, remember?"

"Right." I nod, frowning.

Something's up with Cash tonight. He was quieter than usual on the ride here, brooding almost. But when I asked what was wrong, he shook his head and told me, *What could be wrong? Tomorrow's a new year. Time for new beginnings. It's all good.*

Except, it's *not* all good. From the moment we walked through the door, he's acted up. Acted *out*.

He's always been careful not to get sloppy around Maggie's family, but tonight the Gentleman Jack is flowing like water. He's laughing too loud. Dancing too long. And flirting *way* too much.

A layman would see a guy celebrating the New Year. *I* see forced cheer.

But if there's one thing I've learned, it's that if he wants to tell me what's going on with him, he will. If he doesn't? Well, a pack of wild dogs won't drag it out of him.

A cloud of expensive perfume engulfs me as long, slender arms wrap around my neck. I look up to find Eva, stunning in a slinky silver slip dress, standing behind me. "You made it!" I stand and kiss her cheek. "Maggie May said you were stuck in New York."

"I managed to get stand-by on the last flight." She plops into the chair I pull out for her, snagging the last of Jean-Pierre's canapés and washing it down with his entire flute of champagne.

"Hey now!" he complains.

She lifts a hand. "It's ten minutes to midnight, and it's a tradition that I ring in the New Year with food, booze, and dance. With that"—she motions toward the empty flute and bare napkin—"I've accomplished two out of the three."

"Okay, okay." Jean-Pierre stands and offers her his hand. "You're not exactly subtle, but... May I have dis dance?"

She beams up at him, fluttering her lashes and pressing a hand to her chest. "Why, thank you, Jean-Pierre. Thought you'd never ask."

Before they head for the dance floor, she gives my arm a squeeze. "Happy New Year, Luc."

"Same to you, darlin'." I wink and watch Jean-Pierre swing her into a fast two-step that makes her throw back her head and laugh.

I've retaken my seat when Miss Bea joins me, sliding me one of the two flutes of champagne she brought with her.

"It's almost time," she says, cupping her chin in her hand. The four-carat diamond on her finger catches the lights from the stage and nearly blinds me.

"Indeed it is." I smile. "You sure know how to throw a party, Miss Bea."

She sends me an amused look. "Does that mean you're having fun?"

"Always." I wiggle my eyebrows.

"But not as much fun as *he's* having." She tilts her perfectly styled head toward the front of the room.

I don't need to ask which *he* she's referring to. And since I reckon there's no use tiptoeing around the subject (not with Bea; she's too canny not to recognize BS when she hears it), I admit, "Probably having *more* fun than him, actually. With Cash, especially nowadays, looks can be deceiving."

She takes a delicate sip of her champagne, fingering the double string of pearls that are her signature look. "Maggie hasn't said much. But he's in trouble, isn't he? His head injury isn't improving."

I swallow. "Doesn't appear to be."

"And he's pushing her away because he doesn't want her to have to deal with it."

"So Maggie May claims."

That has her turning fully toward me. Her eyes are shrewd. "And what does *Cash* claim?"

"That he loves her but doesn't want her. Not like that. Not anymore."

For a while, she's quiet. Digesting what I've told her. Then, "Do you believe him?"

I realize I've been holding my breath when a sigh shudders out of me. "Truth to tell, Miss Bea, I'm not sure *what* to believe anymore."

She nods. Then, easy as you please, she adds, "But *you* still want her like that."

For a moment, I'm too shocked to respond. When I finally do, my tone is laced with disbelief. "Did she tell you?"

Her brow wrinkles. Or at least it twitches. Which is about as close to wrinkling as the Botox will allow. "Who? Maggie? You mean she knows?"

"Yes, ma'am. I told her how I felt about her, how I've *always* felt about her, at your Halloween ball."

Her eyes widen. "How'd she take it?"

I shrug. "I think it made her uncomfortable at first. But now she seems to have settled into the idea."

In fact, over the last couple of weeks, she's been pulling away from me less and touching me more. Plus, there's something in her eyes when she looks at me now. I'm not sure what it is, if it's acceptance or affection or simple acknowledgment. But whatever it is, it's a balm to my heart. A salve to my soul.

Bea shocks me with, "I always thought it was the two of you who belonged together."

"What?" I blurt. "Why?"

She lifts a shoulder encased in shimmery gray fabric. "I suppose because it's always seemed easy between you. Effortless. You…click."

I brush aside her words. "I don't think Maggie May wants easy. She's always enjoyed a challenge." I tip my chin toward the front of the room. But instead of finding Cash getting pawed by Scarlet, I see that he appears to be in deep conversation (or, more accurately, a heated argument) with Violet.

"Uh-oh." I go to push away from the table, instinct propelling me to intervene, but Miss Bea stops me with a hand on my sleeve.

"No." She shakes her head. "Let them work it out."

"Work *what* out?" I frown at her. "What's going on?"

"There." She points. "See? All better."

Turning back toward the stage, I see Cash leading the redhead onto the dance floor. Violet is still in the same spot, watching them. She's too far away for me to be sure, but her expression looks…shocked? Or maybe…sad?

Again, I glance around to find Maggie glaringly absent. "What happened to Maggie May?" I ask.

Miss Bea rolls her eyes. "My silly sister had too much to drink. Like she does every New Year's Eve because she parks herself beside the champagne fountain and refuses to budge. Maggie took her upstairs and is putting her to bed with a tall glass of water and two ibuprofens."

I grin, envisioning Miss June all rosy-cheeked and glassy-eyed. But before I can comment, the band leader announces that there's time for one more song before the countdown to midnight.

The crowd cheers and the band picks up their instruments and tears into Ella Fitzgerald's "What Are You Doing New Year's Eve?"

"One more year in the books," I say to Miss Bea, lifting my glass. "Here's to what comes next."

"Here's to us." She clinks her long-stemmed glass against mine.

We both take a sip. She hums her pleasure. I try not to make a face at the taste or the feel of tiny bubbles bursting against my tongue.

Blame it on growing up poor, but I've never developed a taste for champagne. Beer and bourbon are my vices of choice. Proving you can take the boy out of the bayou, but you can never take the bayou out of the boy.

Tonight, however, I've stayed away from both the beer *and* the bourbon and stuck, mostly, with club soda and lime. I'm driving home later. Cash offered to let me stay at his place. But the idea of starting a new year by waking up beside him on that mattress on the floor is too depressing to contemplate.

Plus, I reckon he's drinking enough for the both of us.

"Did you save the last dance for me?"

I turn to find Maggie standing behind me. She's wearing a formfitting emerald cocktail dress that shows off the tuck of her waist, and the spaghetti straps emphasize the creamy skin over her shoulders. Black pumps lift her five inches off the ground, and her hair is twisted up, exposing her neck and the heart-shaped locket she never seems to be without. She's wearing the matching silver filigree teardrop earrings I got her for Christmas.

Hearts and teardrops. The two always seem to go hand in hand, don't they?

"How's June?" Bea asks her.

"Snoring like a chain saw through lumber." Maggie laughs, then offers me a hand. "Well? May I have this dance, Mr. Dubois?"

I plant a kiss on Miss Bea's cheek and thank her for inviting me. "Happy New Year," I whisper in her ear.

"Happy New Year to you too, Lucien, my boy." She pats my jaw, and her smile is affectionate.

I never knew either of my grandmothers. They died before I was born. And looking at Miss Bea, feeling her warmth and caring, makes me yearn for those lost relationships.

Then Maggie jerks me out of the chair and onto the dance floor, and I'm happy to forget about what I never had and enjoy what I do have. Namely, a beautiful woman in my arms who (even though she'll never feel about me the way I feel about her) loves me just as I am.

For a few minutes, we glide around the dance floor, our steps in sync as Maggie gracefully and effortlessly follows my lead. Then Cash and the redhead waltz by us on wobbly legs and I miss a step.

They both appear drunk as skunks. When Cash catches my eye, I do my best to glower him into the ground.

It doesn't work. He feigns confusion and lifts a hand as if to say, *What'd I do?*

"That man's gonna wake up with regrets," I mutter, my hand tightening on Maggie's waist. "Mark my words."

"Oh, I don't know," she says. "He's always had a robust inclination toward self-forgiveness."

I glance down at her, expecting to find her wearing that slightly wounded expression that's always a total gutshot. Instead, her face is...something. I don't know what. Not sad, exactly. Maybe...resigned?

"He's an idiot," I insist. "And his taste in women gets shittier by the minute." I curve a thumb over my shoulder in his general direction. "That one looks like she fell outta the ugly tree and hit every branch on the way down."

"Please." Maggie rolls her eyes. "Scarlet Jensen is gorgeous and you know it. Plus"—she makes a face—"she's *nice*. Cash could do worse."

I search her eyes, frowning. "Are you truly okay with this?"

For a moment, her chin wobbles. Then she firms it. "I have to be, right? I don't want to have any regrets."

I blink because... Has she done it, then? Has she worked her way around to accepting Cash's *friends-only* policy?

If so, I don't know whether to be happy for her or sad. Therefore, I simply nod and pull her close, resting my cheek atop her head.

Unpleasant realities are a part of life. But how we handle them, with grace and aplomb or with whining and petulance, is what separates people into the categories of *emotional adult* or *emotional infant*. Maggie May has always struck me as an emotional adult. Even at the unripe age of fourteen, even when she was so lost in depression and guilt and self-blame that she was hard-pressed to find a reason to live, she was the embodiment of grace.

My heart swells because I've had the privilege to know her. To call her friend.

Unfortunately, that's not the only part of me that swells.

The press of her firm breasts against my chest, the subtle flex and rub of her thighs moving against mine as we dance, has my blood rising. The skin of her hand is soft in mine. Her hair is cool and smooth against my cheek.

She is woman. Everything sweet and supple and mouth-wateringly delicious. Everything a red-blooded man such as myself finds irresistible.

I shift my hips away from her.

The day I turned thirteen, my mother schooled me on the idea of a "consent boner." She lectured me that unless someone agreed (*With words, Lucien. They always have to agree with words.*) to share my hard-on, then I'd best keep it to myself.

Gritting my teeth, I silently begin to list my favorite jazz musicians. Anything to take my mind off the soft, sexy feel of Maggie's body moving in time with mine. But I've managed to think of only six before the song ends and the band leader steps up to the mic.

"Ten seconds till midnight!" he announces, and we're surrounded by a mass of whooping and hollering partygoers as the crowd presses closer to the stage.

A guy in a bright green dinner jacket jostles Maggie, sending her careening into me. I wince when her belly softly cradles the evidence of my desire. Then I make a face of chagrin when she tilts her chin back and looks up at me, her eyes wide with shock.

"Sorry." I shake my head, searching for a lighthearted explanation. "Sometimes the damn thing still thinks it's in American history class."

"Five!" the crowd chants. "Four!"

I expect her to step back, to grab on to my lame-ass joke in an effort to alleviate the awkwardness. But she doesn't move. She stays exactly where she is, pressed against me, hip to hip, chest to chest.

There's a change in the air. It's grown heavy and humid with unexpected pressure.

"Three! Two!"

She goes up on tiptoe as the band breaks into a cacophonous rendition of "Auld Lang Syne," and my heart pounds when her eyes land on my mouth a second before her perfect lips do.

Her breath is warm and smells of chocolate cake and champagne. I close my eyes and convince myself that everything I'm feeling is one-sided. That the vibe I'm picking up is nothing more than wishful thinking.

We're friends. This is a *friendly* kiss. But then…oh…*then* her tongue tentatively grazes my bottom lip.

My eyes snap open in time to watch her jerk away, out of my arms. She stares up at me, a hand covering her mouth as if she's as shocked as I am.

For a while, as the celebration rages around us, neither of us speaks. Then she blurts, "I have to go talk to Cash. Oh my Lord, Luc, I have to—" She cuts herself off, vigorously shaking her head.

Even though people are cheering and blowing party horns, even though balloons are falling down around us, all I hear, all I see, is her.

I don't know what the hellfire is happening, but I feel like I need to apologize again. "Maggie May." I reach for her. "I'm sorry. I didn't mean to—"

"You didn't do anything," she interrupts, avoiding my touch. I curl my hand into a fist and shove it into my jacket pocket. "It's me. I..." She swallows, her eyes as big as saucers. "I *want* you."

With that, she spins on her heel and pushes through the crowd. I would go after her, but I'm dealing with the fallout from the bomb that's gone off in my brain.

I'm reeling. Staggering. Punch-drunk. I nearly fall over when someone stumbles into me. And I blink dully when a woman I don't know grabs my cheeks and kisses me on the mouth before hollering, "Happy New Year!" and dancing away.

I've forgotten where I am. I've forgotten *when* I am or *who* I am or *why* I am. But there's one thing I know.

With those three words, Maggie has changed everything.

CHAPTER SIXTY-ONE

Maggie

You can come to your senses in a blinding flash. Like a tire iron upside the head.

One minute, I was dancing with Luc like I've danced with him dozens of times before. The next minute... *Bam!* Tire iron.

There's no more denying it. No more shrugging it off. And definitely no more pretending it's something it's not.

I want him.

I want *Luc*.

Thinking back, the writing was on the wall, but I didn't see it. It was right under my nose, but I didn't sniff. In short, my body knew long before my mind did.

All those times I touched him and pulled away because something felt...*off*? All that hair-pulling and hand-wringing when I thought he might start dating Eva? Those nasty feelings I had toward Sally Renee? My crazy insistence on trying to set him up with Lauren—a woman I knew wasn't right for him. Yeah. *All* of that was because I wanted him. For. Myself.

But...*how*? How could I? How *can* I?

For twelve years, my whole heart has belonged to *Cash*. Despite the distance that separated us, I've always yearned for *Cash*. Through a handful of relationships, I've always come back around to *Cash*.

And now there's this thing with Luc?

Luc, the boy who used to sit on the front porch swing and paint my toenails? Luc, the first person I complained to when I had period cramps? Luc, the one I confessed my nervousness to about going to third base? Luc, the guy who, six months ago, I would have sworn up and down was the brother I never had?

It feels so wrong.

And yet, weirdly, it feels exactly right.

Lord, I'm confused.

All I know is that I need to see Cash. I need to talk to him. Maybe if I look at him, maybe if I hear his voice, I'll realize what I'm feeling for Luc is a misunderstanding at best. A hallucination at worst. I'll realize that it's *Cash* I love. *Cash* I want.

Like always.

"Thanks for the ride." I hand the taxi driver a twenty from my sparkly party clutch and add, "Keep the change," before stepping onto the curb.

The Vieux Carré is hopping tonight. Locals and tourists alike are out en masse ringing in the New Year. The sound coming from Bourbon Street is a dull roar of drunken debauchery. Smoke from the fireworks the city exploded over the river at midnight lingers in the air, making my nose itch and leaving an ashy taste on my tongue.

After the countdown and kiss, after I ran from Luc like the coward I am, I frantically searched high and low for Cash. He was nowhere to be found, unfortunately. But eventually, I ran into a guy smoking on the veranda. After telling him Aunt Bea would skin him alive if she caught him, I gave him Cash's description and asked if he'd seen anyone who looked like that. He told me he saw a man who might've been Cash climb into an Uber.

I took my chances and called a cab.

Now, standing in front of Cash's house, I'm relieved to see lights burning inside. He could've gone anywhere in the city. To an all-night diner for a burger. To one of the house parties that rage in The Quarter. Or to any one of the hundreds of bars. But, thankfully, he came home.

Blowing out a shaky breath, I head toward the front stoop. After taking the steps two at a time, I lift a hand to knock, only to find the door cracked open.

Palm flat against the wooden surface, I hesitate. Considering the state he's in, now might not be the best time to admit, *Hey, you know Luc? Our best bud? Well, I think I might want to boink the daylights out of him.*

Then again, when *would* be the best time to admit that?

I'm thinking…never.

Shoving open the door, I holler, "Cash!" The word dies in my throat. The *sh* sound is barely a whisper by the time I'm finished.

Scarlet Jensen is up against the wall. The top of her dress is pulled down to reveal the side of one bare breast, and the bottom hem is hiked up over her naked butt. Cash is behind her, his suit pants down around his ankles. He has a handful of her hair wrapped around his fist, and he's hammering into her, his face red with exertion and beaded with sweat.

When he looks over at me, he blinks blearily. I might as well be a three-toed sloth for all the understanding that shows on his face.

Unfortunately, *I'm* not having any trouble comprehending what's going on. Despite the whole room tilting, I can't deny what's right in front of my eyes.

"Sweet Jesus," I whisper, blindly reaching for the door behind me. "Sorry, I—" I shake my head and turn to run.

I don't remember how I got to the sidewalk. Did I skip down the steps or simply jump to the ground superhero-style? Either way, here I am, standing on the cracked concrete, looking up and down the street, unsure where to go.

My heart feels like it's been popped into a pressure cooker with the temperature set to high. My head is a jumble of amorphous, swirling thoughts. There's a pain low in my gut, like someone has taken a fistful of my bowels and is cruelly twisting them.

"What the fuck are you doing here, Maggie?"

I gasp and spin to see Cash standing in the open doorway, doing up his zipper and wiping the sweat from his brow. His hair is a mess. His tie is half undone. And his eyes look surprisingly clear.

"Sorry," I manage even though someone has shoved a towel down my throat. "I came by to—"

Why am I here again? I can't recall.

The scene from his living room is branded onto the backs of my eyelids. Every time I blink, I see it all over again. Scarlet's mouth open and panting. The flex of Cash's butt muscles as his hips piston. The raw *sexuality* of the moment, and the simple, inexplicable truth that I walked in on the man I love making love—No. Not making love. That was fucking—another woman.

I think I'm going to be sick.

"Dammit, Maggie," he growls, shoving a hand through his hair, mussing it even more than Scarlet's fingers already have. "You can't barge in on me like that. You can't—"

My voice is a bare rasp when I interrupt. "I know. I'm sorry." And where the heck is Scarlet? Looking over his shoulder through the open doorway, I can't see hide nor hair of her. Did she escape back into his bedroom? Even now, is she sprawled naked on his mattress, awaiting his return?

I really *do* think I'm going to be sick.

For a while, he says nothing. Simply stands on the top step glaring at me, a muscle ticking in his jaw. Finally, he demands, "For fuck's sake, stop crying. You're making me feel like a total shit-heel when I haven't done a damned thing wrong."

It's not until he mentions it that I realize hot tears are streaking down my cheeks. I scrub them away. To my shame, more erupt to take their place.

"I *told* you all I want is to be your friend," he fumes. "Don't make me feel like you caught me cheating on you."

"No." I shake my head, wanting to get out of here. *Needing* to get out of here. "You're right. You're absolutely right. I only wanted to..." What? What did I want to do? "Wish you a happy New Year," I finish lamely. "So..." I roll my hand, only to find it's shaking. "Happy New Year. I'll...uh...let you get back to it."

Then I turn tail and run.

Shoving my way through the throng on Bourbon Street, I frantically wipe the tears from my cheeks. Then I recall what took me to Cash's house in the first place.

Luc.

Luc, my savior. Luc, my friend. Luc my...one true desire?

A strangled laugh escapes me when I consider the hypocrisy of my situation. I'm upset that Cash is screwing someone else when *I* want to screw someone else? When I specifically went to his house to admit that very thing to him?

What is *wrong* with me? Why can't I decide what I want? When will all of this stop hurting so much? And *how* can any of this be right?

I'm so strung out on adrenaline and nerves that I can't think straight. But I know I need to see Luc. We've got to talk about what happened.

Pulling my cell phone from my clutch, I text him.

Me: Where are you?

I chew on a hangnail and quicken my steps toward home as I wait for his reply. It takes a minute, but then I see three dots appear on my screen. He's typing. And then...

Luc: Almost home. Pulled over 2 side of road. Y'okay? You disappeared from the party.
Me: Fine. In The Quarter heading home.
Luc: Good. You find Cash?

I choke on a half laugh, half sob. Did I find Cash? Oh yeah. I found him.

Me: He's back at his place.

Luc: Glad he's home safe. Listen, don't freak out about what you told me. I'm fine if you wanna forget it. Chalk it up to too much to drink or the party atmosphere or whatever.

Me: Don't want to chalk it up to anything. DO want to talk about it.

Luc: Call me?

I stumble to a halt, staring at those two words. *Should* I call him? Would it be smarter than going to see him?

"Argh!" I wail when someone rams into me, a hard elbow slamming into my shoulder and momentarily numbing my fingers so that I drop my cell phone.

"Ssssorry," a guy in a sequined party hat and a shirt covered in beer stains slurs. He staggers drunkenly, and before I can retrieve my phone, his foot lands on top of it.

A sickening crunch can be heard above the noise of the revelers streaming by.

"No!" I yell, picking up my demolished phone. The screen is shattered, and one whole corner is bent at a precarious angle.

The drunk's slow, lopsided grin makes me consider doing extreme violence to his nether regions.

"Ssssorry," he slurs again. Then he shrugs and rejoins the group weaving their way up the sidewalk.

Hardening my jaw, I continue my march toward home.

The houses in the French Quarter are painted every visible color in the light spectrum. Walking down certain streets, you begin to wonder if a bartender slipped a psychedelic drug into your drink. But I'm in no mood for the visual feast tonight.

As the blocks pass, I try not to replay what I saw at Cash's house. But it's useless. The scene is on repeat in my head. Over and over again, I'm pummeled with the imagery. Battered by it. But oddly, each recital, each echo hurts less than the one before it.

I can feel something happening inside me. A part of me is unraveling. Loosening. Letting go. It's like the tectonic plates in my heart are shifting.

I hate to say it, but it's almost a relief.

CHAPTER SIXTY-TWO

Cash

Dear Cash,

Randy Barker stopped by the ice cream parlor this afternoon. You probably don't remember him since he's quiet and shy and mostly likes to spend his free time with his nose shoved in a book. We had the same study hall our freshman year, and I remember thinking then that there was something sweet about him. And interesting, in an unassuming way. I mean, anyone who reads that much is bound to be interesting, right?

Anyway, he asked me out, and I should have said yes. I opened my mouth to say yes, but my heart wouldn't let my lips form the word.

The silly organ still belongs to you, apparently.

That's hard for Eva to understand. When I called her and told her what happened, she scolded me for being a fanciful fool.

I suppose I am a fanciful fool. It's officially been a full year since you left, and yet here I am, pining for you the same as ever.

Speaking of the year anniversary, Sullivan called me in for questioning again this evening after I got off work. I guess he thought to remind me that Dean is still gone—not that I could ever forget—and I told him what I've always told him. What I CAN tell him.

Like always, he wasn't satisfied. I think he might've tried to get nasty with me, but Aunt Bea was there with her lawyer, and after about an hour, they both decreed that Sullivan's time was up.

I was shaking in my shoes by the time I left.

I'm still shaking now as I write this.

A year, Cash. A YEAR! How can that be?

The flip-book you gave me is sitting here beside me. The Story of Us. I wonder, has our story reached its end?

Love, Maggie

Living with a broken heart sometimes causes you to make broken decisions.

The look on Maggie's face as she stood in the doorway will haunt me for the rest of my days. Never wanted her to see me with another woman. Not like that anyway. Only wanted the gossip and the rumors that I'd been with Scarlet to reach her ears so she'd finally realize I'm serious about the limits of our relationship and give up hoping for more.

God knows I have.

Once and for all.

The email I received before leaving for Miss Bea's party did the trick, and thinking of it now reminds me of my conversation with Violet. That was never part of *The Plan*. But when she came at me, calling me dirty names and accusing me of everything under the sun, my pride wouldn't allow me to stand there and take it.

Now I'm left with the regret of telling her. Not that I'm worried she'll spill things to Maggie. She has many less-than-desirable traits, but being a liar isn't one of them, and she gave me her word that she'd keep things between us. But still. Now someone knows and—

The sound of the toilet flushing precedes the arrival of Scarlet in the living room. She looks at me askance and brushes a self-conscious hand through her hair.

Ever notice how some people can screw a complete stranger without a moment of awkwardness, but the instant they're required to talk afterward, they turn into the world's shyest person?

"Sorry about…" I give the front door a feeble wave. "*That.*"

Her lips twist. "Are the two of you—"

"Friends," I cut her off before she can finish. "Just friends."

"Oh." She nods, clearly relieved. "Good." Then she giggles, her shyness disappearing. "I guess next time we should make sure we lock the door behind us. Although…" She sidles up to me, patting my chest, her expression coquettish. "If next time is anything like this first time, we'll be too carried away and we'll forget again."

We were tearing at our clothes when we came through the door earlier. She's right about that. But she's wrong about there being a next time.

Hate to admit it—especially because I'm beginning to suspect she's a nice woman—but she was merely a means to an end.

"I had a good time tonight." I tenderly kiss her lips, trying to hide my revulsion. In my mind, Scarlet Jensen is now inextricably tied to the look of horror on Maggie's face as she stood inside my front door.

Scarlet leans back, studying the expression I try to keep blank. I feel like a piece of fruit that's hung too long on the vine. I'm rotting from the inside out.

"You're not going to call me, are you?" There's a knowing tilt to her chin and a world-weary glint in her eyes.

I swallow and reach for my flask. My stomach is ice cold, so the booze hits it like a firebomb. "You don't want me to call you," I assure her. "In fact, you want to stay as far away from me as possible."

"Why?"

"I'm a taker. Not a giver." I see her eyes soften. "Don't look at me like that. I'm not a project. Save your time. Save yourself."

Her expression turns contemplative, and I can tell she's trying to decide if I'm worth the risk. News flash: I'm *not*. Then she proves she's not just nice, she's smart too. "Well, it was fun while it lasted. Thanks for a memorable night."

Wish I could say I feel relieved. But the truth is, I'm not feeling much of anything. The more time passes, the more numb I become. Of course, that could be the drugs.

After Maggie left—and while Scarlet was still in the john—I downed three pills. Not so much for the pain in my head, but for the pain in my heart.

"Can I call you a cab?" I ask.

"Nah." She shakes her head. "Think I'll head up to Bourbon Street and see what the tourists are up to. It's too early, and there's still too much to celebrate."

After walking her to the door, I watch her turn in the direction of the sounds of revelry. I try to find peace in the dull roar of voices and laughter and music. In the dull roar of *life*. But I get distracted by a crow in the sweetgum tree on the corner. It cocks its shiny black head, cawing at me.

A portent of danger.

Or maybe that's just in fairy tales.

Then again, when a silver Mercedes careens around the corner and screeches to a stop next to the curb, I think perhaps I believe.

My hands curl into fists when my sperm donor slams out of his car. He rounds the hood only to stand on the sidewalk and glare up at me. "You look like recycled shit."

I snort and hold up three fingers. "Three things to say here," I tell him. "One, so you keep reminding me every time you see me." I curl down my pointer finger. "Two, you're one to talk. Ever think of ordering a salad?" I curl down my ring finger so that just my middle finger remains standing. "And three, happy New Year to you too, you sorry sonofabitch."

"Smart-ass." His face is clenched. Then he dons a fake grin and spreads his arms wide. "Aren't you happy your old man is out of jail?"

"Not particularly," I tell him.

He laughs that oily villain's laugh that I've hated since I was old enough to hear the malice in it. "That damn DA thought he pulled a fast one by arresting me during the holidays. Thinking the courts would be closed and no one would be around to set my bail. But I got friends in high places too."

I sigh, in no mood for his bombastic bullshit. "Why the fuck are you here, Rick?"

"Can't a father wish his only son a happy New Year?"

"A normal father? Sure. But a man like you doesn't show up to dinner without an appetite, so I'll ask again. Why the fuck are you here? What the fuck do you want?"

His upper lip curls. "I want you to tell me who that little cunt and that sonofabitching swamp rat talked to. I want to know which of those rich, fat, pompous pricks had the balls to squeal on me."

I feel a moment's pleasure knowing *I* am the reason he's in this predicament.

"Go fuck yourself, Rick." With a wide smile that invites him to kiss my ass, I turn and walk into the house. But before I can slam the door, he's on me.

A blow lands between my shoulder blades like a sledgehammer, knocking me into the middle of the living room. I manage to keep my feet under me as all the impotent rage of my youth explodes to the surface. Only, this time, it's paired with the overpowering fury of a man who has nothing left to lose.

With a roar, I turn to him, determined to end his reign of terror once and for all.

And this time I don't plan to stop until one or both of us is dead.

Chapter Sixty-three

Luc

Dear Luc,

This will be my last letter.

It's been a year since I penned the first one. OVER a year since you and Cash left. And I have mixed feelings about writing this final note.

On the one hand, I'm relieved. Now I can stop thinking about you every day, since thinking about you makes me miss you, and missing you makes me sad. On the other hand, I've enjoyed sitting down and putting pen to paper. Even though the conversation has been one-sided, I've liked talking to you, imagining what you'd say in return.

Oh, who am I kidding? We both know that even if I'm NOT writing every day, I'll continue to miss you from the bottom of my heart because...well... I think this quote from Hubert H. Humphrey pretty much sums it up. "The greatest gift of life is friendship, and I have received it." You gave me the gift of your friendship when I needed it most.

Thank you. A million times, thank you.

I hope life treats you kindly. You deserve all the good things it has to offer.

Goodbye,

Maggie May

The older you get, the more you come to understand there's no such thing as black and white. Everything is a nuanced shade of gray.

Take, for instance, Maggie's confession. Part of me cringes when I think about it. The three of us got along fine when it was her and Cash pining away for each other, with me stuck on the sidelines. There was a universal synchronicity to it. A *balance*. How will things work if she starts returning my feelings?

I've always hated the idea of a love triangle. Don't reckon I'll take kindly to being a part of one.

On the other hand, I want to whoop with joy and happy dance. I mean, hot damn! After twelve years, it's about time!

And, of course, maybe she would've worked her way around to wanting me sooner if Cash hadn't arrived on the scene when he did, this brash, cocky kid who wouldn't give up until he got what he wanted. (Not that I blame him for falling for her. How could I when that's exactly what *I* did?) Still, it feels like I'm belatedly getting my just deserts.

Then again, maybe this whole line of thinking is moot. Obviously she doesn't want to talk to me about it even though she *said* she did. When she texted *talk* apparently she meant she wanted to explain herself in a few, brief lines, and my telling her to call me scared her off. Which probably means I'm making a bigger deal out of this than I should and—

I pull my earbuds from my ears and cock my head, listening. Even in winter the swamp is alive with sounds. The eerie hoot of an owl. The loud splash of a wild boar tramping through the water. The sorrowful call of the wind through the trees.

The tinny beat of Creedence Clearwater Revival's "Born on the Bayou" issues from my earbuds. But other than that…nothing. I must've been imagining things when I thought I heard a noise that didn't belong.

Popping my earbuds back into place, I hum along to my father's favorite song and watch the stars twinkle over the treetops. The night is dark without the benefit of a moon. And it's cool without being cold.

From my favorite chair on the porch, I spy a pair of eyes glowing about a hundred yards into the water. A gator, watching, waiting, hoping for a fat, orange-toothed nutria to swim by and—

There it is again. That noise that doesn't belong.

Yanking out my earbuds, my socked feet thump against the floorboards when I sit up from my reclined position.

The hairs at the back of my neck lift, and I'm reminded of the tales of the *rougarou*, a cross between a man and a wolf, that supposedly likes to wander the swamp or the city streets at night, assaulting people in hopes that someone will draw its blood. According to legend, once you draw the blood of a *rougarou*, you *become* the next *rougarou*.

Even though I don't believe in any of that, on nights like this, when the swamp is especially dark, it's harder not to let my imagination run wild.

Standing slowly, I turn toward the house.

My pulse steadies, and a relieved chuckle escapes me when, through the window, I don't spot a burglar or *rougarou* or an unwelcome visit from a fuzzy woodland creature (three weeks ago, a squirrel snuck in and I had the devil of a time getting it out) and instead spot Maggie standing in front of my coffee table. She's changed out of her cocktail dress and into a pair of midcalf sweatpants and a long-sleeved T-shirt. But her hair is still styled for a party. And her eyes are still darkened by kohl, giving her a slightly vampy appearance.

There's a strange pressure in my chest. I place a hand over my heart, aiming to quell it. But it doesn't work. Even a long, slow breath doesn't help.

Giving up, I open the porch door. "Maggie May." I'm amazed my voice doesn't betray me. "I reckoned you were gonna call me, not come for a visit. But it's good to see you."

"I couldn't call," she says. "A drunk butthead knocked my phone out of my hand while we were texting and then he stepped on it, smashing it to bits."

Before I can read her expression, she glances down to my open leather-bound journal. Most pages in it are a mishmash of lyrics and stanzas and bits and pieces of poetry. She sits on the sofa and reads aloud a snippet of prose I've titled "The Story."

Her voice is soft. Hearing my words in her throat gives me a strange thrill.

> *I want to tell you a story of a silver moon*
> *that dripped its radiance onto the ground*
>
> *I want to tell you a story of a zydeco band*
> *that played us a melancholy tune*
>
> *I want to tell you a story of a cypress bow*
> *that shadowed us as we waltzed*
>
> *I want to tell you a story of a girl*
> *I loved who didn't love me back*
>
> *I want to tell you a story of a goodbye*
> *that broke my heart into bright, brittle pieces*
>
> *I want to tell you a story, the story, of...that night.*

After she's finished reading, she closes the journal and lifts her face to me. I haven't moved from my spot in the open doorway. But if I clench my hands any harder, my short nails might pierce the skin of my palms.

"Do you ever wonder how things might've been different if I'd let you kiss me that night?"

A chuff of breath escapes me. I squeeze my eyes shut. But, unfortunately, the truth doesn't disappear just because I don't want to look at it.

"Only every day," I admit, slowly opening my eyes, letting them land softly on her face.

"You wouldn't have gone to the truck to fetch your jacket. Dean wouldn't have caught me all alone. I wouldn't have…" She swallows, unable to voice the rest of that thought. Instead, she says, "If I'd let you kiss me, would you have followed Cash into the army or would you have stayed?"

After walking over to the sofa on legs like wet noodles, I take a seat beside her. My weight depresses the cushion, and she slides toward me. Not much. Only enough so that her right knee touches my left.

"Between you and Cash, my choices were the rock and the hard place," I admit. "But what I do know now, what I knew back then, is that Cash needed me more than you did."

"You had dueling loyalties then."

"Hell, woman. I have dueling loyalties now."

She cocks her head. "But you told me you've been holding a candle for me. If you're worried about being disloyal to him, why, after all these years, admit that?"

I sigh. "Maybe 'cause time has a way of obliterating even the best of intentions."

When she frowns, I lift my hands and let them fall. "What d'ya want me to say? I was *tired* of holding it in. I wanted to live my life in the open, in the light."

"You're a spec-ops guy, for Pete's sake," she grumbles. "I thought that was pretty much the definition of a life lived in the dark."

"You're confusing clandestineness with secrets. They're not the same thing."

"Does Cash know?" She chews on her lip and glances down at her hands to pick at a hangnail. Her voice is quieter when she adds, "I mean, have you told him what you told me?"

"I've never come right out and said it, but he knows. I reckon he's always known."

That has her eyes popping to my face. "Always?"

"He said something recently that leads me to believe he's known since the first day when he sat down at our booth."

She blinks myopically. "And yet he still made his move on me?"

I smile and spread my hands. "Can you blame him? He didn't know me from Adam, and you were so young and fresh, with this sparkly, shiny way about you. He was a moth drawn to your light. We *both* were."

She swallows and looks away. "I never *felt* sparkly or shiny. I felt...lost. And alone. And so scared of everything, especially myself."

"Not all that glitters is gold, Maggie May. Sadness can have a sheen to it too," I tell her. "Loneliness can have a certain luster."

A puff of air escapes her. "Pretty words."

There are a million questions I want to ask her. Starting with, *Did you truly mean what you said at the party?* But the chasm between what I want to ask and all the complications and repercussions of the answer seems impossible to cross.

Eventually, she asks, "Why didn't you tell me back then how you felt?"

I shrug. "It wouldn't have changed anything."

She shakes her head. "But how do you know that?"

"'Cause I was *there*, remember? I saw your face when you looked at him for the first time. In that moment, it was all over for me. So I decided not to fight a losing battle. I decided to accept what you were willing to give."

She clutches her locket in her fist. After a while, she admits quietly, "I think I needed someone like him. Someone *not* from around here. Someone who hadn't suffered the terror and trauma of Katrina. Someone I could forget with. But now? Now I think he's the opposite of what I need."

I wish I could think of something profound to say, but that pressure in my chest from earlier is growing, making it impossible to breathe, much less speak. It's hope. Voluminous, ever-expanding hope.

I feel so damned guilty for it.

"He still loves you," I remind her. But maybe I'm reminding myself.

"Yeah, but he doesn't *want* me."

I shake my head. "How can you be sure? He might just be *saying* that 'cause—"

She stops me with a raised hand. "I'm sure." There's a certainty in her voice I haven't heard before. "And the truth is, it doesn't matter if he does or doesn't want me, because I think *I've* stopped wanting *him*."

"You don't mean that," I scoff.

"Don't I?" She searches my eyes. When she sighs, it sounds like letting go. "When I was young, I didn't understand that Cash's brand of love can be self-serving and careless. I was blinded by his confidence and his life-force. But I can see things clearly now. *You've* helped me see things clearly."

My chin jerks back. "What did *I* do?"

"You've been *you*."

I shake my head, not understanding.

"When I think back on it, you've always been my one true thing."

I can't let myself believe her, even though I want to so badly.

She fiddles with her locket. Watching me. Waiting for me to say something.

I don't know *what* to say. This is my biggest fantasy and greatest nightmare all rolled into one. My heart is a time bomb waiting to explode. There's a rushing river in my ears.

Eventually, she sighs. "It's pretty simple actually. Happiness isn't an accident that either crashes into us or doesn't. Happiness is a *choice*. We have to *choose* the things in life that bring us pleasure. He doesn't make me happy, Luc. He *hasn't* made me happy in over ten years. You do. Every day you've been back in my life has given me joy."

"What are you saying, Maggie May?"

"I'm saying I want to see if there might be something more between us. I'm saying..." She swallows, and her cheeks flush an adorable cotton-candy pink. "I want to kiss you, Luc." She makes a face. "Maybe I've been listening to too much Cher, thanks to Jean-Pierre, but I feel like if I kiss you, I'll know if we have a chance."

My whole body flashes hot and cold as the old lyrics about a kiss proving whether it's love spin through my head. I try to lighten the mood (and also I'm stalling) when I say, "You know Cher only covered that song, right? It was originally sung by Betty Everett."

"Luc, come on," she pleads helplessly.

I rake in a deep breath, as if filling my lungs will somehow make what I'm about to say more bearable. "Are you sure you're not feeling this way 'cause you're upset with how Cash acted tonight at the party? 'Cause you're feeling rejected by him and looking for a way to make yourself feel better?"

Her mouth twists. I can't tell if it's with humor or pain. And then she clears everything up when she smiles that smile that lights her up from the inside out. "Maybe 1 percent is about that."

"And the other 99 percent?" I ask anxiously.

"It's about you being wonderful and amazing and sexy as hell."

All the hope inside me bubbles to the surface. My decision is made; my loyalties are no longer divided. This time it's *my* turn. "I can live with that," I tell her.

Cupping her jaw, I lean close, overwhelmed by the proximity of her. I search her eyes and see her tense, as if she's having second thoughts. Then she glances at my mouth, and her expression loosens. When her eyes return to mine, her curiosity, her *hunger* is unmistakable. Before I can overthink things, I claim her mouth.

It's as soft and sweet as I thought it'd be. Eager beneath mine. Following my lead.

I take my time, learning her taste, her texture, teasing the pleasure out of her, showing her all I've learned over the years until my head grows light and my blood grows hot.

This right here, kissing Magnolia May Carter, is what I was born to do.

I didn't know it until this moment.

Her hands spear into my hair, and she groans, opening wider, inviting me in. Instantly, our soft, searching kiss turns wanton and wicked. It grows deep and wet. A kiss I feel in my belly. In my bones. In the hard, incessant throb of my blood.

"Luc," she whispers when I let her up for air.

"Maggie May," I answer quietly, lost in her. Lost in this. Lost in *us*. But before I can reclaim her mouth (that mouth that is the end and the beginning of all things), the sound of tires crunching over gravel invades our privacy.

At first I'm too confused to place the noise. But when she pulls back, blinking at me, I come to my senses.

The first things I notice are her delightfully rosy cheeks, slightly dazed eyes, and wonderfully kiss-swollen lips. So this is what she looks like when she's been good and snogged? She's even more beautiful than I imagined and—

The slam of a car door reminds me why my tongue isn't currently inside her mouth.

"Are you—" She has to clear her throat. Please don't judge me too harshly for feeling a kick of pride at that. "Are you expecting someone?"

"No." I stand from the sofa. Walking over to the window above the sink, the one that overlooks the back of the house, I squint into the darkness beyond. My fingers instinctively curl around hers when she comes up behind me and slips her hand into mine.

"Who is it?" She tries to peer over my shoulder.

My heart, so full and swollen a second ago, drops onto the floor like a lead stone.

"Go lock yourself in the bathroom," I tell her.

"What?" She blinks in confusion as I let go of her hand to open a cabinet drawer. I pull out my Colt .45 and press-check the chamber to make sure a round is loaded. "Luc?" There's a terrified edge to her voice as her wide-eyed stare turns from the gun to my face. "Who is it? What's happening?"

"Go to the bathroom, Maggie May."

"Who *is* it?" she demands.

"It's Sullivan." Even in the dark of the swamp, I can't mistake the hulking outline of his Dodge Ram pickup truck or the sparkle of its cattle guard.

The sound of boot heels thumping across the wooden walkway leading to the back door is like an aural assault. The hairs on the back of my neck lift in warning, and adrenaline sizzles through my bloodstream.

"The bathroom, Maggie May."

"No." She shakes her head vehemently. "I'm not leaving you. We're in this together."

There's no time to argue. "Stay behind me, then," I tell her.

Opening the door, I aim my weapon at the brim of Sullivan's cowboy hat. He's halfway down the walkway and gaining ground fast. Starlight glints off the chrome plating of the six-shooter in his hand.

I'd be a liar if I said I've never been scared. There were plenty of times in the army when the shit had hit the fan and my life was most definitely on the line. But I was always with a team of men as tough as I am. Now my only backup is a pipsqueak of a woman. And even though she's got plenty of gumption, she has zero firepower.

So, yeah, it's safe to say that, right here, right now, I'm more scared than I've ever been.

I'm also more determined.

Having the love of my life here means there's no give in me. I'll do whatever it takes.

"Stop right there, Sullivan!" I shout, and he skids to a halt, his beady eyes landing on the menacing black hole at the end of my Colt. If you've ever stared into the business end of a weapon, you know it absorbs all light.

"You're on private property," I growl. "And it's obvious you aren't here on police business. So I reckon you better lay that there hand cannon on the ground before I put you *in* the ground."

To be continued…

ACKNOWLEDGMENTS

Huge thanks to my clever, funny, ever-supportive gal-pal, Amanda Carlson. I couldn't have done any of this without your reassurance, your wisdom, and your patient guidance. You've been there for me during the hardest moments of my life. Put simply, you're the best.

Thanks to Joyce Lamb for taking the lumps of coal that were the first drafts of these books and helping me turn them into things that (hopefully) now sparkle like diamonds. Your nit-picky editorial eye and your refusal to blow smoke up my ass makes for a dynamic duo. Here's hoping we write many more books together.

Wider thanks to all the folks who do the hard work of getting a book into readers' hands, Marlene Engel, proofer extraordinaire, Amy Atwell, formatter for the stars, and Sofie Hartley at Hart and Bailey Design Co. for the beautiful covers.

And last, but certainly not least, to my amazing family who never fails to support and encourage me. You're a wild and crazy bunch, but I wouldn't have you any other way.

The story continues in this sneak peek of

In Moonlight and Memories:

VOLUME THREE

JULIE ANN WALKER

CHAPTER SIXTY-FOUR

Luc

Snuffing out someone's candle doesn't make your own light shine any brighter. In fact, it steals a bit of your glow.

I learned this the hard way in the Green Berets when circumstances forced me to end a life. I'd hoped, once I was out of the service, I'd never have to make another of those terrible decisions. I'd hoped I'd never have to lose another ounce of my luster.

But George Sullivan has a look in his eye.

One I recognize well.

I saw it in the mountains of the Hindu Kush on the faces of enemy combatants. I saw it on the eyes of the men in my unit when we were pinned down behind enemy lines and taking fire. And I saw it in Cash's expression the day he came to drop off his Dear Jane letter for Maggie. It's fatalistic. A killing look.

Someone's leaving here in a body bag.

Unless I can find a way to defuse the situation.

"Look, man." I never break eye contact with Sullivan, willing him to read the sincerity in my gaze. "I know you're hurting over the loss of your son. I know about waking up in the morning with a smile on your face 'cause for a split second you forget that the one you love is gone, and then feeling like you've been hit by a

Mack truck when you remember. I *know*. I lost my dad. Maggie May lost both her folks. We *understand*, and we—"

"Spare me your Kumbaya, we're-all-in-this-together bullshit." Sullivan's tobacco-stained teeth gleam yellow beneath his mustache when his upper lip pulls back into a snarl. "Your parents died. My boy was *murdered*. The difference between those things is bigger than the journey from here to hell."

"Dean wasn't murdered." I beg him to hear the truth in my words. "Leastways not how you're thinking."

"Yes, he *was*!"

"No! He *wasn't*!" I realize I'm matching Sullivan's volume when Maggie tangles the material at the back of my shirt into her fist.

Right. Never has a shouting match lessened the tension of any situation.

Taking a deep breath of damp swamp air, I hope it'll tamp down the molten desperation bubbling inside me. One of us has to keep our cool. And it's certainly not going to be Sullivan.

The man looks unhinged. (Although, I don't reckon he was ever hinged to begin with.) The side of his face not shadowed by the brim of his cowboy hat looks splotchy in the starlight. And a big vein pulses in his neck.

It's at this moment he makes his second mistake of the night. (His first was coming here looking for revenge.) He lifts his Magnum .44 and aims it straight at my chest.

The muscles in my jaw turn to stone at the same time I harden my heart. If I allow him to pull his trigger, the caliber of his big-bore weapon is enough to send a bullet clean through me and into Maggie May.

I wish she'd gone to hide in the bathroom like I told her. Then again, it takes a woman with snap in her garters to stand with me and face down a stark raving gunman. So I'm full to bursting with pride for her too.

I've had my finger pressed against my trigger guard. (One of the first things the army taught me was never to touch the trigger until I'm damn good and ready to fire.) But now, with infinite care, so as not to draw Sullivan's eye, I slip my pointer finger around the cool metal mechanism. When squeezed, it promises to discharge hot lead death.

Isn't that crazy? To think that a piece of metal barely an inch long can be the catalyst that snuffs out a life in a fraction of a second?

The night breeze plays with the wind chimes on the front porch, sounding a discordantly sweet note. The dry, decrepit odor of the pecan husks that have fallen from the tree next to the house tunnel up my nose. And the poisonous atmosphere that's gathered around us is harsh on my tongue, like Creole bitters.

In life-and-death situations, all my senses come into sharper focus.

"Tell me once and for all what you did to my boy!" Sullivan shakes his six-shooter in emphasis, and my index finger tightens around my trigger. But I don't squeeze. I haven't reached the point of no return. There's still one thing left to try.

"If I tell you," I say, "will you finally leave us well enough alone?"

Behind me, Maggie sucks in a startled breath. "Luc, no."

I don't dare take my eyes off of Sullivan when I say to her, "I know we swore to take this to our grave. But this secret has been festering for years. The only way I know to stop the spread of the rot is to lance it open and expose it to the air. We'll deal with whatever he tries to make of it afterward. After all, the *truth* is on our side. And we have more power to fight him now than we did when we were kids."

"Tell me!" Sullivan barks again, taking a step toward us.

I feel my trigger give the tiniest bit as the muscles in my hand instinctively react.

"Not another step," I warn, my voice taking on the authoritative ring I used when aiming to get my unit to fall into line. (Everyone but Cash was always quick to comply.)

Sullivan's Adam's apple travels up the length of his throat and seems to lodge there like a fish bone. But he doesn't say anything more. And he stops his advance.

It ignites a small spark of hope that maybe, just maybe, there's a way we can all come out of this thing alive.

Softly, slowly, so as not to spook him into doing something foolish, I relate the tale of prom night 2009. How Dean followed us into the swamp to spy on us. How he attacked Maggie after I'd gone to retrieve my tuxedo jacket from Smurf. How she defended herself by clocking him clean unconscious with one well-placed blow from a rock. How I found her struggling on the ground beneath his limp body. How I yanked him off her and told her to run.

"After she was gone, he came to," I say. "He stumbled 'round for a bit before falling back to his knees too close to the water's edge. You know as well as I do how dangerous it can be there."

Even before I say the words, Sullivan is shaking his head. Not wanting to believe what he knows comes next. Not wanting to hear it.

"A gator got him," I say, not couching my words. Letting the horrible truth speak for itself.

Maggie gasps and pokes her head out from behind me. I can feel the force of her gaze, although I don't dare return it.

"Wait." Her voice is tremulous. "Are you..." She swallows noisily. "Are you saying Dean was *alive*?"

My brow pinches in confusion. "'Course he was alive," I say. "You knocked him for a loop, but—"

"Oh sweet baby Jesus!" The sharp hitch in her voice shoots a jolt straight through me, stopping my heart. When it starts beating again, a rush of blood goes to my head.

"What is it, Maggie May?" I demand, completely flummoxed.

"Why didn't you *tell* me?" Her whisper sounds harsh, and the second-to-the-last word is cracked in two like it was slammed against a hard edge. "All these years I thought I killed him!"

"Wait. What?" I must look a sight with my eyes bulging from my head. "When I met you back at the truck, I *said* he was gator food."

"I thought that meant you'd thrown his body into the swamp! I didn't know that meant he was *literally* attacked by an alligator!"

The record player of my mind scratches to a stop. I can't think. Can't breathe. All I can do is stand there, staring down the barrel of Sullivan's .44 as more than ten years of misunderstandings flash in front of my eyes.

There's a loud buzz in my ears. I'm pretty sure it's originating in my brain.

Forcing a swallow, I find my voice. "Dean was whole, if not exactly hale, when you ran off that night."

The sound she makes is awful. Pitiful. A wounded sound. Like a tendon tearing free from bone.

All this time, she's been living under the impression she's a killer? It's untenable. *Unthinkable.* How could I not have known?

Oh, right. Because I ran off to join the army soon after and cut off all communication with her.

If I didn't have to worry about Sullivan and his chrome-plated bang stick (which he hasn't lowered, even after my explanation) I'd be tempted to kick my own ass.

"If he was alive, if it was an alligator that killed him, why have we been lying about seeing him that night?" Her voice is steadier now, but it's still thick with unshed tears.

"You think he would've believed us?" I hitch my chin toward Sullivan.

"I don't believe you now," he snarls, proving my point.

"We all knew about that girl from St. Bernard Parish who accused Dean of raping her," I say to Maggie, ignoring Sullivan. "And we all knew what happened after ol' Georgie boy got finished with her. Her reputation was ruined, and her name was mud."

Something passes over Sullivan's face. Maybe it's simply remembrance. But it looks a lot more like satisfaction. He seems *pleased* to have saved Dean by destroying an innocent girl.

"If we'd come forward to say Dean attacked you, do you really think *he*"—I hitch my chin toward Sullivan—"woulda let that stand? He'd have come after you just like he went after that other girl. Only it woulda been worse 'cause of what happened to Dean afterward."

"Enough! This is bullshit! I don't believe any of it!" Sullivan snarls again.

Except, he does believe it. There's acceptance in his eyes.

Unfortunately, there's also determination. The truth hasn't made the slightest difference. He's still resolved to put an end to us.

I try one more time to change his mind. To save him.

"I want you to know neither of us ever wished Dean harm," I say calmly, "even after the way he treated us. And that night, I did everything I could to help him."

The memory of Dean Sullivan's last moments has, time and again, appeared in my path like a piece of broken glass. When it does, it stabs into the bottom of my foot, leaving me sick with pain and regret.

The same two questions always plague me.

If I'd shouted instead of standing in mute horror when I saw the alligator lunge, would it have given Dean enough time to escape its gaping jaws? Is there something more I could've done once the beast grabbed him?

When the reptile shot out of the water like a rocket-fueled missile, I thought I was hallucinating. It was the biggest damn gator I'd ever seen. At least fifteen feet and weighing what had to be three-quarters of a ton. A wily old swamp monster if ever there was one.

Maybe it'd been lured to the water's edge by the commotion. Maybe it'd been the smell of Dean's blood that drew it in. Or maybe it'd simply been bad luck. The wrong place at the wrong time with the wrong Louisiana yard dog waiting to pounce.

Regardless of how it happened or why, when it clamped down on Dean's thigh, the force of its bite nearly severed Dean's leg. Blood spurted. Flesh tore. In my nightmares, I can still hear the awful sound of Dean's choked whimper, and I've often wondered why he didn't scream his head off.

Maybe he was in too much shock? Maybe the pain had paralyzed his vocal chords? That's all I can figure.

I ran for him, grabbing his outstretched hands and pulling with everything I had. But the soles of my rented patent leather shoes were slick. Getting traction was impossible. Falling backward, my hands slipping out of Dean's desperate grip, I hit the spongy ground with enough force to bruise my tailbone. (I couldn't sit right for weeks afterward.)

Scrambling to my hands and knees, I looked up to find terror, and the awful inevitability of the situation, written all over Dean's face. In that moment, he wasn't the dickhead jock who called me names, or the soulless rapist of teenage girls. He was a boy who knew this was the end of the line.

The giant wasted no time dragging him into the water. Dean fought the entire way, his hands ripping up roots and soil and vegetation. I ran after him, aiming to get a hand on him again. But I wasn't fast enough. And Dean, for all his hulking football bulk, wasn't strong enough.

Soon, boy and beast were in the swamp, getting farther and farther away from me with each passing second. I didn't stop even when the water was up to my waist and I was in danger of being grabbed by another gator or bitten by a water moccasin. I didn't stop until I was chin-deep and didn't dare go a fraction farther.

Look away! my mind screamed. And oh, how I wanted to. But I couldn't let Dean face his gruesome fate alone.

I never broke eye contact with him. Not once. So I saw the instant the reptile's big body tensed. And knowing what would come next had stomach acid burning the back of my throat.

When the gator barrel-rolled, the night came alive with the awful sound of massive amounts of water being displaced. Great plumes of tea-colored liquid arced into the air, catching the light of the moon and sparkling like strings of diamonds.

Over and over again. Roll, roll, roll. So fast it was a blur. And with each passing second, the circle of blood floating atop the water grew like an oil slick. Until, eventually, the monster stopped.

Where there had been motion and chaos, stillness reigned. And Dean? Well, he was as quiet as the grave.

For good reason. He'd gone to his.

Scrambling backward out of the water, I crab-walked up on the bank, shivering despite the warmth of the night. Sitting there in the mud, all I could hear was the raggedness of my own breaths and the rapid *chug-chug-chug* of the runaway freight train that was my heart.

As quickly as it'd arrived on the scene, the alligator sank beneath the surface of the swamp, dragging Dean's lifeless body with it. I knew it would tuck Dean beneath a submerged log, letting the water go to work on Dean's flesh, making it tender enough to tear off in great, meaty chunks.

Closing my eyes, I tried not to envision it. But the images assailed me nonetheless. By the time I opened them again, I had to put a hand over my mouth to keep from screaming.

I have no idea how long I stayed there, watching the eddies atop the water expand and swirl. Time seemed to have no meaning. (I know now I was in shock.) But eventually I managed to drag myself to my feet and set about using a big, dead branch to obscure our footprints.

All I was able to think was, *No one will believe me about what happened here. George Sullivan will go after Maggie May like he did that girl from St. Bernard Parish. I gotta save her.*

Fat lot of good that did me, though. Here we are, ten years later. Still faced with George Sullivan's wrath.

"Even if what you say is true," he says now, "that doesn't change the fact that Dean wouldn't have been in that swamp if it weren't for you two. Maybe you didn't kill him outright, but you're still the reason he's dead. And I aim to get justice for my boy, right here and now."

Here it is. The moment I hoped to avoid. The moment I hoped the truth could prevent.

I give it one last-ditch effort. "There's a fine line between justice and vengeance, George." I purposefully use his first name, making what I'm saying more personal. "If you do this, you'll cross it."

"Fuck you, you filthy swamp rat!" His aim steadies, and my vision tunnels to a single spot. It's the place where his trigger finger meets his hand.

"Don't—" That's all I manage before I see the muscles in his firing hand twitch.

Of the two of us, Cash has always been the better marksman. He claims it's because, thanks to Rick, he has a particular thirst for blood that I've never acquired. But just because Cash is better, that doesn't mean I'm not still damn good.

I don't miss what I aim for.

I get off two shots to Sullivan's one, and the air is rent by the roar of gunfire. The smell of spent propellant blooms inside my nose like an acrid flower.

Luckily, speed of fire isn't the only difference between me and the superintendent of the New Orleans Police Department. There's a big disparity in accuracy too. While his shot ranges wide, whizzing by my shoulder and lodging into the corner of the house, both of my bullets find a home inside Sullivan's big, barrel chest.

He goes down like a ton of bricks, his cowboy hat flying off his head and getting stuck between two balusters. (It's a weird thing to notice at a time like this, but he's bald except for the thin ring of reddish-brown hair that starts above his ears and circles the back of his head.)

His six-shooter slips from his hand and skids along the boards of the pier before coming to a rest near the edge. Now that it's not in his hands, the weapon is no more a threat to me than a child's toy. And yet the sheen of its chrome plating continues to sparkle menacingly.

I drop my own pistol to my side. It suddenly weighs a hundred pounds. Letting my head fall back, I gaze at the glistening underbelly of the night sky.

Deep winter in the bayou means deceiving stillness interrupted by bursts of volatile life. Wild boars crash through the underbrush. Egrets take unexpected flight from the water's edge. A coyote ambushes a cottontail and drags it away while it squeals and wriggles. But right now...silence, as if the entire swamp is watching as a bit more of my light disappears. As a bit more of my soul dies.

I know from experience the necrosis will continue to spread in the coming days.

A fluttering sensation against my back has me lowering my chin. Maggie still has a hold of my shirt. She's shaking like a leaf. Her skin is the color of milk glass. And her mouth is open, revealing the gap between her two front teeth.

No words issue from her throat, but her eyes ask, *How did this happen?*

I shake my head. If everything happens for a reason, I can't figure the hows and the whys of this. It seems so pointless.

Cupping her jaw, I run a thumb over the tender skin of her cheek, wiping away the lone tear glistening there.

"It's okay, Maggie May," I tell her. But we both know that's not true.

"S—" she tries, but has to stop and swallow. "Sullivan?" she finally manages.

Even though I know what I'll find, I tuck my pistol into the back of my jeans and walk over to the police superintendent.

He's faceup on the pier. Blood that looks black in the night continues to grow around him. It drips between the wooden slats and falls into the swamp below.

The iron-rich smell will draw the night hunters from their hiding spots soon. But for now, there's only the hushed whisper of the breeze in the trees.

Pressing a finger to his neck, I check for a pulse even though there's no point. My first shot blew apart his sternum. My second exploded his heart. He was dead before he hit the pier.

"Is he—" Maggie can't seem to finish the sentence.

"Dead," I assure her.

She stumbles to the railing and wretches over the side.

Turning away, I give her privacy. I lost my lunch the first time I saw a gunshot victim too. But the years, and the things I've witnessed since then, have forged my constitution into a thing of tempered steel.

When she's finished, she wipes the back of her hand over her mouth. "Sorry," she whispers, holding on to the rail to steady herself.

"Nothing to apologize for," I assure her, my mind spinning through the details, sorting them into a list.

Funny how your brain can continue to function normally even when your whole world is falling down around your ears.

"I need you to go grab my cell phone. It's charging on the bedside table." Her eyes are wide and empty, like her mind has run somewhere to hide. She needs something to do. Inaction only strengthens shock. "Call the cops," I instruct her. "Tell 'em to get here quick. Once you're done with that, find Abelman's number in my contacts. Ask him to meet me at the police station. I'm gonna need a good lawyer."

The vein snaking up the center of his forehead swells. "Careful what you say to me, boy."

"Or what?" The noise I make is rude. "You'll beat the shit out of me? Been there. Done that too many times to count. Don't you ever get tired of the same old song and dance?"

"I won't get tired of it until you finally learn to show me some fucking respect. That's something my old man taught me. Your woman and kids should damn well respect you."

Your woman and kids. As if Mom and I were his property.

Never met my paternal grandfather. He died before I was born. All I know about Big Joe Armstrong is that he worked his whole life in a factory that made radios for military jets. And, apparently, that he was as much of a sonofabitch as my own father.

"Please tell me it's not as simple or clichéd as that," I say.

Rick's brow wrinkles. "What the fuck are you talking about?"

"I'm talking about you beating me and Mom because your own father beat you. I'm talking about a textbook case of perpetuating the cycle of abuse."

He snorts. "Don't try to psychoanalyze me, you little shit. I don't have any deep, dark emotional wounds that need healing. I wasn't a stranger to the sting of my father's knuckles, that's true. But he only gave it to me when I deserved it. And unlike you and your mother, I learned pretty quickly not to deserve it."

I stare at him, but it's my mother's face I'm seeing. All the black eyes. All the fat lips. "You think Mom *deserved* what you did to her?"

"She was a dirty slut who got me drunk and screwed me without a condom. Then she had the bad sense to turn up pregnant and whine to my old man about it. The bastard made me marry her, and then he up and died not two months later. If I'd known he had a time bomb for a ticker, I could've waited him out. You and your mom wouldn't have been my problem. I could've lived the life I wanted."

I know it's useless to argue with him. But I can't help myself. "I seriously doubt Mom got you drunk. You never seemed to need any help with that. And what life were you so anxious to live anyway?"

"Doesn't matter." He waves a hand. "What matters is she should've been grateful for the roof I put over her head and the food I put in her belly. But she never could come around to it. All she ever did was cry her eyes out and let her looks go to shit."

"Because you *beat* her!" I yell.

He sniffs, unfazed by my reasoning. "You're just like her." There's disdain in his voice.

"Which explains why you started kicking the shit out of me, I guess." There's sarcasm in *my* voice.

"Bah! This is a ridiculous conversation. I didn't come here to talk about our dysfunctional family."

"Oh, so you admit it's dysfunctional?"

He ignores my interruption. "I came here to talk about your friends and who they got to squeal on me. You better think twice before telling me to go fuck myself again. You may've gotten in one good shot." Again, he touches his jaw. "But I think we both know that when it comes to this"—he shakes a fat fist—"I'm still the better man."

"You want to know who sicced the DA on you?" My rage has been replaced by a feeling of detachment. I want this to end. I want it *all* to end. I want to be free of him, finally. "You really want to know?" He narrows his eyes. "It was me. *I'm* the one who gave the DA the goods on you."

It should feel good to admit that aloud. To prove, once and for all, that *I* will be the one to come out on top. But all it does is drain me further.

Rick's eyebrows lower. I see the intent in his eyes. So when he comes for me, I'm ready.

Even though fighting is his MO and even though I'm feeding into his illness by engaging, I have to defend myself. Once you're in the barrel of a rifle, there's only one way out.

When he takes a swing at my head, I duck and drill him in the gut with all my strength—which, unfortunately, isn't what it used to be. Still, my fist sinks into the overabundance of his flesh. When he doubles over, making a strangled *oomph*, his hot, tobacco-rank breath puffs against my cheek. I immediately add an uppercut to the mix. A flawless one-two combo.

Sailing backward, he lands on his back with enough force to shake the house. The new windows rattle in their frames, and the silver picture frame—the one Maggie gave me for Christmas— jostles on the mantel.

Instinct propels me to go after him while he's down, to punch and kick and mutilate in every way possible. But that's what *he'd* do.

So instead, I cross my arms and watch dispassionately as he rolls side to side like a turtle stuck on its back. Eventually, he gets his knees under him. Sweat drips from his brow to stain the newly sanded floor as he hoists himself upright with a mighty grunt.

His eyes are ablaze with a lifetime of hatred when he looks at me. Blood seeps from the corner of his lip.

A few minutes ago, the sight of him bleeding would've filled me with joy. Now all I feel is a strange, all-encompassing apathy that I attribute to a few things, not the least of which is the combination of booze and pills.

"I should've forced your fucking cunt of a mother to get an abortion." He gnashes his ridiculous veneers, using the back of his hand to wipe away the blood. Thanks to the sweat pouring off him, it leaves a pink streak across his cheek.

This isn't the first time he's said that to me. Those awful words used to cut deep. Now, the damage has long since scabbed over and the scab has long since fallen off. What's left in its place is a layer of thick, protective skin.

"Nothing you say can hurt me," I tell him. "And I think I've proved I can kick your ass if I want to. But see, here's the thing. I don't want to. You're not worth it. So we're done here. Get the fuck out of my house."

I point to the open door as a group of revelers stumble by outside. The light inside draws their attention. They salute me with their go-cups, blowing party horns and drunkenly calling, "Happy New Year!"

Right. It *is* a new year. Time to let go of past grievances and make a fresh start. Except, here I am right where I've always been, squaring off against the bastard who supplied my Y chromosome.

The instant I have the thought, I'm defeated by it.

"This isn't over between us." Rick points a finger at my face. "Not by a long shot."

"But see, it *is*. Soon, you'll be serving a nice long prison sentence, and I'll be—" I stop and shake my head. "It doesn't matter where I'll be. *You'll* be where you've always belonged."

"You truly did it, didn't you? You weren't just blowing and blustering. You truly are the reason the DA is coming after me."

I nod. But I don't feel any real satisfaction in it.

"Do you hate me that much? So much you'd turn against your own flesh and blood?"

After everything he's done to me, after all the pain and suffering, how can he be surprised?

"Ten years ago, I hated you. Hell, ten *minutes* ago, I hated you. But now?" I shrug. "Now I realize I can't face my future while holding on to my past."

As soon as the words are out of my mouth, I feel their weight. Their unassailable truth.

"So I'm going to let go of it," I tell him. "All of it. What you did to Mom. What you did to me. What you've done to so many good people. I'm going to forgive you, Rick. Not for you, but for me."

He stares at me in disbelief, his too-wet mouth opening and closing like a fish out of water.

The whiskey in my pocket sends up her siren's call. The mattress in the master bedroom joins the chorus. This entire night feels like I've been awake in my own worst nightmare.

"Just go," I say with a heavy sigh. "We're even."

"How the hell do you figure *that*?" he demands.

I search his eyes. Those eyes that are mirror images of my own. "You stole my childhood," I tell him evenly. "Now I've stolen your future."

"You sonofabitch," he snarls.

I laugh. "As many times as you've called me that, I should have it tattooed across my chest."

As if to prove me right, he adds, "You sorry, ungrateful sonofabitch."

This time I don't respond. Not because there aren't a million things I could throw in his face, but because I don't have anything left in me to give to him. "I'm going to bed," I say. "You can show yourself out."

I make the mistake of turning my back on him. Just for a second. Truly, it's only an instant.

That's all he needs.

I hear his heavy footfalls and swing around to see the bulky silver picture frame raised high in his hand. I have enough time to lift my arms and yell, "No!" before the hard metal corner connects with my temple and it's all over for me.

White-hot pain explodes.

The world goes dark.

MORE BOOKS BY JULIE ANN WALKER

BLACK KNIGHTS INC. ROMANTIC SUSPENSE SERIES...
Hell on Wheels
In Rides Trouble
Rev It Up
Thrill Ride
Born Wild
Hell for Leather
Full Throttle
Too Hard to Handle
Wild Ride
Fuel for Fire
Hot Pursuit
Built to Last

DEEP SIX ROMANTIC SUSPENSE SERIES...
Hot as Hell (prequel novella)
Hell or High Water
Devil and the Deep

About Julie Ann Walker

A *New York Times* and *USA Today* bestselling author, Julie loves to travel the world looking for views to compete with her deadlines. And if those views happen to come with a blue sky and sunshine? All the better! When she's not writing, Julie enjoys camping, hiking, cycling, fishing, cooking, petting every dog that walks by her, and... reading, of course!

Find her online at
www.julieannwalker.com

Made in the USA
Columbia, SC
15 July 2019